BY DONALD HONIG

Sidewalk Caesar

Walk Like a Man

The Americans

Divide the Night

No Song to Sing

Judgment Night

The Love Thief

The Severith Style

Illusions

I Should Have Sold Petunias

The Last Great Season

Marching Home

The Plot to Kill Jackie Robinson

Last Man Out

The Sword of General Englund

DONALD HONIG

THE
GHOST
OF
MAJOR
PRYOR

A NOVEL OF MURDER
IN THE MONTANA TERRITORY, 1870

SCRIBNER

SCRIBNER
1230 Avenue of the Americas
New York, NY 10020

DESIGNED BY JENNIFER DOSSIN

Set in Sabon

Manufactured in the United States of America

1   3   5   7   9   10   8   6   4   2

Library of Congress Cataloging-in-Publication Data
Honig, Donald.
The ghost of Major Pryor : a novel of murder in the Montana territory, 1870 /
Donald Honig.
p.   cm.
I. Title.
PS3558.05G48   1997
813'.54—dc21   96-45048
CIP

ISBN 0-684-80322-4

FOR CATHY AND MICHAEL LABELLA

ONE

Barley Newton didn't believe in ghosts, even though he might have been entitled to such indulgence, having been amid the dead and dying at stopping places like Antietam and Chancellorsville and coming out of the engagements not knowing whether he himself was dead or alive and at times not even knowing which he preferred. You saw it, you heard it, and worst of all you remembered. Those memories became like living organisms, and a man had better be acutely aware of that. A man had to be alert to the mischief those memories could provoke.

So it was a long-resolved matter with Barley that there were no such things as ghosts; he wasn't just a skeptic, he was more than that, because he had actually thought soberly and rationally about the matter (a man who had spent years, and much of that time solitudinous, in the Montana Territory goldfields had time to think about a lot of things that were not normal everyday things) and come to what amounted to a scientifically convinced conclusion: there were no such things as ghosts. He was as convinced of this as only a man haunted by unkempt memories and floating voices could be (what a man might see when he was in his cups didn't count).

The nearest thing to a ghost in Barley's life was actually a very substantial metal known as gold, which over the past few decades had become probably the most evocative word in America, a stirring, image-conjuring sound. Barley's search for the metal, the word, was almost spiritual; it didn't have as much to do with dream or aspiration as it did with finding just the right patch of ground somewhere on the vast and alluring continent and unlocking one of nature's secrets, one of God's secrets if you would, though there certainly wasn't anything presumptive or sacrilegious about looking for it because if the Almighty didn't want you to find it and take possession He wouldn't have buried it there within reach in the first place.

Barley had headed west right after the war, as much to try to get away from the echoes of terminated thunder as to follow the seductive whisper that seemed to come gleaming from the word *gold*. He rode west away from Abilene and its noisy end-of-the-trail cowtown hilarities, went north to Nebraska, crossed the Platte into Wyoming, followed the old Pony Express trail beyond Fort Platte, crossed the Powder River, and kept going, into the Montana Territory, swimming his horse across the cold Yellowstone waters.

Along the way he rode in and out of mining towns (some of them little more than rows of tents lined up on either side of a street that was a street only because there were tents lined up across from one another), staked a few modest claims, had a bit of luck here and there but never enough, and kept going. He arrived in Baddock, in the Montana Territory, in 1869, still animated and motivated by the resolution behind the malady known as gold fever.

If gold fever was probably incurable (if it was anything, it was highly contagious), it did at least have one palliative—it enabled ex-Sergeant Barley Newton, long-term veteran of a much-bloodied New Hampshire volunteer regiment, to suppress (not forget) the torments of war's clashing anvils and replace them with a different kind of passion, a different kind of accompanying night-thoughts. Of course this passion generated its own torments, in that Barley never could be quite sure if he wasn't riding across or walking upon or even sleeping on or near that which he so strenuously believed in and sought.

So the ghost was more than a ghost; it was a stunning leap at him from out of a nightmare past he thought had securely folded up and gone away for good. And it was more than a ghost because it wasn't spectral or evanescent, wasn't afloat on some moonlit landscape, wasn't something smokily skeletal or that came dripping from some putrefied bed of earth, nor was it some lapse of mind into antic imagination, even though Barley knew that the one fertile pasture open to these visions was the human mind.

The ghost appeared to Barley on Baddock's Main Street on a July afternoon a year or so after he first arrived in town, within the shadows of another mountain sunset as another Montana day was going to rest under a panoply of imperial scarlets and purples, borne by a warm breeze he would swear contained no sinister whisper. The ghost was unlike any he had ever heard of (and he had heard of plenty of them while sitting around campfires with men who had spent too many, not days or weeks, but months alone). This ghost was solidly boned and held blood and exhaled breath, and its boot heels made sharp rhythmic noises on the raised plank sidewalk as it came at him under the extended wooden awnings with brisk stride. It was wearing a black high-crowned wide-brimmed hat and dark broadcloth jacket and trousers and leather vest and gun belt and holstered pistol.

At first, from a distance, the approaching figure evoked a faint, involuntary memory, a vague similarity of size, shape, stride, and then more; as it neared, something in the face. Barley was of course well versed in the rules and codes of the unfettered West, and one of them was never stare too closely at a stranger. But he couldn't help it; as the distance between the two men closed he became more curious and then almost transfixed. As the man came abreast of him Barley almost stopped, did, in fact, hesitate for a moment, and then felt a cold chill when the other man did the same, eyes taking full measure of not just Barley's face but of what Barley might be seeing, thinking, remembering. What felt to him like sternly perceiving eyes made Barley feel almost paralyzed even as he continued walking.

The apparition-turned-flesh-and-blood so unnerved him that Barley, almost as he might of a stranger, had to ask himself if he believed it. And he answered his own incredulous question of himself by not turning around to stare after the striding man, whose rapping boot heels he now listened to as though they were sounds levitating from beneath the earth. He knew he believed it by knowing how much he did not want to, by knowing that it would be too much even to begin to try to understand.

Barley paused at the end of the boardwalk, his hand touching the short spray of graying whiskers that hung from his chin. A flat-bedded wagon filled with sawed logs rolled unsteadily over the wheel-worn ruts and gullies of Main Street, making a soft rumbling clatter that he hardly heard. Then, abruptly, he moved again, stepping down from the raised boardwalk and crossing the street to the Honest Eagle, his saloon of choice in Baddock, not because it looked or smelled any different from any of the others but because it generally was trouble free, which was a substantial inducement for a saloon in a mining town.

Barley stepped up onto the planks on the other side of the street and headed for the saloon. He entered through the open door and went directly to the bar, where he slapped the oaken surface several times with the flat of his hand, not loudly or urgently but merely to announce his presence. Several men were slouched at the bar, a few others scattered around the tables drinking or playing cards. There was a permanent odor of tobacco because of the low pinewood ceiling where the smoke seemed to purr and eddy endlessly. The stool at the corner piano was empty, the player and his headful of tunes bouncy and melancholy not yet there. The bullet hole in the piano's front—the Eagle had bought the instrument in that condition—was a source of jibes for the player, who was constantly assured he would be safe as long as he played, that in Baddock nobody ever got shot in the back, but that when he turned around all bets were off.

"Whiskey," Barley said to the bartender. "Whiskey."

"Heard you the first time," the bartender said mildly. "And the second."

"Then put it down," Barley said, tapping the bar with his forefinger.

He emptied the shot glass with a single toss, then leaned heavily forward on his forearms, squeezing his eyes shut for a moment, remembering what—who—he had just seen, trying to fix it in mind with absolute clarity. *Can't be,* he told himself, the words silent on his moving lips but clearly auditory inside his head, as though there were another, more rational self in there trying to restore balance. It just couldn't be, it was impossible, *Yet I could have reached out and touched him.* He gazed at his work-hardened large-knuckled hand as if reassuring himself of its real and solid actuality, the hand that could have reached out and touched and not lied to him. He picked up the shot glass and cradled it against his palm, then closed his fingers tightly around it.

Gold fever was not an idle phrase, Barley thought. It was not an ailment to be found in medical histories, and people back East might speak of it jocularly. But it was real and it could be subversive. It began as clearly as hope, then misted off into dream, wherein it became susceptible to delusion and nightmare and hallucination—he had heard stories. It could become whimsical within the mind—anything based on hope was easy prey because it began so openly, innocently. Maybe he had been out there for too long now, maybe the hope was gone and he was simply toiling not because he any longer had it but because he remembered it. Too many times he had dug and panned laboriously because he believed something was there, only to prove that it wasn't. And now maybe he had begun to see things that were not there. Gold fever.

Jesus Christ, he thought dismally, they'll be sitting around the camps in the hills telling about the poor jackass who became so possessed by it he began seeing ghosts. He would become a cautionary tale. Sardonic chuckles from those who

were still living confidently with their own sanguine expecta-
tions, unaware of the subtly entwining tentacles, the mists
forming at the borders of their own minds. Somebody would
douse the fire with water and when the steam rose hissing
would say, There's his ghost now.

Barley looked up and recognized a friend who had just
entered.

"Patterson," he said, signaling the man to join him.

"Barley," Patterson said, coming over. "How long have
you been in town?"

"Never mind. I need to buy you a drink."

"Need to?"

"Yes," Barley said. "Need to. I've got something funny to
tell you."

TWO

It had been a slow and monotonously uneventful day for Captain Thomas Maynard, sitting at his desk at the War Department waiting for someone to come through the door with a word or some bit of business or even a breeze of gossip, and finally he would have settled for a rumor. But it was summer in Washington, D.C., a time of year that seemed to belie that majestic fact of history being a perpetual rolling forth. History, it appeared, possessed its own fine sense of tidal progress, knew when it was summer in Washington, D.C., when Congress was out of session, when the summer's heat seemed to have woven a mesh that forestalled or repelled that supposed inevitable and irresistible forward flow. Or so it felt to Maynard as he sat morosely inactive at his desk, listening to the occasional footstep pass along the corridor on the other side of the blank wooden door.

Behind him, the office of General Northwood, on whose staff Maynard served, was empty, the General having taken the day to go off riding with some high-ranked colleagues along the trails beside the Potomac. The army, in far cry from the massed blue legions of a few years ago, were today mere blue threads traversing the hills and plains of the Western territories in pursuit of roaming bands of Sioux and Cheyenne warriors.

Occasionally he received letters from a fellow officer campaigning out West with Sheridan's army filled with wryly expressed envy for Maynard and his "cushion" at the War Department, letters that told of long marches, dust storms, broiling heat, driving rain, stony ridges, knapsack rations, river crossings, and other satiric "amenities" of frontier service. These letters (he strove to imagine it) had been written by campfires under prairie skies inlaid with a million soft stars, or in a candlelit tent, or maybe even, as he himself had sometimes done, in the saddle during a tedious ride. Because of his own current stagnant immobility it was easy to envision and at odd moments even to envy, though from his own experience with Kiowas and Comanches on the Southern Plains he knew there was little to envy. The satisfaction derived was largely personal and intimate: you served, awake and asleep, and therefore you belonged. To Maynard, it was the belonging that mattered.

He left the War Department's grandly porticoed building at six o'clock and faced the torpor of an August evening in the nation's capital. He was wearing a dark blue single-breasted frock coat that hung to the bend of the knee, with a single row of nine highly polished buttons running from just under the stand-up collar to his oval belt buckle, and dark blue trousers. His blue forage cap, with its bugle emblem signifying its wearer as infantry, was worn slightly forward. Maynard had grown his bristly dark mustache after the war, feeling that it provided the needed serious maturity befitting a man who had survived what, in retrospect, seemed like four years of slaughterous nonstop battle (as well as affording him the dignity necessary as a member of a general's staff). He had enlisted as a teenager during the winter before Sumter, a runaway from his Adirondack Mountain village, grown up with shocking rapidity within the whirlwind of fire and blood, earned promotion after promotion and decided to stay on when the mayhem was done.

Dinner at his boardinghouse would only extend the routine, he thought now, walking under the scorched sky from which daylight seemed to have been burned out. He knew who would be at table. His fellow lodgers, for the most part government clerks and junior officers, were earnest and likeable, but the conversation and then later the post-dinner ramblings under cigar smoke on the back porch were thin and predictable, and this evening that wasn't good enough.

He headed away from the Federal buildings with their huge architectural sobrieties and intimations of eternity, and walked toward Willard's Hotel on 14th Street. The clipclops of the horse-drawn carriages and omnibuses sounded listless on the cobblestone streets, and around the gaslit corner lights clouds of insects up from the Potomac tidal flats spun and swarmed.

Willard's, with its six-story-high quadrangular mass of rooms, was normally a center of political dealing and scheming, but at this time of year was so quiet its chief preoccupation seemed to be virtuous reflection. The gaslit marble-floored oyster bar with its high ceiling and long mahogany bar appeared much larger for being nearly three-quarters empty. Maynard put one polished shoe up on the brass rail and ordered a whiskey and water, watching with patent uninterest as the bartender spooned a few chips of ice into the glass. After shutting his eyes softly to the first sip, he turned to study with the jaundiced eye of the veteran several young lieutenants with their fresh epaulets who were sitting with two attractive young ladies at a nearby table. The coy feminine laughter struck Maynard like a decisive confirmation of something he hadn't realized he'd been brooding about.

A half hour later, after a quick meal of bean soup and green salad, he was back outside, walking briskly now, his blue-sleeved arms swinging in cadence with what was almost a jaunty step. As always, Maynard carried his shoulders square, implying to the casual observer a pride of confidence, achievement, capability. But at the moment he was being motivated by none of these; this time it was something else: a purpose. It seemed that society in its wisdom had thus far been able to devise but two escapes from what was besetting him: either let the mood dissolve into intoxication or else seek the succor, at once soothing and explosive, of a compliant woman. He chose the latter.

Mrs. McCoy's House of Entertainment was located in a boxlike three-storied redbrick building on Vermont Avenue, where in the evening draperies slid across the windows like thick embroidered shadows and remained in place until morning, which by Mrs. McCoy's timekeeping was seldom much before noon.

A tall gray-haired woman of dignified bearing, Mrs. McCoy was amiable, well-spoken, and was said to have elevated discretion to an art form. She was also of no known antecedents, with even the "Mrs." and the "McCoy" themselves being of uncertain provenance. In return for the lush gratifications offered in her small, well-appointed, feather-bedded rooms she insisted on decorum; drunkenness and rowdyism were not tolerated, with the rules of the house overseen by a six-and-a-half-foot, 300-pound giant named Hughie, who sat in the downstairs parlor with a Bowie knife in his belt and a pair of feral black eyes in an otherwise stolid, short-bearded face.

Maynard mounted the three brick steps to the front door, turned the brass knob, and entered, removing his forage cap as he closed the door behind him. Like the rest of the house, the entrance foyer was thickly carpeted, the maroon velvet–covered walls decorated with large framed paintings of an embryonic turn-of-the-century Washington, D.C.

Maynard found Mrs. McCoy and several of her elaborately gowned and coiffed young ladies gathered in a knot at the foot of a staircase whose carpeted stairs seemed to roll down like a pleated waterfall. The women were staring with evident anxiety up toward the second floor. Following their gaze, Maynard could see nothing up there.

"Ah, Captain Maynard," Mrs. McCoy said, turning to him, her ringed hands clasped under her small, firmly set bosom.

"Is there a problem, Mrs. McCoy?" he asked.

"I believe there is," she said. "Yes, I believe there is."

"Isn't your Goliath attending to it?" Maynard asked, referring to Hughie.

"That man," Mrs McCoy said, more with dismay than annoyance. "He stepped out some time ago and hasn't returned."

"And you wish he were here now?"

"He's a settling presence," Mrs. McCoy said of the giant with his Bowie knife and murderous eyes.

As if to punctuate her remark, a brief, sharp yip of pain flew out from upstairs, almost like a physical passage of flight. Maynard found all of the women staring at him.

"Is someone in distress up there?" he asked.

"Frankly," Mrs. McCoy said, "we don't know what to do. There've been intermittent cries over the past ten or so minutes. We don't like to enter a client's room when he is in the act of business, but . . ."

"Well, you make the rules here, Mrs. McCoy," Maynard said, "which means you're entitled to break them as well."

The madam's soft pink mouth compressed for a moment.

"Or," Maynard said, "you can authorize someone to do it for you."

She expelled a despairing breath. "Captain," she said, "you are so authorized. But for God's sakes . . ."

"I know," Maynard said, trying to contain a mischievous smile. "Discretion." He handed his hat to her.

"It's the third door along the corridor, to your left," Mrs. McCoy said, watching Maynard begin mounting the stairs. He rode his hand up along the fur-covered banister, inhaling a perfumed aroma that grew stronger when he reached the landing, where he turned and then completed the ascent. When he arrived at the second-floor corridor he heard another cry of pain, again brief, sharp, almost like a shrill bark.

At the third door on the left he paused, aware that this was going to be no casual intrusion, that either way, if Mrs. McCoy was correct about something untoward going on, or not, he was going to be the man in the doorway, with either an embarrassed apology or—he didn't know.

When he opened the door—at first by several inches and

then until there was clearance enough to see within—he had
a whiff of warm air thickened by stale perfume and then saw
the disheveled bed with its covers driven back to the foot and
bunched like collapsed ramparts, and then the white soles of
two bare feet tensely upright.

"Don't." That was the woman's voice, terse but within it a
strain of painful expectation.

The man was straddling her, leaning forward as if confid-
ing something, his backside spread wide in the tight knee-
length long johns he was wearing. His broad, bare torso
seemed headless as he bent his face close to the woman's.

Maynard moved the door aside and stepped into the room.
He cleared his throat. The head appeared, snapping up into
view, and then the face, wheeling around, filled with querulous indignation, made the more vivid by the wide waxed
gray mustache that seemed to slice it in halves.

"What in God's name?" the man demanded. "Who the
hell are you?"

Now Maynard saw the small dagger in the man's right
hand, the bone handle tightly gripped.

"What are you doing?" Maynard asked.

"Doing?" the man, now fully pivoted around, asked. "I'll
give you a taste of it if you don't back off."

Moving closer, Maynard saw the woman's distressed face
glaring up from the pillow, in the lamplight shining with per-
spiration, her brown hair swirled around her head and in a
few scattered strands across her face. Several small, fresh-
blooded cuts were gleaming on her shoulder.

"For God's sakes, man," Maynard said.

With his free hand the man struck angrily at the bed and as
if the blow had released the mechanism of a catapult he suddenly bounded from the bed to the floor, his limber, barely clad,
narrow-chested figure poised maniacally as he raised the dagger, his eyes fixed upon Maynard with lurid intensity. Behind
him on the bed the woman moved fingertips tentatively to her
wounds, slowly turning her naked body on its side.

"You had better put that down," Maynard said, taking short steps to his right in order to lengthen the dagger's sweep, if it should come. And come it did, aimed toward his left shoulder, missing Maynard's sidestepping body completely and throwing the man into an off-balancing spin, long enough for Maynard to seize him by the wrist and whirl him in a semicircle and then release him to crash into a chair. As he fell, his grip on the dagger loosened and Maynard gave it a quick sideways kick that sent it under the bed.

The man rose and, hunching his shoulders, charged at Maynard. *Damn him,* Maynard thought, taking a backward step as he rolled shut his fists and drove his right hand flush into the maddened face, the force of the blow knocking the man aside, where he staggered drunkenly as his eyes swam, and then he dropped to the floor, falling amid the litter of clothing that had gone over with the chair. It was then that Maynard became aware of the blue uniform, and more: the silver eagle insignia on the frock coat's shoulder straps.

Jesus, he thought. *I've leveled a colonel.*

THREE

The general had the window shade in his office drawn against the morning heat, which didn't seem so much to have returned as never faded, as if it had remained unstirred and unspent within the night and simply been not restored but unveiled with daylight. Given entrance through one side of the shade, the sun was running an antic stripe across the desk and its papers and blotter and pens and inkwell and ashtray and then continuing on across the thinly carpeted floor so that it looked like a ribbon stretched out for use in wrapping the desk.

A grandfather clock measured time's passage from the corner, sounding staunchly loyal, almost like a human retainer. A framed photograph of President Grant and what seemed his single, unrevealing facial expression hung on the wall behind General Northwood, whose large, nearly hairless head was bent as he studied a written report on his desk, a cold, half-smoked cigar between the fingers of one hand. Then he looked up, removing his spectacles as he did and placing them on the desk so that they were like another pair of eyes studying Maynard, who was sitting on a straight-backed chair set a few feet in front of the desk. (That he had been asked to have a seat suggested to him that this might not be as bad for him as he feared, as it could be.) The general had come in at nine o'clock, given Maynard a glance of no perceivable expression, and said, "I'll see you in thirty minutes, Captain." It was almost always "Tom," so Maynard had a fairly good idea of what might be on the general's mind.

"Had you ever met Colonel Zachariah before last night?"
the general asked.

"Was that his name, sir?" Maynard asked.

"Frederic Zachariah. No 'k' at the end of Frederic. I
assume someone else knocked that off of him. But a colonel
of the United States Army, in which you serve. As a captain."

For how much longer? Maynard wondered as in a repen-
tant's voice he said, "Yes, sir."

"I'm sorry this happened, Tom, and I'm sorry I had to hear
about it, but it was inevitable I would. You know how these
things carry. There's more privacy in a Sibley tent than there
is in this city. A secret has as much chance in this city as a vir-
gin does among the Hottentots. If you want to be sure something has the widest possible dissemination all you have to do
is mark it secret. Everybody around here feels he can keep a
secret; it's the fellow he spills it to is the one who's not reliable. And the lascivious will travel faster and more greedily
than even a declaration of war. And when a captain sees fit to
bash a colonel—in a house of ill repute no less—then the
information sprouts wings."

"There were circumstances, sir," Maynard said guardedly.

"I'm sure there were, Tom, because I know you well
enough. I've heard four versions already and in one of them
you were said to be acting chivalrously."

"The man was cutting the woman with the point of a dagger."

"In the midst of . . ."

"Well, at the beginning of the midst of . . ."

"I understand," the general said, waving off further detail.

"General, he might have murdered her."

"Colonel Zachariah wouldn't have gone that far."

"You know him, sir?"

"I know him," Northwood muttered. "Well enough. An
eccentric man. A teetotaler no less, so he doesn't have that
excuse."

"No, sir."

"In the version favorable to you, it's said you acted valiantly."

"Yes, sir."

"But unfortunately that version comes from the lady of the house, and Mrs. McCoy's testimony is not going to carry much official weight, even though she could probably fry half of eminent Washington if she chose. Colonel Zachariah's version is that you attacked him in a drunken rage, without reason. And of course he's doubly provoked, in that not only was he knocked cold by a junior officer but that it happened in a bordello with a naked prostitute in attendance. Think of what that's done to the blood pressure of a churchgoing family man."

"That'll take some explaining, sir."

"Well," Northwood said sourly, "a man doesn't attain the rank of colonel in the United States Army without having imaginative resources. I'm sure he'll think of something to bank the home fires. But that's his problem; it's your problem that I'm concerned with. You're a member of my staff."

"I regret causing you this trouble, sir."

"I'm sure you thought you were acting properly, Tom."

"Yes, sir."

"You weren't drunk, were you?"

"No, sir. The only reason I went there in the first place . . ."

"For Jesus' sakes, Tom, I know why you were there. Do I look like a choirboy?"

Maynard studied the rough but not unkind face in front of him, the eyes bright with indignation as they stared out over the drooping mustache that hung down in a shaggy crescent.

"No, sir," he murmured.

The general glanced at the stump of dead cigar between his fingers and then tossed it into the round brass ashtray. He got up and went to the window and raised the shade, flooding the room with a glow of rich molten sunlight. Then he raised the window as far as it would go.

"Won't make a damned bit of difference," he said, gazing out. The view was the Navy Department straight ahead and, at an angle, Lafayette Park and beyond that the executive mansion. "Damned heat sticks to everything like paste." He returned to his desk and resumed his seat.

Maynard watched him, waiting. Normally under these circumstances the junior officer would have been standing there in complete circumspection, with little if any eye contact with his superior; but not here, not with these two. The six-year bond between the two men was close and mutually respectful, ever since Maynard, little more than a boy at the time, had hauled the wounded then-Colonel Northwood onto his back and carried him to safety through the blazing battle-chaotic thickets of the Wilderness. The colonel had then spent months tracking down his anonymous savior, raised him in rank, and added to his staff the young man who was not only tough and courageous but also proved to be bright and resourceful.

"Dammit, Tom," the general said, "you can't go around bashing colonels. Not even one who's a horse's ass. Generals don't have that privilege, so why should captains?"

"The man should have been arrested, General."

"Never mind what should have happened; we have to deal with what did. And the matter isn't helped any by the close associations he happens to have."

"Sir?"

"Colonel Zachariah, it seems, has a web of associations and relationships that has spun itself through the halls of Congress and other various corridors of government." The general sighed. "I hate when that happens," he said. "It gives a man a wholly unearned and undeserved influence on things. A mule can be turned into a thoroughbred just because he's able to bend somebody's ear or get a signature scratched onto a piece of paper. This particular mule happens to have kinfolk in Congress. It's probably how the fool got eagles to begin with," Northwood added in what sounded like an aside.

"You'd think the man would want to keep a thing like this quiet."

"I'm sure that would be his preference; but I told you, Tom, it's all over town now. As we used to say back home, he's got his pecker caught in the stirrups of a runaway horse."

"Painful, sir," Maynard said, suppressing a smile.

"So I would imagine. His only way out is to make trouble for you."

"Yes, sir."

"Which he will try to do."

"Yes, sir."

"But he's not going to be allowed to, if I have anything to say about it. If a man wants to indulge in sadistic perversions, that's his business; but the unjust harassment of one of my officers is another matter. All right," the general said, laying his hands flat on the desk for a moment. "We'll move all that to the side for the time being; there's something else that has to be taken under consideration, a matter that only recently has come to my attention."

General Northwood leaned back in his chair and looked toward the window. The sun, with its wall of heat that felt almost touchable, drew keen glints of light from the buttons of his blue tunic.

"Something very peculiar has come up, Tom," he said, turning back to Maynard. "Very peculiar indeed, and it's been disturbing me. I've conferred with some colleagues about it and, frankly, we are of many humors on the subject: we are puzzled, we are perturbed, and we are more than curious—we are intrigued. We've talked it through and through, formally and informally, we've opined and speculated, to the point where we've decided we want an answer. It seems," the general said ruefully, "you can just plain talk yourself out onto that particular branch of the tree. But it does legitimately fall under our aegis and should be investigated. You'd be a good man to undertake it, and under current circumstances, I think the ideal man."

"The undertaking, sir, I take it, would carry me beyond the city limits?"

"That's a very correct assessment, Captain Maynard," Northwood said, gazing across the desk with an expression so impassive it bordered on collusion. "Beyond these city limits. The situation concerns a certain Andrew Pryor, formerly a major in the Army of the Potomac, and by his record a damned good officer. Served with distinction in many of the purgatories that army was subject to. He was a West Point graduate, class of fifty-two. When the war broke out he helped raise a New Hampshire regiment and, as I say, saw a lot of holy hell. He seems to have been a by-the-book stickler, but his men followed him, and I mean followed, because he was always the man in front. But then in the spring of eighteen sixty-four he was killed, while riding his own reconnaissance in Virginia. I emphasize the fact: his *own* reconnaissance. Alone."

"He sounds like a bold officer," Maynard said.

"Maybe. Or maybe not. But anyway, he was off in a wooded area when he was bushwhacked and brought down. Shot in the face, according to the records: another fact I emphasize for your benefit. His men found him and buried him nearby, after cleaning his pockets of personal belongings and sending them on to his family in New Hampshire."

Maynard said nothing, did not even nod his head, merely sat and listened, because so far he had not a scintilla of understanding as to why he was being told this story of a Union officer dead these six years, though his mind had taken hold of those two facts verbally underlined by the general, that Major Pryor had chosen to reconnoiter alone and that he had been shot in the face.

"So," General Northwood said, "*sic transit* Major Andrew Pryor of the Army of the Potomac, quiet hero and leader of men, one of six hundred thousand killed, who matter in the great scheme only when you count them one at a time." Maynard had heard this lamentation from his superior before.

"But," the general said, raising one finger for a moment like a man testing the wind, "was it really *sic transit?* Maybe not.

A letter has come in stating that Major Pryor has recently been seen alive and well and walking on top of the ground on his own two feet just like anyone else. What do you make of that, Captain Maynard?"

"I would first question the witness of this, sir: his sobriety, his veracity, the basis of his claim. How well did he know the major, did he speak to him, was it night or day?"

"Fair questions. According to the information we have, the man was sober, of decent repute, he did not speak to the major—under whom he had served during the war—and there was daylight enough."

"Then could he have simply been mistaken?"

"He could have. But what was conveyed in the letter made him sound quite positive of what he'd seen. Believe me, I'm not sending you out to the Montana Territory because some damned gold-fevered miner might have seen somebody who reminded him of somebody. If that's all it was I'd see to it that your friend Colonel Zachariah was dispatched. But, dammit, Tom, we're talking about a commissioned officer who, if this report is correct, deserted in time of war."

"You did say the Montana Territory, didn't you, sir?"

"You know damned well what I said."

"Yes, sir."

"The man who claims he saw Major Pryor was a former sergeant of Pryor's regiment named Barley Newton. Moments after the sighting—on the streets of a mining town called Baddock, in the aforementioned territory—Newton, genuinely shaken, went into a saloon and had a shot of whiskey in the company of a man named Simon Patterson, to whom he confided what he had just seen. Patterson is the man who wrote to me. I knew the fellow, you see. He's a good man. Trustworthy. During the war he was a correspondent with the *New York Herald* and he followed us around quite a bit. Apparently he's switched from digging for news to digging for gold, which in my opinion is a far more respectable occupation. Patterson says there was no doubt in Newton's mind about whom he'd seen. Patterson says Newton seemed badly shaken, and not just by what he'd seen but because he felt he himself had been recognized."

"But no words had been exchanged?"

"Between Pryor and Newton? No. I guess Newton was so struck cold by seeing someone risen from the dead that he had no words of greeting. In fact, I'm not sure if those words have been written yet. So he did the most sensible thing— what you or I would have done—he went into the nearest saloon and burned his tonsils a bit."

"But, sir, you're still relying on what Newton saw."

"What you're saying, Tom, is the Montana Territory is very far away," General Northwood said with a mild smile.

"Not at all, sir," Maynard said, he hoped with conviction.

"Look, Tom, if this fellow is alive, then he was a deserter. I restate: this man was a commissioned officer. West Point. There are some things we don't take lightly. I want you to go out there and touch up with Patterson, who'll introduce you to Newton, and then you can take it from there. If it turns out the man was mistaken, then so be it. At least we'll know."

"And if it is Major Pryor?"

"You'll turn him over to the nearest military garrison, which is at a place called Bear Creek, which is about thirty miles from Baddock. It's a small outpost."

"I know of it, sir. Shall I report to them?"

"No, not until or unless you have something to report. I don't want anyone to know who you are or why you're out there, except Patterson, of course. And stop frowning, Captain. While you're enjoying the amenities of the Montana Territory I'll be back here dealing with the wrath of Colonel Zachariah."

FOUR

There was a man who might be of some assistance, General Northwood told Maynard, and he worked in that very building.

Samuel Mark occupied a tiny first-floor office toward the rear of the building. The high-ceilinged room looked as though it was constructed of paper; the desk was awash with it and the high-rising wall shelves filled with it, most of it tied into thick packets with pieces of blue string.

"Statistics," Mark said. "That's the job here. Collecting them, writing them down in neat columns, and putting them away, against the unlikely event someone will want to look at them someday. I always had a head for numbers and this is where it landed me." He seemed cheerful enough about it.

"It would set me to sleep," Maynard said, sitting in the narrow wooden folding chair in front of Samuel Mark's paper-ridden desk.

Mark, apparently a resolutely genial man, laughed. His thin, open face was run on either side by thick reddish muttonchops, which on a different, less pleasant face might have been too solemnly decorative but which here only added to the man's lighthearted amiability.

"The government likes to have a number alongside things," he said. "It's like an official stamp proving that something truly exists. There's a certain sanctity to numbers."

"Whether they're right or wrong," Maynard said.

Mark shrugged. "That almost seems not to matter. The secret of getting along in this job, my particular job, is not to question any of the numbers. That's up to someone else, if they see fit. I just make my notations in a clear hand and pass the stuff along. But anyway, that's not what you've come in to talk to me about. General Northwood sent down a note instructing me to help you in any way I can."

"What I want to talk to you about has nothing to do with numbers."

"Then it'll be refreshing," Mark said with a laugh. "And in that case why don't we find a bench and sit outside. It'll be at least one degree cooler."

As Maynard rose, Mark leaned over and picked up a curve-handled wooden cane from the floor and used it as he walked with a slow, severe limp.

The limp, he informed Maynard as they walked outside into the hot, steady sunlight, was the consequence of a Confederate bullet that had shattered his leg during a brief skirmish in northern Virginia in 1863. The wound ended his war and when he came out of the hospital he found himself assigned to the War Department, where he had been ever since, now as a civilian employee.

"I'd appreciate it," Maynard said, "if you'd indulge me while I ask you some questions and indulge me still further by not asking any yourself."

"Ah," Mark said with a conspirator's smile, "a confidential matter. I understand."

They were sitting on a bench in elm shade in the small parklike area behind the building. The bench was narrow, backless, and Samuel Mark sat straight up, hands resting on the handle of his upright cane as old men in the front row of group photographs often posed.

"During the war," Maynard said, "you served with a New Hampshire regiment."

"That's correct. An all-volunteer group."

"And you served under Major Andrew Pryor."

"Ah yes, Major Pryor. For two years. A very fine officer. Why do you mention Major Pryor? Am I permitted to ask that?"

"Oh, Mr. Mark, you can ask anything you please," Maynard said.

"And you can choose to answer or not, eh?" Mark said with a smile. "I have an inquisitive nature, Captain. Fountains of curiosity, I'm afraid. But I'll do my best to stem the flow."

"I want you to tell me about Major Pryor. All that you can remember."

For several moments Maynard could fairly hear that curiosity coming to foam as Mark sat in pondering silence, no doubt puzzled.

"He's dead, you know," Mark said finally.

"Tell me about that."

"It occurred, as I recall, about a year after I left the regiment. I heard about it in a letter from a former tentmate, himself later killed at Cold Harbor, poor fellow. The major had been scouting some countryside when he was shot."

"Riding alone."

"That's correct. I remember that letter very well. I remember them all, as a matter of fact. They never seemed to write unless they had some bad news to tell. Or share."

"Was it unusual for Major Pryor to ride out alone like that?"

"Ah, Captain, after several years of war, what remains usual and what becomes no longer so? And who soon notices the difference? Major Pryor was certainly a brave man, at times a heroic one, but never one who seemed convinced of his own immortality."

"You mean he wasn't foolhardy?"

"You were in it, Captain Maynard. Did you know a foolhardy man who lasted long enough for his coffee to cool?"

"Tell me about him."

"In what regard?"

"Any regard. The view from the ranks, which I understand is where you were."

"I'd made corporal two months before my misfortune."

"Look, just to ease a bit of your curiosity before it hits high tide, we learned that you'd served with Major Pryor and here you were, sitting in our laps, in a manner of speaking."

"I'm probably the only member of the old regiment living in Washington. As a matter of fact, there probably aren't too many who knew Major Pryor well living at all. Whole ranks were wiped clean at Cold Harbor. One of the old fellows wrote and said, 'Never curse your wound, Sam; it kept you out of Cold Harbor.' God, it must have been hell, if I'm to be grateful for an unbalanced stride." Mark glanced at Maynard and smiled uneasily.

"Major Pryor was dead by then, wasn't he?"

"Yes, killed before the whole Wilderness campaign started."

"What kind of officer was he?"

"Strict," Mark said, "but fair. I think he felt he deserved to be brevetted up—he was West Point, as you no doubt know—but that elevation never came. He was something of a disciplinarian, but not beyond the point of reason. He'd send you up for court-martial though, if he thought it warranted. He was particularly hard on looters. Oh, I don't mean if you lifted somebody's pig or chicken; but if you invaded someone's home and made off with their treasures, he could be very hard about it. You might find yourself wearing the ball and chain in the guardhouse, or standing on a barrel all day wearing a placard announcing your dereliction, or forfeiting pay, or whatever else."

"I take it he was hard on deserters."

"He had them shot. With great ceremony."

"Was he a spiritual man?"

"Not any more or less than the rest of us, though I would wager that promotion was high up on his menu of prayer. Not to speak disrespectfully, you understand."

"I understand."

"I suspect every officer has at one time or another believed that promotion was good for the soul."

"Do you, Mr. Mark?"

"I take it you're not West Point, Captain?" Mark asked, looking at Maynard for a moment.

"No."

"Up from the ranks? Nicely done, Captain. Severely earned, I'm sure."

"So you may be."

Mark held his cane straight out for a moment, as if aiming at something, then turned it in several lazy circles before replacing it in its upright position and settling his hands once again upon the handle.

"Was Major Pryor a tippler?" Maynard asked.

"Not to my knowledge. All this talk about a dead man," Mark said with a shake of his head. "I don't understand it. Is he up for canonization or something? Pardon me for asking."

"Was he married?"

"I believe not."

"Did you have much conversation with him?"

"I can't recall ever having any."

"Can you give me a physical description of him?"

Mark pondered the question, tapping with the cane for a moment, as if it might aid his thought.

"Nothing beyond the ordinary," he said. "An average-looking man. Not unduly tall or short. A bit of character in his face—as befitting an officer in time of war," Mark said, turning to Maynard with a pleasant, momentary smile—"but nothing there that you would remember forever. Large beard."

"He was bearded?"

"Luxuriantly. Dark hair."

"Had he ever been wounded?"

"Not to my knowledge, no."

"Any unusual quirks of manner?"

"Only those common to most officers. I mean West Pointers, of course."

"Such as?"

"The usual military bearing. Very crisp and precise. I often wondered whether they actually thought that way or it was how they wished to be seen."

"I wouldn't know."

"I didn't mean to be critical," Mark said.

"Is there anything else about him you can bring to mind? If he was walking along that path there right now, fifty feet from us, in civilian clothes, would you know him today?"

Mark squinted out at an imaginary Major Pryor, then said, "I couldn't rightly say, Captain."

"Then there was nothing truly distinctive about him?"

"I don't recall anything, which is not to say there wasn't, but certainly nothing out of the ordinary. Except when he went into battle, of course."

"And then?"

"He'd become galvanized; the life would seem to pour into him."

"You think he relished it?"

"Not in any particular sense," Mark said. "I think he felt that as an officer it was expected of him."

"A man who took his responsibilities very seriously."

"On all occasions; but most particularly when we were going in."

"Well then, Mr. Mark," Maynard said, "I thank you for your time."

"You're a cruel man, Captain."

"How so?"

"To ask me this battery of questions and never tell me why. What can an honest soldier have done to merit such interest six years after his death?"

"What indeed," Maynard said.

FIVE

How do you look for a shadow in a dark room?

Never mind, Maynard thought; he supposed he ought to consider himself fortunate to be getting out of Washington, and not just because of a summer heat that seemed permanent and indissoluble, but also because of whatever consequences might derive from his encounter with Colonel Zachariah.

The whole matter of Major Andrew Pryor he found annoyingly mystifying for its lack of sense and clarity. The only way a man could die and be resurrected was not to have died in the first place, and if that was the case, then what logic could there be for it? A major in the Army of the Potomac (and West Point, no less), by all accounts a sound and capable officer with a good performance record, did not just light out—the word was *desert*—in the middle of a war and years later reappear in the Montana Territory. And what about the fact that it had been his own men who planted him in Virginia? Didn't men who had marched with Andrew Pryor for years know who he was?

Maynard thought: I could be looking for a man who has been dead for six years, who was buried by those who knew him best. I'll be looking for a man who, by Samuel Mark's account, was average and ordinary in every seeming apparent way, whose most distinguishing feature was a large beard, which, if he was indeed Andrew Pryor trying to conceal his identity, had long since been shaved away.

General Northwood himself was not unmindful of the

improbabilities inherent—it was improbable that Andrew Pryor was alive and it was just as improbable that he would be found if he was. Nevertheless, the general said, the matter could not be ignored; the army simply could not accept the possibility of an officially dead former officer (who had been splendidly eulogized and buried with honors, the general pointed out) floating about in the Montana Territory. The matter must be investigated. And, Maynard asked with what he hoped was discretion, for how long ought the investigation go on (the implication being that this was going to be a long launch into futility)? And was told: Until your best judgment tells you to terminate it.

There had been, Maynard recalled, going back to his boyhood years, an itinerant preacher who had followed a circuit of the small Adirondack villages, who would appear suddenly and unannounced in Maple Creek, sitting upon a creaky nailed-together wagon that was drawn by an ancient brown horse of such doleful lack of spirit it amounted to dignity. The preacher would park in the center of town, remove a small platform from the wagonbed, and step up onto it and begin his sermon in a low rasping voice that sounded like it was coming through sandpaper, talking to no one at first but gradually drawing an audience that came and stood more in curiosity than piety. Tom, not yet a teenager, would be among them, listening only fitfully, intrigued more by the white-bearded old man and his flat-crowned black hat and sad frock coat than by the words, although one thing he did hear and remember: *For everything there is a reason.* This the boy believed because in Maple Creek, where things happened simply and directly and which was the only place he had ever known, it seemed so. But then, later, four years of war altered his belief in what in an isolated mountain village had been indisputable. In war too many things seemed to happen for no reason at all—and no ordinary things either—unless you thought of luck or chance being a reason.

In the years since the war his consideration of the old ser-

mon and its most memorable line of text had reverted somewhat. In peacetime most events were traceable down to their
roots (or maybe it was only because you had had returned the
tranquillity of mind to think so). So as he made his long and
tedious journey by rail across the continent he thought again
of the old message, which through its simplicity had been
made indelible on a mind young and open and thus far free of
doubt, though in its untutored capacity to believe still too
ingenuous to realize that there were bad reasons as well as
good, which the preacher had left for him to work out for
himself. If there was a reason for everything, then about his
journey he came to this conclusion: Barley Newton, sincere
enough no doubt, had been mistaken. So, Maynard thought,
I'm going out there to prove that someone who wasn't there
in the first place doesn't exist.

Farms, meadows, prairie, rivers, mountains, the full American topographical variety, ran past his window, sometimes
with a monotony so changeless it acquired a kind of
grandeur; a world still at primal mold, so much of it still so
wild, beautiful, and unvisited as to evoke not so much the
awe and wonder of the living as to ratify the bold dreams of
the anciently dead.

As per instruction from General Northwood, he was going
as plain Tom Maynard, uniform and captaincy left behind.
The general's friend and correspondent in Baddock, Simon
Patterson, for whom Maynard carried a letter of introduction
from the general, alone would know his full identity and purpose. Patterson, Maynard had been assured, was a man of
character and trustworthy.

Appropriately for a man detached on private inquiry for
his government, he sought privacy during the long train ride.
He had with him for companionship a slim volume of Emerson's essays, which he read slowly and carefully, phrasing certain sentences from the elegant flow over and over in his
mind and sometimes silently with his lips as he sought not
just to get under the ideas but also to connect them with

things already in his knowledge and fuse it all into greater understanding. So deeply would he become transfixed by Emerson's New England transcendentalism that he would look up and be startled by the sight of buffalo herds or grasslands in flow to the horizon, jarred by the juxtaposition of nature's pure majesty and the mind's intuitive spirituality.

Men gathered in the parlor car at night to smoke cigars and indulge in the garrulousness of strangers meeting strangers far from home. He sat back and listened, the onetime teenage runaway and current professional soldier, with no true home to be far from, with no need to comfort himself with talk. Army barracks, wartime encampments, and a Washington, D.C., boardinghouse provided a history without nostalgia.

Sometimes the surrounding talk found its way into the war, with former soldiers hoisting the sails of their experience. He listened intently, and with private amusement thought that none of them had it just right, that no man's war could geminate with his. He fell asleep on that thought one night: only Thomas Maynard had seen and fought the true war.

SIX

The tedium of rail journey with its manifold inconveniences soon seemed like regal luxury to Maynard when he began the final leg of his way to Baddock by stagecoach. He doubted if there had ever been, or would again be, a mode of transport as incessantly variable as this. From roads smooth-worn and flat to others gouged and stony and wheel-rutted, to mere trails climbing at increasingly severe angles up into hills and mountains, splashing across streams and skirting forests, rolling along canyon rims where an errant foreleg might take them over the side, enduring rain and high wind, and at night as the two teams of horses ran on under a sky prodigiously crowded with stars the weird feeling that you and your few companions were the lone reasoning creatures for thousands of miles around.

When it had first appeared among these pristine immensities, the Concord stagecoach (so known for its New Hampshire origins) was an unlikely intruder into a wilderness still intact in its Day-of-Creation integrity. With its expertly carved contours and its paneled doors with their hand-painted floral designs, it had come from the workshops of New England artisans if not to tame then at least to integrate, a bounding horse-drawn trumpet of a strong young nation in massive expansion.

Sitting in the upholstered interior with a half dozen other men—the passengers came and went, boarding or getting off at any time of day or night at isolated stations or at nondescript hotels amid clusters of buildings that called themselves towns—Maynard sat at one corner of the padded bench seat, arms folded, legs crossed. The canvas curtain was pushed aside and he was watching it all pass, trees, boulders, sudden fields of grass, occasional ranches, cabins. He had found it unexpectedly easy to sleep, particularly when the way was reasonably smooth. The coach's thoroughbraces—the thick steer-hided straps that suspended it from below—allowed the oval-shaped vehicle to sway to a lulling effect. A half dozen or more passengers—capacity was nine—helped provide the stabilizing weight, giving the balanced coach its easy, elastic side-to-side oscillation. The driver's seat, where Maynard sometimes climbed and sat when the conversation or the cigar smoke inside became too bothersome, protruded in the front and the baggage boot extended from the rear like a lady's bustle, carrying its load of mailbags, express boxes, and personal baggage.

"You'll want to think again about sitting up front in a day or two," the driver said to him. This was during the second day of the five-day journey from Salt Lake City on the coaches of the Territorial Stage Line. They were at the moment following a long, gentle upgrade through foothills, where the wheel-rutted road looked as though it had been pressed through the surrounding rocks and scrub pine.

"Why is that?" Maynard asked.

"Road agents," the driver said. He was wearing a stovepipe hat and a linen duster that came halfway to his calfskin boots. His fingers seemed to be communicating through the reins to the four blinkered mustangs trotting at moderate speed, maintaining the ordained five-miles-per-hour pace. Next to him on the seat lay a tassel-handled whip with which he could slice the air above the horses' ears with snapping reports when more speed was desired.

"Do they operate heavily?" Maynard asked.

"It seems so," the driver said, "when you're stopped. And there's all sorts of them. Some are polite, some are very twitchy, and some are outright murderers. That's why I'm obliged to warn you about sitting up here. You might be taken as a shotgun escort and be picked right off. It's happened."

"To you?"

"To others. Are you armed?"

"I have a pistol," Maynard said.

"I'd wear it," the driver said, glancing across at him. "In fact, when we hit the station tomorrow morning all unarmed passengers will be offered weapons. The stationmaster hangs them in the slings inside the coach."

"I wondered about those slings."

"You got to be ready, in case those bastards come out shooting, which they'll sometimes do. A man's got to defend himself."

"It's that bad then?"

"The closer you get to Baddock, the worse it gets. I don't go up that far myself, but everybody knows the situation. A gold strike, a mining town, diggings scattered all over the hills, stages sometimes carrying bullion—it'll always draw the scum of the earth out into the sunshine. No offense, mister."

"Then there's not much law up there, I take it."

"Law is as law can do," the driver said, "and there's not much it can do about those who are skulking around in hills and canyons. So the company does what it can. Juggles the schedules about now and then. And sometimes they'll put an armed man up next to the driver."

"Does that help?"

"Depends on who's coming out of the bushes. They see an armed escort sitting up here they figure the vehicle is carrying some real value, and they might get an appetite to start shooting. They'll be shooting at the escort, but, Jesus, I'm sitting next to him, ain't I?" The driver sighed as he jostled the reins about the lead team, which responded with an extra leg of speed. "It's a nice sweet job," he said wistfully, "but there's always some worrying, isn't there?"

On the evening of the fourth day out of Salt Lake City, Maynard was sitting in the coach with only one other passenger, a young Philadelphian named Edson, who had boarded that morning at one of the stations. A stomach ailment had taken him out of the journey for several days, he told Maynard, or else he would have been in Baddock by now.

"Those stations hardly provide high-class accommodations, do they?" Edson asked.

"I wouldn't know," Maynard said, a smoking cigar tucked between his teeth. His dark brown Stetson was pushed back on his head. He was wearing a buckskin jacket over a flannel shirt, his trousers tucked into his boots, sitting with his legs crossed, the foot of his crossing leg rocking with the coach's motion. He was wearing his gun belt now, the holster's tapered bottom edge peeping out from under the flap of his jacket. "I haven't stopped over at any of them," he said. "I've been traveling straight on through."

"Well," Edson said, "you haven't missed much, believe me. All those cots laid out in a single room—and you don't have to bring your own lice, either, I can tell you. Men, women, and children, all under the same roof, and too bad if you're overladen with modesty. But then I reminded myself that this was untamed country, and I said to myself, 'This is where you wanted to come, boy, and this is now where you are.' "

He laughed. He didn't appear older than twenty-five. Everything about him seemed too new and fresh, from his broad reddish mustache to his Western clothing that still looked to retain some of its on-the-shelf creases.

"I thought about it and thought about it," he said, looking out the window at the passing terrain, a bright, ingenuous look in his eye. "Gold in the ground, just waiting there to be taken out—by me. I imagined it. I imagined digging or panning for it, and finding it, of course. You always find it when you're dreaming, don't you? That's what starts the push, doesn't it—the dream? I suppose if our dreams were honest with us we'd never get anything started and less done. The richest veins of misinformation come right from our own heads, right?" Edson said with a light, self-disparaging laugh.

"Anyway, it got to the point where the obsession began to ventriloquize through my lips to such extent that my friends would cross the street when they saw me coming. So there was only one thing for it."

"And here you are," Maynard said.

"Six months, I told my fiancée, or a year at most, depending on the thick or thin of my luck. I don't want to be the fellow who quits one day too soon."

"That can be a deadly idea; if you keep at it to its final conclusion, it can mean you never leave."

Edson laughed good-naturedly, the reddish mustache expanding over the open, friendly smile.

"I take your point," he said. "But no, it's my own obsession; I grew it and I'll shrink it back when the time comes. But I'll tell you what I told my little lady before I left—when I return home I'll be either rich or disenchanted, and no matter which, a better man for it."

After sitting silently for a while, Edson went on.

"The way I look at it," he said, "I missed the war, and now this may well be the last great adventure of my time. I'm tired of sitting back and listening to other men's tales. Are you heading for the diggings?"

"No," Maynard said.

"But you're going to Baddock?"

Maynard nodded.

Edson laughed self-consciously. "I was told by someone back home, who claimed some knowledge of the matter, that it was poor form to ask questions of strangers out here."

"I think you received some very sound advice there."

The two men sat silently for a time inside the swaying coach, Maynard amused by the curiosity that remained vivid in Edson's face as the latter watched out the window, seemingly mesmerized by every tree and stone and patch of ground.

The coach began slowing. Maynard glanced at his watch; it was well before arrival at the next station. Though they were winding through foothills the trail here was fairly level, running along the edge of a fall-off of hostile ensnaring growth and boulders, dropping a hundred feet or so to the sharp outcroppings of lava beds. On the other side of the trail trees grew thickly, some of them swung at angles, arrested in death fall by their neighbors.

"Driver's probably got to answer to nature," an unconcerned Edson said.

"Maybe," Maynard said. He unbuttoned his jacket, pushing the open flaps back across his holster. "Are you armed?"

"Armed?" Edson asked with a puzzled smile.

"Yes or no?" Maynard asked, sitting forward now, looking through the window as the coach continued to slow, until the wheels were barely turning.

"I've never held a gun in my hand in my life."

"Then you'd better take one out of those slings."

"Listen, I wouldn't know which end to point."

"All right," Maynard said, "then you'd better not."

"Listen, what's going on?"

Maynard rose and pushed the door partially open.

"What is it?" he called up to the driver.

"Trail's blocked," the driver called back. The coach had stopped now.

"What's he mean?" Edson asked.

"Stay here," Maynard said curtly, opening the door wide and getting out. He walked as far as the wheel team and looked up at the driver, a gray-bearded man in a long yellow linen coat, whose face under the sagging brim of a slouch hat was gazing steadily ahead. About two hundred feet along the trail a tree had pitched forward dead across, its thickly leaved branches creating a complex barricade, its crown hanging out over the edge in thin air.

"Not good," the driver muttered.

"Not an act of God, you mean," Maynard said, looking ahead.

"Not unless He used an ax. That baby's been chopped. It's lying too perfect."

From inside the coach Edson called out, "Can't we clear it?"

"Oh, we can clear it all right," the driver said, speaking quietly to no one in particular. "It's what comes before is what worries me."

"Do we make a fight of it?" Maynard asked.

"Don't be brash, sonny," the driver said. "You don't know how many of them there are, nor where they might be in those trees. The way to live through this is to figure there's a rifle aimed at you the whole time."

Standing there in the suddenly breathless preternatural silence of the foothills of the Montana Territory, in sharp cool sunlight, Maynard realized it was a feeling he'd never had before, not through four years of war when there had been thousands of rifles in front of him, not at Antietam or Gettysburg or anywhere else; he had survived because he had never believed that anyone was aiming specifically at Thomas Maynard, that it was all too impersonal for that. It was the only way: to believe in your own deliverance, even as men close enough to touch were dropping around you. And now this new moment, when the way to live was to believe in the imminent possibility of sudden death.

Maynard saw the rider coming up from the rear first, and then the other, the horse moving from out of the trees ahead. The one ahead might have been riding toward a mirror, for all the difference in them. Both wore long black woolen coats, both were masked with large black bandannas, both wore slouch hats with the brims pulled forward so that they had faces with only their eyes visible. And both were riding slowly, as if with infinite self-absorption, each with rifle raised and aimed.

"Good morning, gentlemen," the one coming from the front said. "You know what it's about. So let's have it done without any talk."

"You picked a thin one," the driver said. "I'm carrying only two men and no express boxes. You can read my waybill if you like."

"We'll see," the rider said. He fixed his rifle on Maynard. "Lift the pistol out—and need I tell you, carefully—and drop it on the ground."

Maynard did so, with calculated slowness, holding the weapon lightly with his fingertips for a moment and then letting it fall to the ground, and then, following a command to do so, kicking it away.

"Empty your pockets," the rider said. His voice was low—trying to keep it unrecognizable, Maynard reckoned—and neither friendly nor unfriendly but almost casual, as if knowing it would be obeyed.

"I sent my packet up ahead," Maynard said. "All I've got is some coins and a few greenbacks. But you're welcome to them."

"Just turn your pockets over."

Maynard did so, dropping to the ground what money he had spoken of, along with his handkerchief, pocketknife, and watch; the latter he bent over and put down gently.

"You're a poor day's work," the rider said, a mild contempt in his still casual voice. "Now just go around to the back there and untie the boxes and tumble them down."

Maynard never got to the boot to undo the luggage. He had barely turned round, still feeling that rifle's aim upon him like a pressure point, when all at the same instant he saw the second rider come abreast of the coach door—still swung out from Maynard's exit—and heard him shout, "Son of a bitch!" and then fire his rifle into the coach. And then two more things: the man's horse, startled by the shot, swinging its hindquarters around, and the rider struggling for a moment to hold it steady, yanking at the reins with one hand and holding a sky-aimed rifle with the other, as the horse conducted a brief, agitated, dust-rising dance. And the other thing: a brief, barely noticeable shudder from the coach, as though something had been thrown about inside of it.

Now Maynard felt both rifles aimed at him, front and back, and to appease the second rider, whom he was facing, he raised his hands, but only to shoulder height, subconsciously (or maybe not subconsciously) unwilling to raise them higher, too proud to demonstrate the hot fatalistic fear he felt. Still trying to control his horse, the second rider was holding the rifle in one hand, the barrel with its wisps of smoke still curling out, weaving slightly as the horse gradually settled.

"This is shit," the rider in front said disgustedly. "This is all shit." Then, to the driver, "You say you're not carrying express boxes."

"I tell you no," the driver said. "Have a look for yourself and then shoot me dead if I'm lying."

"I ought to shoot you dead anyway, for wasting my time."

"Your time?" the driver said irately. "I'll be hours trying to shift that goddamned tree."

"I could save you the effort," the rider said, pointing the rifle at him, then, turning to Maynard, said, "Kick that pistol over the edge."

Maynard did so with a swipe of his boot, watching for where the weapon would approximately land. Then he stood, arms still partially raised and, not wanting to provoke the riders further, eyes intently and purposefully on the ground.

The second rider dismounted, his eyes, sinister looking between the tightly tied high-worn bandanna and the drop of the hat brim, watching Maynard. He stepped up into the coach, emerging a few moments later with a drawstring leather bag, which he held up and rattled for the benefit of his companion. He dropped the bag into one of the pockets of his coat and then remounted, swinging the horse around. Without another word the road agents began galloping back down the trail. Lowering his arms, Maynard watched them until they had disappeared around the trail's long bend. Then he retrieved his belongings from the ground and walked to the coach's open door.

Edson was sprawled back on the upholstered seat where the rifle shot had thrown him, awkwardly twisted, both feet on the floor, head fallen to one side. His hat, apparently having flown back with him, lay crushed under his shoulders. He had taken the bullet in the chest, his white shirt filled with blood. The cause of it, the revolver he had inadvisedly lifted from one of the wall slings and probably tried to aim, was still gripped in his hand.

There was a slight tremor from the coach as the driver left his seat and descended.

"Got him, did they?" he said, standing next to Maynard and peering into the coach. "Damn fool should never have pulled. He could've started something that got us all killed."

"He told me he'd never held a gun in his hand in his life."

"Then he picked the wrong occasion for the first time."

"He was just a pup from back East come out to try his luck," Maynard said.

"Well," the driver said, "he's probably been spared a lot of heartache. Anybody that foolish would never have stood a chance. Come on, I'll get a blanket and we'll wrap him up."

The driver spread an old coarse gray woolen Confederate army blanket on the ground and then they lifted out the body and laid it at the edge of the blanket and began slowly rolling man and material over and over until they had made a narrow bundle. Maynard bound it with rope at the head and the foot and they placed it back inside the coach, on the floor between the seats to spare it the indignity of being thrown there by the coach's unpredictable turns and descents. (Maynard would spend the rest of the trip sitting up with the driver.) Then the driver pointed to the fallen tree.

"We'd better put our backs to that," he said.

"Do you have an ax on board?" Maynard asked.

"I do."

"Then you'd better set to hacking. Cut it up from the middle and I suspect the top half will drop off the edge on its own. We'll be able to swing the rest of it."

"You'll divvy the labor with me, won't you?"

"As soon as I retrieve my shooter," Maynard said.

It took him nearly a half hour of exasperating searching among the thick, prickly bramble and the old savagely embedded boulders that had been there eons before history's dimmest reckonings. As he searched he heard the driver's steady chopping, punctuated by the frequent, hopeful, "Find it yet? Hey?"

When he finally climbed back up to the trail, Maynard relieved the driver of the short-handled ax and it took nearly another half hour of steady chopping before the tree was at last severed and, as Maynard had foreseen, the top-heavy upper section dropped and tumbled with a series of soft splitting and crackling noises partially down the hillside. Then they lifted the remaining half and swung it aside, reopening the trail.

"I'm getting too old for this sort of business," the driver said morosely when they were up on the front seat, reins in hand.

Maynard didn't think any age was right for it.

SEVEN

Maynard had heard about these mining towns. Spawned by the gold-veined mountains that had taken on the imagery of glittering temples in the minds of the men who came charging across river and plain to get to them, these abrupt eruptions of hammered-together ramshackle buildings that came to face each other across a lumpy tract of land called Main Street were the latter-day El Dorados that had first burned in the minds of sixteenth-century conquistadors. Earthbound though they were, there was still about them a cometary aura, for the suddenness of their appearance, the boldness of their duration, and then the lingering ghostliness of their departure.

The Baddock strike was proving to be, by most boomtown standards, a long one, the first discoveries having been made more than four years ago. A place no doubt primitive to the eyes of an easterner, it had become, by mining town reckonings, a veritable metropolis, from the time the first dwellings had seemed to shoot straight up from the ground, beginning with frames of light scantling and tack-fastened cloth and crudely dug fire pits to help a man ward off the fierce Montana Territory winter.

Lying in a bowl created by the surrounding mountains with their—sometimes—running golden streams, Baddock had stores and saloons and restaurants and livery stable and its own newspaper; it had a doctor and a dentist and an attorney and a minister and a schoolteacher and an undertaker and a sheriff and a small jail. It had all the services, licit and otherwise, that were endemic to these places, and that saw to

the wants and needs of the miners when they came in to
carouse or resupply or to winter. Scattered around and
beyond the Main Street buildings were private homes ranging
from the rudest cabins to well-carpentered two-story houses
with white picket fences and even here and there a garden,
and a flat-roofed one-room schoolhouse and further out a
steepled gray-timbered church and near that a fenced-in
cemetery, most of whose occupants were moldering away
around lead slugs, and beyond that some outlying ranches.

Compressed into its remote deposits, the seductive gold
had power enough to rend all common sense and good reason and transform them into miasmas of self-justification.
Because its very idea (much less its presence) could destabi-
lize, it meant that these towns and their scattered claim sites
played host to the most impetuous and unpredictable of men,
men lately taken by a religious fervor without the bindings of
spiritual center. They were men suddenly unrestrained by the
laws and rules of the society they had not just come from but
seemed to have willfully abandoned, law being too slow and
too self-pondering to keep up with the heights of dream and
the celerity of pursuit. To try to reason one's way through a
dispute in a gold-struck environment could be a fatal error of
judgment, where men seemed out to prove that civilization
was an imposed rather than a natural condition. Right and
wrong were too frequently determined by the preponder-
ances of good and bad locked into a man's nature. Here was
a place where the dream dominated the reality, where failure
was too easily temporized, where Golconda could be a mere
shovel's thrust away. A man who had hitherto been able to
resist naturally any temptation here found himself striding
with conviction into a particular fascination.

Across the jouncing backs of the mustangs, through four
sets of perked buoyant ears, Maynard watched Baddock
grow larger as the Concord coach came skirting around the
foothills the following morning. While it might have seemed
puny and irrelevant under the breadth of blue Montana sky

and the bulk of wild mountains, the town nevertheless projected a certain singular, hard-nut stubbornness, as though it had a charter to endure.

The trail had nowhere been as joltingly irregular as Baddock's ridged and rutted Main Street, whose hard dry surface looked and felt like it had been dug and hacked and gnawed. The traffic moved every which way with a spontaneous independence. There were lone horsemen and one-horse hooded chaises and light traps and wagons of all sizes, some open, some hooped and canvas covered like the old prairie schooners.

As the coach rolled along the street Maynard looked from side to side, amused by the fact that there was virtually no architectural resemblance from one structure to the next, each the work of an entrepreneur concentrating upon himself alone. They all seemed to have come to Baddock, or at least one of each and in some cases more: there were signboards, hammered to storefronts or hanging out from supporting timbers, that announced Groceries & Provisions, Pies & Cakes, Milk & Beer, Restaurant, Barber Shoppe, Dry Goods, Drug Store, Tin Shop, Liquor, Dentist, Bank, Lawyer, Hotel, and of course Saloon, at least three or four. A whole slapdash society of basic needs and wants excitedly put down, as if it had been not so much built as commandeered.

And who among the men riding past or striding along the plank boardwalks, Maynard wondered, might be—if he existed at all—Andrew Pryor, former major in the Union Army? And if the man was not dead and buried in the Virginia earth, as the official records so stated, then why not? Questions to be answered, certainly, he thought. But right now all he could really think about was a room, a hot bath, and about ten undisturbed hours on a good mattress.

When the stage rolled to a stop it was not at the office of the Territorial Stage Line but that of the sheriff, where it was met by a half dozen men. The town fathers, Maynard guessed, from their clothing and from the sober concern in their faces. Then the sheriff appeared in the doorway. He was a tall, overly filled-out man, his thick drooping mustache turning an already rueful face almost dolorous. No doubt a fine physical specimen in his day, he was now fronted by too much belly, putting a strain on his gun belt.

"Hours late, Sam," one of the men said, looking up at the driver.

For response the driver simply jabbed a thumb backward over his shoulder. The coach door was swung open and the men gathered around to look inside at the bound-up bundle on the floor. Turned in his seat to watch them, Maynard took note of the reaction: not shock, but flat, almost wordless anger.

"Coming up the foothill trail," the driver said, to no one in particular. "Late yesterday afternoon. Two men. The fellow drew on them and was shot down." When he was asked what they looked like, he made a sardonic noise. "They wore masks," he said, looking down at his questioner, "and long coats, and their horses looked like horses," he said, the sarcasm rising in his voice.

"Take it easy, Sam," the sheriff said from the doorway. He had come no further than that, standing there with his thumbs in his belt, as if recalling some old belligerence.

"There's too much taking it easy," the driver said, venting an anger Maynard hadn't seen before. "I don't like having passengers shot dead in my coach."

"We'll get at it, Sam, don't worry," one of the men said. "We're as torn off about it as you are. This is our town, remember."

"You may live here, cousin," the driver said, "but it sure ain't your town. And it's not going to be anybody's town until a man can ride through those mountains without worry."

"And what did you see, mister?" This was the sheriff, moved to the front of the group now, looking up at Maynard.

"Same as he did," Maynard said.

"The fellow drew on them?"

"He panicked," Maynard said.

"Did you know him?"

"Only from the ride. He boarded a couple of days ago. Said he was from Philadelphia."

"All right," the sheriff said. "Let's haul him out and get him over to the undertaker. If he's got any papers on him bring them over, and whatever's his in the boot. Then box him up and plant him." He spoke it quietly, dispassionately, as Maynard could remember certain officers talking after a particularly costly battle. He was never quite sure whether they mourned in private or not, and if so, what it did for them. He guessed that grieving for strangers was an abstract emotion, ameliorating if nothing else.

"What'd they get, Sam?" someone asked the driver.

"The fellow had a drawstring, but I wasn't carrying anything," the driver said. "I'd already off-loaded back down the road. Wasn't much of anything coming up here."

"Well, hell then, Sam," someone said. "Come on down from there and have yourself a drink."

"Well," Maynard said, offering the driver a handshake.

"Welcome to Baddock," the driver said laconically, giving back a limp, unenthusiastic shake.

Maynard found a room at The Brothers Hotel, the largest building in town, which from its three-storied, somewhat asymmetrical and multiform structure indicated that it had undergone several enlargements.

"We hit Baddock in the early days," said Oscar Lamont, one of the pair of eponymous brothers who ran the place. "My brother Willard and myself. We could see it coming."

"See what coming?" Maynard asked uninterestedly as he inked his name into the overlarge ledger on the desk, which Lamont had swung around for him.

"A boom town, just what you see," Lamont said cheerfully. He was a short, round man whose red cherubic face smiled out from between a pair of full-grown white muttonchops. He wore a fresh yellow wildflower in the lapel of his black cutaway that matched the color of his silk vest. "When the presence of gold is announced, you look ahead. You look ahead. If you make the first footprint, I told my brother, and if you make it wide enough and deep enough, nobody else will dare follow. When we got here they were sleeping in sheet tents or inside sugar barrels or crockery crates or under wagons. We hammered this place together and in the beginning all we had to offer was horse blankets and empty rooms and the boys was damned glad to have them. Damned glad."

"You do have beds now, I presume?"

"In every room, yes, sir. Clean sheets, feather pillows, fresh water in the pitcher, clean chamber pots. And a hip tub in the room at the end of the hall. You just whistle down and I'll see it's filled with hot water for you, no extra charge. We're the best hotel in town. We're the only hotel in town, in fact, but even if there were five we'd still be the best."

"I'm glad to hear that."

"Service," Lamont said. "Competition is a good thing, but you're better off without it, don't you think?"

"I'm too tired to think," Maynard said.

"Long journey, eh, Mr. . . ."—Lamont turned the ledger back around—"Maynard?"

"Long and hard."

"Well, you can sleep it away right upstairs." Lamont held up a key attached to a number-inscribed slat of wood. He shook it like a temptation.

Maynard gathered the key into his hand, picked up his strap-tied leather suitcase, and began heading upstairs.

"Dining room's always open," Lamont called up to him from behind the desk, a still larger smile broadening his face.

"I'll bear it in mind," Maynard said. He paused on the landing. "I'll be looking for a friend."

"I know most everyone in town."

"Mr. Patterson."

"Well known to me," Lamont said. "I'll get a message to him."

"Much appreciated," Maynard said, going on.

"Service," Lamont said, opening his arms as if he was going to sing an aria. "Service."

Maynard wasn't expecting any frills in his room, nor were there any, beyond a clean-swept floor and wallpaper that was hung straight. There was a single bed with an iron bedstead, two straight-backed wooden chairs, a three-drawer bureau mounted by an oval-shaped kerosene lamp, and the usual bowl, pitcher, and chamber pot, each of white porcelain, with the side of the pitcher showing a small jagged lightning-bolt crack. The mattress was stuffed with straw and the cleanliness of the sheets could have been debated, but the pillow was soft, and minutes after he had stripped down to his long johns and stretched out and closed his eyes, Maynard was asleep.

EIGHT

It wasn't until after six in the evening that Maynard came back downstairs, rested, bathed, shaved. He had satisfied some of his nagging hunger with a few deep swallows from the bottle of whiskey he'd bought in Salt Lake City, which he was beginning to feel was going to become a steadier companion to him out here than he would have liked. His life these past ten years had swung back and forth between the genteel amenities of Washington, D.C., and the rugged camaraderie of the battlefield, the two contrasts sharing the one familiar—an organized and conforming existence, which for a man without family or true home was almost life-giving.

As if reality had been being numbed by his sense of duty since leaving Washington, he now found himself feeling peeved at having been sent out here. If General Northwood had been trying to get him out of the way of the well-connected and vindictive Colonel Zachariah, surely a less onerous assignment could have been found. The feeling of being a soldier under orders, of being slotted into some carefully wrought design, did not here obtain. If Washington had been stifling and at times soporifically monotonous, at least there he had been part of the machinery of government, occupied at work that someone of more exalted standing believed needed doing. Here he was a lone man doing the unsoldierly work of pursuing what might, quite literally, be a ghost. Here, the message of his uniform was lost.

Well, he thought as he came down the staircase of The Brothers Hotel, perhaps he ought to look at the positive side

of it and be flattered for having been chosen for what General
Northwood obviously felt was a needed investigation, or at
the very least, that the general was concerned enough to get
him out of the way of any grapeshot that might come from
the direction of Colonel Zachariah.

"Ah. You must be Mr. Maynard."

And this, Maynard reasoned (even as he thought how flat
and uninteresting his name sounded without its "Captain"
prefix), must be the other Lamont brother. This one was tall
and as thin as a shinbone. The sides of his face were decorated with muttonchops, as his brother's were, these grayish
and somewhat tattered, like some natural growth that desic-
cated with seasonal change. Impeccable in a swallow-tailed
coat, he stood with regal formality behind the registration
desk, his bespectacled face slightly raised as if he had just
heard the distant call of a royal trumpet.

"My brother," he said, "undertook to locate your friend
for you." He sounded as if he had been rehearsing it.

"That was kind of him," Maynard said, approaching the
desk. The carpeted lobby was empty, its padded chairs standing around in plump expectancy.

"We give service."

"That is quite apparent."

"It's absolutely essential for a hotelier," the other Lamont
said, standing erect behind the desk as if he had been planted
there years ago and grown from the floor just this way, like
the proud epitome of a species. "Especially in a mining town,
and most especially a gold mining town, because in a gold
mining town the prevailing sense of the mind is obsession—
the single occupation, ambition, topic of public conversation,
and subject of private thought. When that is occurring, it is
the obligation of the hotelier to see after the needs of his
guests, whose concentration is frequently—"

"Thank you, Mr. Lamont," Maynard said, at the desk
now. "Do you have a message for me?"

The other Lamont paused, compressed his lips for a

moment, then said, "Mr. Patterson will be expecting you at the Honest Eagle saloon."

Maynard rapped his knuckles lightly on the desk and smiled as he turned to leave.

"Thank you," he said.

The Main Street traffic had cleared considerably, with only a few high-wheeled wagons or lone horsemen coming and going. Most of the stores had closed down for the night, though the saloons seemed well attended. He could hear, as he passed one of them, bouncy piano tunes and a fiddle. He crossed the street, stepping carefully over the deeper ruts, then mounted the opposite boardwalk and went on. He had noted that morning that many men walked around here armed, and so he was wearing his gun on his hip, thinking, *Might as well be stylish.* A sharply defined half-moon was just rising over a distant mountain crest, looking polished and inlaid upon the purity of a darkening, cloudless sky. The air was keen with the first faint breaths of a Montana winter gathering somewhere beyond the mountains.

His boot heels clumped on the raised plank surface as he strode forward, arms swinging lightly. As he approached the sheriff's office he noted the bulky, mustached man of the law standing outside noting his approach. The big man looked even bigger in his buffalo coat.

"Good evening," the sheriff said. Maynard sensed an invitation to stop. "We buried your friend."

"He was a nice fellow," Maynard said, "but hardly a friend."

"He'll be sticking in memory longer than most friends."

"I don't doubt that, Sheriff."

"His name was William Edson."

"I knew that much."

"Was to be married when he got back home, according to the letter he'd half written to the young lady."

"So I understood. I take it you'll see the family is notified?"

The sheriff nodded. His mustache came down mournfully

around the sides of his mouth, like a pair of sewn-together dog tails.

"We're getting very practiced at that," he said. "These goddamned mining towns bust out like cannonballs, and all you can do is wait for all the pieces to come down."

"I suppose that's all you can do."

"That fellow should have stayed home."

Maynard allowed a chiding smile. "We all have a 'should-have' in our lives, Sheriff."

"And some of us with more than one. What's your name?"

"Thomas Maynard."

"You have business out here, Mr. Maynard?"

"Not especially."

"Just askin'."

"You're the sheriff."

"Doesn't seem to mean Jack shit out here," the sheriff said, looking away for a moment. "What can you tell me about those road agents that Sam couldn't?"

Maynard shrugged. "Two men in masks," he said.

"Nothing unusual about them?"

"I couldn't say, Sheriff; they were my first road agents."

"Well, you came off lucky. Smarter than the other fellow."

"I'm not much of a fighter," Maynard said.

The sheriff appraised him for a moment, one eye narrowing at the corner.

"Perhaps," he said, turning away and entering the office.

The Honest Eagle occupied a single unattached building near the north end of Main Street, the name arced in raised brass letters across each of its broad half-curtained windows, a double-doored entrance of frosted glass in the center. An outside flight of stairs ran up one side of the building, leading to rooms whose windows overlooked the flat wooden awning supported by four posts wedged between the board-walk and the awning's underside. About a dozen horses stood at near portrait immobility at the tie rail.

Inside, the place smelled of stale beer and tobacco, the

familiar ambiance establishing itself at the first intake of breath. The bar ran nearly the length of one wall, with several dozen men leaned into it, serviced by a pair of bartenders in identical striped shirts with sleeve garters and the plastered-down shiny hair Maynard had seen on bartenders in Washington and New York. Away from the bar were tables and chairs, with another row of tables against the opposite wall, these covered with green cloths, for the higher-stakes games, Maynard reasoned. An unattended piano stood in a corner at the back wall. Some drinking was being done at the tables, under the hanging lamps and illuminated webs of smoke. Several card games were going on, and some quiet conversation. It was generally quiet, with, it seemed, a minimum of motion.

One table stood alone, at the far wall near where the bar ended and next to a backroom door, positioned so it commanded a view of the entire place. There was but a single chair at the table, and in it, back to wall, an insouciantly poised man sat, watching, not with undue interest or curiosity but with that steady, detached air of ownership, with a face that suggested that smiles and congeniality were strictly obligatory and had nothing to do with what he might or might not be feeling.

Maynard felt himself come under observation from this table the moment he walked in and closed the door behind him, and he paused, his quest for Simon Patterson suspended for a moment by those unconditionally inquiring eyes. He understood immediately the import of their reading: he was new, unknown, and therefore subject to intuitive judgment, to be weighed and measured, graphed from innocuous to troublesome.

Maynard didn't particularly care for the cool, uninhibited assessment, and he stared back. The man sitting in such compelling isolation at the far table was hatless, clean-shaven, his light brown hair neatly combed. He bore no resemblance, either in style or manner, to anyone else in the saloon and gave the impression that he had striven to do just that. His even-featured face was as unrevealing as a covered mirror and seemed designed that way, to mask any thought or current of emotion, holding itself to this steady advantage. He was wearing a black frock coat and gray silk vest over a white shirt, with a string tie delicately in place.

Not more than five seconds elapsed as the two pairs of eyes ran one to the other across the quiet saloon, until the man at the table smiled faintly, and, Maynard thought, inwardly, as if smoothing an edge of judgment, then turned away.

Maynard went to the bar and called out a whiskey, then had an involuntary glance at the far table, but the smooth inquiring face had turned its attention elsewhere.

"I'm looking for a man named Patterson," Maynard said as the bartender filled his glass from a leveled bottle.

When the bartender had finished pouring he set the bottle down and looked out across the bar.

"Is there a Mr. Patterson here?" he called out.

Maynard turned as a man sitting alone at a table near the window looked up and smiled, then waved Maynard over.

"You're Patterson?" Maynard asked, standing over the table.

"And you?"

"Maynard."

"From—"

"Washington." It was spoken barely audibly.

"Sit down," Patterson said. He was anywhere between forty and fifty, with a worn, pleasant face that looked to have absorbed more turmoil and cynicism than an inherently genial and uncomplicated disposition had been molded for. He had a salt-and-pepper mustache that appeared to have grown in temperamental spurts and white hair that grew thickly out from under his hat and thick black eyebrows that looked like they had been borrowed from somebody else. He had a slow, mischievous smile that suggested he took wry pleasure in the sardonic humors the world had imposed upon him, as if he had been given dispensation not to feel responsible for them.

"They're careful around here," he said when Maynard had seated himself, drink in hand. "He didn't know who you might be; and as a matter of fact, though I drink in here all the time, he doesn't know who I might be. It's all part of the frontier melodrama." He smiled his weary smile. "So you're Northwood's man."

"Tom Maynard."

"Rank?"

"Captain."

"Which of course you'll drop as long as you're here."

"That's right," Maynard said. "Plain old Tom."

"I'll bet there's nothing plain about you," Patterson said. He was sitting back, his hand wrapped around a tall glass of beer. "Not if Northwood sent you out."

"It could have been punitive."

Patterson laughed. "Yes," he said, "it could, couldn't it? Loosened from the comforts of the nation's capital and sent out here."

"You're here."

"That's more an indictment of my jumbled self than an endorsement of the Montana Territory, believe me."

"Frankly, I don't care why you're here," Maynard said. "I just want to find out what I have to and get the hell back."

"And how is the general?"

"He's well."

"You were in the war with him?"

"Toward the end," Maynard said.

They were speaking quietly. Maynard was facing the window, where hatted upper torsos kept passing on the other side of the pleated half curtain that hung from a metal rod.

"I've been out here for more than a year now," Patterson said, "though it's not much different from the place I was before, and probably not from the place I'll be next."

"Am I going to get your hard luck story?"

"I haven't told it in a while," Patterson said with his slow, sad smile. "When a man is in the mood to tell his tale of woe, it's really cruel to deny him."

"The single point of view is never very interesting."

"I didn't say it was."

"If it has anything to do with the war," Maynard said, "I don't want to hear it."

"Maynard," Patterson said, "right now if you eliminate the war from honest discourse the country will fall silent. Anyway, that's one of the few gratifications of this place—the war might never have happened. Nothing stands a chance in the face of avarice. There is but the single obsession. It can be quite instructive for the student of human nature, if he doesn't fall victim to the fever himself, which he almost inevitably will, since he is apt to forget how absolutely human he himself is. Too many men often become the worst part of what they study most."

Maynard sipped his whiskey. He could hear cards being riffled, the sound of a silver dollar being dropped onto a table, voices in short-sentenced conversation, some growled laughter.

"Don't let the fever catch you, Maynard," Patterson said, "or you'll never go back. Don't smirk; it's happened to better men; it's one of those things that not a good mind or a fast horse or a quick six-gun can protect you from. There are men scattered around through those mountains now with their souls in bondage. They've got the same quality of conviction as those people who swear they saw Christ's face in a pillar of smoke. I tell you, it's worse than any addiction; at least the addict doesn't have to break his back for his intoxication. But for me it wasn't an obsession but an excuse. I just wanted to get away, don't ask me from what."

"I have no intention," Maynard said.

"You're an unsympathetic man, Maynard," Patterson said with a reproachful shake of the head. "I know you've come a long distance . . ."

"And sat through a murder along the way."

"Yes, you were on that stage, I heard of it. My regrets."

"Save them."

"All I wanted to say was—"

"Christ," Maynard said, "is everyone in this place a bag of wind?"

"I beg your pardon?"

"My innkeepers seem intent upon wearing out either their throats or my ears."

"Is that where you're staying?" Patterson laughed. "Those idiots will talk you to death, Maynard. Don't worry, I've got something for you; it's private, reasonably comfortable, and won't cost you a penny."

"That's the first thing you've said worth listening to."

"What did Northwood tell you about me?" Patterson asked.

"He said you'd been a correspondent for the *New York Herald* during the war."

"Correct. I spent quite a bit of time with Northwood. He had the gift, or maybe it was the misfortune, of always being at the center of the action. Very candid fellow. If I'd printed everything he said, he'd be a corporal today. But I daresay I saw more of the worst of it than any soldier, and then had to write about it, which meant seeing it all over again in order to give it accuracy. I think the return trip to hell is the worse, when it's quiet."

"You poor fellow," Maynard said flatly, so without inflection that Patterson felt stung by the mockery.

"All right," Patterson said defensively, "it may not be the same as being shot at, but it's got its own bite of misery, and when misery is in close fit on a man no other man can imagine how bad it is. I'm afraid I'm a sensitive soul, Maynard."

"Then you should have stayed out of the way."

"I had a job to do. But enough was enough and I quit right after Cold Harbor; it was that or take the next few steps over the edge into complete lunatic despair. I'd seen years of brutality and savagery; but once that Wilderness campaign got into full flower it got worse. There was an anger in it."

"We were on the home trail then," Maynard said. "Impatient."

"You were crazed. The whole goddamned army. Anyway, I didn't come west to look for gold; I'd recovered too much of my calm reason to do a thing like that."

"Where is Barley Newton?"

"Barley is dead," Patterson said.

Maynard knew he'd heard correctly, but it sounded so absurdly and stunningly wrong that he refused to believe it. His incredulity must have been vividly apparent, because Patterson nodded and said it again.

"He's dead, Tom."

"You'd better start talking precisely to the point, Patterson. And don't tell me that the ghost of Barley Newton came to you and told you that he saw the ghost of Major Pryor. I've come a long way and—"

"I guess my second letter arrived too late. Barley was shot dead the day after he told me what he'd seen."

"Shot dead by whom?"

"By a hand in the night," Patterson said. "Nobody knows. People are shot dead around here with uncivilized frequency, and by the expression in your face I fear I may be next."

"There's a temptation."

"Which I hope you'll keep in quarantine. I'm sorry, Maynard."

"What am I supposed to do now?"

"Try to make the best of it. Either way, you're here."

"You're asking me to make a meal from an empty plate."

"Not entirely empty. Though it's pretty thin gruel, I'll admit."

"So all I have to work with is what he told you. Exactly what was that?"

Patterson shrugged unhappily. "Simply that he had just walked past a man he believed to have been killed in the war, a Major Andrew Pryor."

"How certain was he?"

"I tell you, Maynard, he was trembling with it."

"Sober?"

"As a sermon. I walked in—it was right here—and he signaled me over and said he'd buy me a drink and that he had something 'funny' to tell me, funny in the bizarre sense. He said, 'If I saw a ghost, then I'm damned. If I only think I saw a ghost, then I've been turned around.' "

"Well," Maynard asked, "which was it?"

"He swore it was the man, and he was certain, too, that the man had recognized him. He said that the cold chill he'd felt on his spine was evidence enough of it."

"But he didn't speak to the man?"

"A very strong instinct, he said, advised against it."

"Newton was in no way a frivolous man?"

"Not at all," Patterson said. "He was a good friend, as good as I had in this place. We used to sit here and drink and play checkers, when he was in town. He'd come in now and then to resupply and such. He was working a small claim up in the hills. I think he was beginning to get lucky, too. He was a good, sane fellow, Maynard."

"Did he see his ghost again after that?"

"No, and I'm sure he would have told me if he had. I saw him again the next day; I rode out to the cabin he used when he was in town. I guess I teased him a bit about it, and he said, very sternly, 'It was him, Simon. That's all there is to it. It was my major.' "

"Did he seem concerned about it?"

"How do you mean?"

"Well, Christ, he was gunned down soon enough."

"No, he didn't seem concerned; and anyway, we don't know if there was a connection. People *do* get shot around here."

"Always for a reason, I assume," Maynard said. "Look, did Newton have any ideas about this, what might be behind it? Any explanation, any theories?"

"No, or at least none that he offered up. It puzzled him

and upset him, but I don't think he was going to chase it down. He was getting set to return to his claim the next day."

"Did he give you a description of the man?"

"Not to any great detail," Patterson said.

"General Northwood said you were a pretty good journalist."

"So?"

"Powers of observation."

"I didn't see the man," Patterson said pointedly.

"But whatever Newton told you—can't you see that inside your head now?"

"You're asking me to examine what another man saw."

"What he told you he saw. It's somewhere under your hat and between your ears. Get in there, Patterson."

"I can tell you—it wasn't anything out of the ordinary. A well-dressed man, he said. But he wouldn't tell me his name."

"Then he knew him, I mean from here in Baddock."

"Oh, Barley knew him all right," Patterson said. "He'd seen him before, but this was the time he recognized him. Called him a 'nabob.' "

"Say that again, Patterson."

" 'Nabob.' "

"Barley said he was a 'nabob.' "

"I remember that."

"How did he use the word, was it respectfully, contemptuously, how?"

"I don't really recall. He might have been slightly impressed. I'm not sure," Patterson said. "I don't remember the context. The word just sort of came up and then slipped away."

"You didn't push it?"

"He didn't want to tell me, Maynard," Patterson said somewhat defensively. "Maybe because he wasn't one hundred percent sure or maybe out of an old loyalty, or maybe it was the discretion you learn to observe out here."

" 'Nabob' would imply that the man is of some local prominence, wouldn't it?"

"Unless he was referring to him as an ex-major."

"No," Maynard said, "that doesn't sound right. I think there was probably a bit of sarcasm in 'nabob.' "

"Barley was not normally a sarcastic person."

"Not a normal situation, Patterson. He sees a man he's believed was dead, is shocked, startled; he doesn't want to give him away, but he can't help making some commentary. The dead man not only isn't dead but he's made something of himself out here."

"Possibly. Maybe the gruel isn't so thin after all."

"I want Barley's tone when he was talking to you," Maynard said. "Was he positive, stubbornly positive? What was he?"

"I follow your meaning," Patterson said. "Stubbornly positive would mean . . ."

"That he saw more than a resemblance or even a powerful resemblance; what he saw was a man who had somehow altered his appearance but who was still that man."

"Altered how?"

"Pryor had a full-grown beard. No doubt it's long since been cleaned off. That can change night into day, as far as a man's appearance is concerned."

Patterson had been thinking. "Stubbornly positive, I'd say," he said. "I've been trying to bring it back, and I think that's how it was."

"All right," Maynard said. "We have a man who was well dressed, which from what I've seen around here narrows it down more than a little bit. 'Nabob' means he's probably prominent and prospering."

"It also means he's been here for a while."

"Pryor would be about forty years old, so we have an age range to work with. I'd say we've trimmed the herd a bit," Maynard said with some satisfaction.

"Well, there's a fingertip's worth of grip anyway. At least you won't be going around looking up every mule's ass."

"How many nabobs do you have here in town?"

"Not so many. There's the doctor, but he'd be too old.

There are some prosperous ranchers who come into town, but I wouldn't describe any of them as well dressed. And Pearson, who'd qualify as a nabob, since he runs the bank. He fits into the age square."

"Beard?"

"No beard. Then there's Abbot, who owns the general store and a few other things. Civic activist, self-important. He's of the right age, and has a clean chin. There's Carson, who runs the newspaper, for which I do a bit of writing now and then. But he's too old. Then there are the Lamont brothers."

"I think we can eliminate them," Maynard said with a smile.

"I think they'd make fine officers," Patterson said facetiously.

"I can see them renting tents."

"There's Turner, who's the superintendent of this division of the stage line. Big, blustery, and very belligerent. Probably too old to be your man, and too crude, and anyway he's got a beard."

"What about miners? There must be some wealthy ones."

"The really successful ones only come down to winter; otherwise they're always up there, overseeing their strikes, which is probably why they're successful."

"Let's try and narrow down 'nabob,' " Maynard said, elbows on table, gnawing at his thumbnail for a moment. Then he lifted his glass and sipped some whiskey. "You said this man Turner was too crude. All right. What would 'nabob' mean to a man like Newton?"

"To a man like Barley, probably a bit of distinction."

"Maybe pomposity."

"Possibly."

"Who would fit into that?"

"Pearson, the banker. He's a bit starched."

"And who did you say was self-important?"

"Abbot," Patterson said. "The merchant. But that wouldn't fit O'Connor."

"Who's he?"

"Didn't I mention him? He's the lawyer. Definitely a nabob, by local standards. Right age—high thirties to early forties. A small, pointy beard. Just a touch of pomposity, but only when he's expounding legal matters; otherwise an affable sort, certainly more than the other two."

"Pearson and Abbot?"

"Yes."

Patterson drummed his fingertips on the table for several moments, then rubbed his face.

"But," he said, "thinking back, there was something odd. Maybe it's all this talk—I certainly gave it no thought at the time—but a day or two after Barley was shot, O'Connor came around to the newspaper and just sat down and had a chat."

"Was that unusual?"

"Well, it didn't strike me as so. But he'd never done it before, nor since."

"I know what you're thinking," Maynard said. "You were known as Barley's closest friend, right? And you're wondering now if O'Connor—if he happens to be a certain ex-major—wanted to come in and try you on for size, to see if he could guess whether Barley had told you about him or not."

"I would say that my mind has leaned toward that interpretation, yes, though it didn't at the time."

"What did he want to talk about?"

"Nothing in particular. He said he was just passing, saw me sitting there—I was by my lonesome—and thought he'd stop in and be neighborly."

"Did he mention Barley?"

"No. Just talked about the town, about business. About nothing, frankly. Then he went out and I never thought of it again from that day to this. Jesus, Maynard, it takes nothing to plant a suspicion, does it?"

"They can grow right out of stone."

"Well, if he is your man," Patterson said, "then I passed the test, since I'm still drawing breath."

"I'm not saying anybody is anybody," Maynard said. "But if somebody is somebody, then I want him."

"Well, it's not going to be easy, since you don't seem to know a hell of a lot about the man to begin with."

No, he didn't, Maynard had to agree; not much more than the shadows that had fallen from Samuel Mark's memory, and these conformed with any number of men: neither tall nor short, dark beard (the latter no doubt long gone), no particular characteristics, nothing memorable about him at all. A totally unremarkable man. It was disconcerting, Maynard thought, when you realized how vast the category was, how lamentably ordinary most men were.

Few of Pryor's fellow officers had survived the war, the final carnage of the Wilderness campaign taking a brutal toll. Nor could Maynard make inquiries of what family Pryor had left behind in New England; for one thing, such inquiry could only be baffling and alarming for them, and for another (and more importantly), if he was indeed still alive, Pryor might well be in surreptitious communication with them.

"It seems to me," Patterson said, "that unlike a private soldier, who's really just a civilian in a uniform and who is only too eager to chuck it all when he musters out, a major might be inclined to take some of it with him. The fact of having been a major, I mean. For most men it'll always be the best beans they ever tasted."

Possibly, Maynard thought. He knew plenty of officers, retired, who had never lost the eye and carriage of command. It was pride's grip, and in Pryor's case might be immune to mask or caution. But for God's sake, Maynard thought, am I supposed to walk around looking for somebody who's striding about like an officer? Too many proud men had that stride. And remember: this man was running away from something, so could be desperate; he was hiding, so could be cunning; of all the world's Edens he was in this place, so could be mad; or he could be here with gold fever, which would mean he's not going to be or act differently from any other obsessed mountain rat. Or he could be a rancher or a lawyer or a banker or a merchant, newly respectable and thoroughly different. Or he could be buried in Virginia.

"The expression on your face," Patterson said, "tells me you wish Barley had kept his mouth shut. Or that I'd never written that letter."

"Why did you?"

"I thought Northwood might want to know. And after Barley was shot . . . well . . ."

"I just wish I knew if he was shot down because of what he saw."

Patterson smiled. "That's the possibility that's going to keep you out here for a while, isn't it?"

"The man could have been shot down by anybody. This is hardly a place of genteel manners."

"Ah," Patterson said, nodding indulgently. "That makes some sense, but how comfortable would you be telling that to General Northwood after sitting out here for just two days?"

Not very, Maynard thought dejectedly.

"But of course you have to take it into consideration," Patterson said. "As you point out, this is not the most genteel of places. Barley could have gotten into some dispute, or he might have been killed by claim jumpers who were after his stake. That's a live hazard around here. He told me that he'd had to run a couple of them off at rifle point not so long ago."

"There doesn't seem to be much law around here, does there?"

"We have Mr. Dunlop, our sheriff. A good man in the wrong place, and maybe a bit along in years. But there's not much he can do if a crowd of roughnecks ride in looking for a good time, and there's not a damned thing he can do about what goes on along the trails or out at isolated claims. Out here, a man measures what law he gets by what courage he's got, and I have to tell you, Maynard, that most of our courageous ones are lying in the boneyard outside of town. Being sheriff in a town like this is like being a butterfly in a beehive."

"So the road agents operate with impunity."

"Pretty much. Until they're stopped."

"Stopped?"

"There's a lot of anger," Patterson said, lowering his voice. He leaned forward. "I wouldn't be surprised if sooner or later—sooner, I'd say—we don't see some law improvised."

"You mean a vigilance committee."

"As they had in California some years ago."

"That's a damn ugly business," Maynard said.

"No uglier than honest men being robbed of their labor, and sometimes murdered for it."

"Well, it's got nothing to do with me."

"You saw a man murdered."

"His own fault," Maynard said.

Patterson smiled slowly, with more indulgence than Maynard cared for. "Really?" he asked.

Maynard felt uneasy. He finished his whiskey and put the glass down on the oval tabletop with self-conscious softness. He had been trying to keep aside the murder of the unfortunate Edson, trying to tell himself that he had already in his life seen so many men die and that the young gold-dreamer was just one more, a brief extension of past slaughters. But it wasn't; it had been murder. So it was a different kind of death, one apart and vivid. He hadn't been fighting alongside this time, having his share. He had been standing there with his hands in the air, and no matter how objectively he relived the circumstances, there was at the end the disquieting fact that he had done nothing to prevent it. His inaction had been understandable, beyond reproach. But one edged and restless corner of his mind refused to settle with it.

"You wouldn't mind," Patterson said, "seeing those men swinging in the air, would you?"

"If it was done legally," Maynard said.

"I'll buy that principle," Patterson said, "but I don't think it's going to be up for sale much longer."

"Would you be part of it?"

"I don't know. I wouldn't want to take an active role, but I am one of God's natural-born observers."

"In this case, Patterson, the actor and the observer would be equal partners."

Patterson smiled uneasily. Then his face relaxed for a moment, as if to allow his mind a retreat into thought. "I suppose," he said, "that a thing happens only if it's witnessed. But I'll tell you, Thomas, I don't know if I'm equal to anything these days. The war burned me down to the bone. There's nothing left inside. I tell you, if I swallowed a penny you'd hear it clip against each rib and land with a ring."

"Incidentally," Maynard said, swaying the talk away from something he was not interested in hearing, "when I walked in, there was a man sitting alone at a table against the far wall."

Patterson glanced across Maynard's shoulder.

"He's still there," he said.

"Who is he?"

"The proprietor. Lucas Bell. Why?"

"He has an impolite way of staring."

"Actually, he's a very polite man; but I wouldn't play cards with him."

"So that's what he does," Maynard said.

"Impressively. The previous owner of this place sat down at the table with him and when he got up he was no longer the owner. They say the game—it was stud poker—went on for thirty-six hours. The fellow lost all his money and then what he could borrow and then the saloon, a quarter interest at a time, and then the whole building, including the furniture upstairs, and then finally when he offered to wager his lady friend, Bell told him that was undignified and threw him out."

"That sounds like quite a run of luck. Does he play a square game?"

"Well, if he doesn't, I wouldn't want to be the one to tell him so."

"He's like that, is he?"

"The truth is, nobody knows what he's like and nobody seems to want to be the first to find out. But I'll tell you why I drink here—because there's never any trouble. If anybody starts any roughhousing, one of the boys will come over and say, 'Mr. Bell asks will you please refrain from making any excitement.' The 'please' is the interesting part. There's no threat or ultimatum. It touches up on a man's self-respect, I imagine. The house is asking you to 'please' stop. It seems you have a choice in the matter. That's easier to accept, especially when you know that you might have five seconds to live if you don't."

"Has that happened?" Maynard asked.

"Nobody has called Mr. Bell on it yet. Sometimes I wish they would. I'm curious."

"If he's the gambler you say he is, then he's probably prepared to back himself."

"I don't doubt he is."

"Do you know him well?"

"I don't know if I do or not," Patterson said. "He can sit there all night like a sphinx, and at other times he'll suddenly turn gregarious and have a few with you, on the house. So who knows? But he's an interesting man, seems to have some education."

"The good gamblers are like that," Maynard said. "The easy charm is part of it. You're supposed to feel like you're privileged to be sitting in with them. It takes some of the sting out of the losing."

"Well," Patterson said, "I say if you come away with the drips it doesn't make any difference whether the woman was cultivated or illiterate."

Maynard laughed. "Speaking of which . . ." he said.

NINE

Well, Maynard was thinking, the last time he was in one of these places he'd been compelled to prevent a woman from being perhaps cut to ribbons, and then ended up knocking a senior officer ice cold, which act of chivalry was probably partially (at least) responsible for his being now in Baddock, Montana Territory.

As an occasional ironist who liked to string things together in the interest of charting the symmetry of cause and consequence, he couldn't help think of it now as he lay next to the woman under a thick but lightweight feather-stuffed blanket that held the estranging odor of too many episodes of paid-for ardor. This place may have lacked the refinements of Mrs. McCoy's House of Entertainment—no perfumed air of spurious gentility, no carpeting, no fur-lined banister—but he missed none of it, none of it mattered when what he needed and what he had begun creating inside him started raising their own steamed and ever-closing walls of intimacy.

If you must, Patterson had told him, then this was the best place in town for it, as long as you avoided thinking who might have been in the bed before you, because a bath wasn't always the first thing the mountain rats thought about when they hit town. The place was called Paradise West and it was directly across the street from Lucas Bell's saloon, so that that staring face could have been watching not just his saloon but the whorehouse as well, which was also under his ownership.

Because there were so few of them out here, it didn't take much for a woman to have airs, or appear to, which was all right and in fact preferred. The last thing a lonely man wanted was a prostitute who acted like a prostitute. The ladies of Paradise West were dressed almost sedately in rustling silk dresses, with combed hair, lightly rouged cheeks, and they avoided tawdriness and vulgarities as if they had been lectured about it, and Maynard assumed they had been, very carefully, by their employer across the street. (This enterprise hadn't been won at cards, Patterson told Maynard, but had been bought and paid for by Bell, who insisted on a high standard of decorum from those on both sides of the house's transactions.)

"Is that your real name?" Maynard asked. "Theodora?"

"Do you doubt it?" she asked.

"No. I'm simply asking."

"If you're asking, then you must doubt it."

"In that case," he said, "I'll withdraw them both, question and doubt."

"If you start asking me questions," she said, "then I might do the same of you."

"And you'd rather not."

"No."

"And why is that?"

"Because I'm always going to hear the same things, most of them untrue."

"You're probably right."

They were lying side by side on the single pillow, naked under the feather blanket. The half-moon had covered a lot of sky and was now positioned to allow a bit of light through the shadeless half-open window, which faced out of the rear of the building onto nothing but prairie and a few distant cabins. It was quiet except for the occasional steady beat from an adjoining room where someone else was doing what Maynard had already done twice.

His eye had lit upon her the moment he'd come through the front door into the parlor where they were sitting, three of them. He liked her because she didn't immediately remind him of any woman he'd known. She appeared to be around thirty, which probably meant she was younger, with thick black hair swept up from the neck and neatly piled and a full, sensuous body. Where the others had given him practiced smiles of artificial seduction, she had sized him up as the commodity he was and then turned away, which he in his vanity took as invitation. He liked her face in profile, with its flat planes and small nose; he liked thinking that she was trying to present a truer image of herself than the others were, even though he knew this was part of the fantasy a man spun out for himself when entering these places.

"Do you remember my name?" he asked.

"You told it to me, didn't you?" she asked. He was holding her hand under the covers.

"That was an hour ago."

She sighed; there was a faint note of impatience to it. When he turned to her on the pillow she closed her eyes. She had large dark eyes that seemed self-protective, sensitive guardians of what remained of her privacy.

"This is always the worst part of it, isn't it?" he asked.

"Of what?" she asked, not curious, not interested, but polite.

"The job."

"Job?"

"What you do."

"I suppose it's a job," she said.

"Not a profession."

"God no. If you think it's a profession then it becomes one. Anyway, I don't know what you're talking about."

"I'm talking about talking," he said, turning his head away and staring straight up at the ceiling, feeling oddly self-conscious about what he was saying. "That's got to be the worst part of it for you, when they start talking."

They, he thought. That must have sounded odd to her, as it did to him.

She didn't say anything. He could tell her eyes were still

closed, as though she were in some painless endurance, listening with almost palpable lack of interest.

"I suppose," he said, "they want to give you a catalog of their troubles; some men seem to take comfort in their own sad sounds, whether anybody's listening or not. And I guess others are just lonely because of what is and what was, and listening to them drone on about it can be damned depressing."

"Scary," she murmured.

"And then there are your would-be redeemers," he said, "the older ones mostly, I would imagine, who want to know what got you into the game and would like to rescue you from it."

"And which one are you?" she asked after several moments' silence.

He released her hand now and brought his up from under the blanket and folded both his hands on his chest.

"I just want to know if that's really your name," he said. "Theodora."

"Yes it is. People call me Theo, which happens to be the Greek for God. Or so I've been told."

He didn't say anything.

"And you're thinking," she said, "what is a prostitute doing with such a name."

He said nothing, though he was offended by what he felt was a judgmental remark. And as if she sensed this, she said quietly, "And your name is Tom."

"Ah. You remembered. I'm flattered."

"Because someone remembered your name an hour after hearing it? That's very sad."

He smiled pensively.

"How long have you been in Baddock?" she asked.

"Since yesterday."

"From where?"

"East," he said.

"Shall I ask you any more?" She had moved her head slightly toward his.

He laughed uncomfortably. "I don't want to sound mysterious," he said. "Or ornery."

"Then I'll take my choice," she said. "It's either a wife or the law or some kind of funny business somewhere, which means anything you tell me will have been cooked in the oven for a while."

"That makes me a liar even before I've said a word."

"I heard once," she said, "the only man who tells the truth is the one who tells you he's a liar."

He rolled over and rested up on his elbow, gazing amusedly at her. She slid her eyes and stared back at him.

"You're quite the lady philosopher," he said.

"You'd better be, in a town like this."

"Why do you stay?"

"I won't be here forever."

"But you're here now."

"That's right," she said, "and I don't want to go somewhere just for the purpose of sitting there and trying to decide where to go next."

"That makes sense."

"What's your whole name?"

"Thomas Maynard."

"Is that the truth?"

"Do you think I'd lie to you?" he asked.

She studied him, as if the question went deeper and was more profound than he intended or she wanted it to be. She in fact seemed perturbed by it and turned her face away, fixing her eyes as though determined to outstare something in the semi-darkness. He watched her wonderingly for several moments more, then lay back down and formed a steeple of fingers on his chest.

"Well," he said, "I suppose it's time to vacate."

After several moments' silence, she asked, with a puzzled frown he could not see, "Will you be back?"

It called for a slap on the rump and a hearty acquiescence. But what he did was say, "Yes," and nod his head.

TEN

"I'm not a habitué of those places," Patterson said, "but certainly, I know Theodora. I wouldn't account myself much of a man if I hadn't taken notice of her."

They were riding in the small trap he had borrowed from his sometime employer at the Baddock *Newspaper* (the name whimsically given it by its elderly editor-publisher, who managed sporadic editions when newsprint was available in sufficient supply). They were following the stage road out of town, passing a scattering of cabins and a few one- and two-story clapboard houses with fenced-in front yards and even a few tended gardens here and there. The morning was cool, sharp with drafts of air that felt pristine and never breathed. Caravans of white clouds in huge inflation passed over the mountains from one blue horizon to another.

"I'd say she's a real lady," Patterson said, holding the reins in his hand, watching the brown mare trot along the uneven road, hooves making some clucking sounds, "in spite of how she's earning her bread."

"How long has she been here?" Maynard asked.

"Less than a year. Simply turned up on the Territorial one day. According to the story the driver got from the stationmaster where she boarded, she appeared at the station with some man in a wagon, who kissed her good-bye, let her down, and drove away. God knows what was behind that. She rode the stage for two days, right on into Baddock. But this was no shrinking violet, according to the driver. It seems one of the passengers made some suggestive remarks to her

and she pulled a derringer from her purse and sat there holding it on him until he yelled up to the driver to stop so he
could join him up on the seat. The fellow said she had her finger right on that trigger and he was afraid some jolt from the
road might impel a discharge. I hope you didn't make any
out-of-the-way remarks to her."

"How can you make out-of-the-way remarks to a woman
when you're lying in bed with her after having already been
done up twice?" Maynard asked.

"I suppose you're correct," Patterson said.

"What did she do when she hit town?"

"She surprised everybody, that's what she did. Everybody
thought she must be somebody's sister or daughter or what
have you. I happened to be at the stage line office when she
pulled in and I remember thinking, after having a look at her,
that by God civilization is starting to come to Baddock. She
was decked out in some mighty nice finery and had a keen
look about her. Turner, who runs the Territorial in these
parts, carried her bag and escorted her across to The Brothers
Hotel and when he came back told everyone her name was
Theodora Diamond, and that's when we began to look at one
another, thinking, No woman has a real name like that. Well,
sure enough, Bell soon had her settled in a room upstairs
from the apothecary and she was working for him in Paradise
West."

"How did he get to her?" Maynard asked. "Had he
known her before?"

"I don't know. Maybe."

"She didn't strike me as being a professional."

"What did she strike you as?" Patterson asked.

"Somebody who's down on her luck."

"I don't know, Tom; she doesn't have that grim look."

"Maybe her luck's gone sour," Maynard said, "but not her
spirit."

"I'll grant you, she is out of the ordinary. But if she is a
professional, then she's of a different stripe. She's the only

one he lets live out of the house; all the others stay right there."

"What's that mean? They can't be paired up."

"I wouldn't think so," Patterson said. "A man like Bell wouldn't want his woman doing what she's doing."

"Then what?"

Patterson shook his head. "You don't ask questions. It is what it is, that's all."

"Do you know her?"

"Not in the Biblical sense. She's come into the office a few times to buy a paper. We've talked. She's well spoken."

"What do you know about her?" Maynard asked.

"You've taken an interest, it seems," Patterson said, glancing across with a sly smile.

Maynard said nothing.

"Well," Patterson said, "if you've been to the sheets with her at least you know she's not Major Pryor in pretend."

"I asked what you knew about her."

"She doesn't tell much, Tom. Jesus, you spent intimate time with her."

"What I learned you'll have to pay to find out."

"Then maybe I will," Patterson said.

Maynard found himself resenting that, and then annoyed with himself for it.

"She's traveled around a bit, I know that," Patterson said. "We talked some little bit about Denver and Salt Lake. She knew those towns. I got the feeling—and that's all it was— that she's from back East somewheres, and probably with the usual hard-luck story. Some of these bed-squeezers will talk your head off, looking for sympathy or for you to explain their lives to them; others are like Theo: it's none of your business, mister."

The road took them near the church. It was a small building nailed together with unevenly hewn gray boards, standing on a slight rise. It had a small A-framed-roof entrance, atop which was fitted a modest cupola with small shuttered windows and a three-foot-high carved steeple tapering off into the sunlight. The rest of the building was gable-roofed. Another claim being staked in the Montana Territory, Maynard thought, looking out at it with an incurious eye.

"That's the minister out front," Patterson said.

"Then let's say hello," Maynard said.

Patterson turned the trap toward the church and rode it up to where the minister was standing. He was of medium height, with sparse reddish hair, clean-shaven. He was wearing dark trousers and a buttoned-to-the-neck tieless white shirt that looked starched and pressed and seemed to gleam in the morning light. He raised one arm slowly and placed a pipe between his teeth as he watched the trap roll to a halt before him. He acknowledged Patterson's greeting with a nod of the head.

"This is to introduce Mr. Maynard," Patterson said.

The minister stepped forward and extended his hand. "Arthur Wynston," he said, "minister to this church."

"Tom Maynard," Maynard said, leaning back after the shake of hands.

"Will you be joining our congregation, Mr. Maynard?"

"I'm not sure, sir; but it's a comfort knowing it's here."

The minister nodded his head once and smiled, his pale brown eyes staring straight back into Maynard's inquiring gaze.

"You're new to Baddock then, Mr. Maynard?"

"Just arrived."

"Are you here to test your good fortune?"

"In a way," Maynard said.

"Well, whatever your way is, I hope you'll find your way here."

"It's Mr. Wynston's message," Patterson said, "that if you strike it you'll need to pray not so much for thanks as for wisdom."

"Too many people," the minister said, "suffer the disastrous judgment of thinking that wealth and wisdom are one and the same."

"I've found that fallacy extends to rich and poor alike," Maynard said.

"If gold made you wise instead of rich," Patterson said, "I wonder how avidly it would be sought."

"If a man was wise enough to appreciate the fact," the minister said, "I daresay he'd be too wise to go in pursuit of it."

Maynard was looking beyond the church to the small fenced-around cemetery.

"You had a funeral here yesterday," he said.

"An unfortunate young man," the minister said. "Did you know him?"

"Enough to feel sorry," Maynard said, gazing through the sunlight at the near but remote-seeming patch of land. "Did they put up a board?"

"It will be seen to."

"His name was Edson."

The minister nodded several times, watching Maynard's outgazing face with a curiosity that remained unchanged even when Maynard looked back to him.

"Having a morning ride?" Mr. Wynston asked.

"We're heading up to check out Barley Newton's claim," Patterson said. "What's to be done about it, I don't know; but I don't want anybody jumping it until what's to be done is done."

"Did you know him, Mr. Wynston?" Maynard asked.

"Barley Newton? I don't believe I did. Was he a friend of yours?"

Maynard shook his head.

At that they said their farewells and rode on.

"Is that how you're going to do it?" Patterson asked as the trap began following an off-trail leading up toward the gulches. "Ask everybody if they knew him? That'll get you nowhere, or shot, which is about the same."

"It was a reasonable question."

"Not the way you were asking it. The *minister*, Thomas. For God's sake."

"Why can't a major become a minister?" Maynard asked.

"I suppose he could; it's a mere matter of transferring your authority, the difference being that one profession is dedicated to slaughter and the other to salvation. Anyway, are you a churchgoing man, Maynard?"

"I never answer that; there are too many levels of explanation."

"Well," Patterson said, "neither am I. But he knows."

"Who knows?"

"Wynston. He's already marked you off. They can spot a potential parishioner a mile away. But I'll tell you something," Patterson said as he flicked the reins for the steepening trail, "I think that little church building makes a lot of people uneasy. Do you know why? Because you've got men up here breaking their backs against the ground and in the streams hoping to achieve a big, wonderful, exciting pageant of change in their lives; a new world of living and conjuring for themselves; and then they come back into town and there it is, standing there in embodiment of the eternally unchanged, unchanging, and unchangeable. Very sobering. Very depressing."

They reached Barley's claim in late afternoon. It had been staked in a particularly unattractive place, part of it under a series of beetling ridges mounted with some precipitously poised boulders. The irregular ground was studded with rock outcroppings and coils of gray bramble that looked mean enough to snare the wind. A narrow creek channeled through the claim.

"This doesn't look like a place where fortunes are made," Maynard said as they walked across the hard inhospitable ground. They had covered the final half mile on foot, having tethered horse and trap below, where the last semblance of trail had given out.

"The making of a fortune begins in the imagination," Patterson said. "A good enough imagination can make even ground like this start to glitter. Anyway, he worked the gulches. All he needed was a common pick and shovel, water to wash the dirt, and a sluice. And a strong back, of course. It was all simple enough to keep the imagination going. But you wanted to see it, and here it is."

"What I wanted to see," Maynard said, "is whether it was worth killing a man for."

"Barley thought it might be. He'd come on back to town every so often to resupply, with his little sack of glitter, and people saw that. I told him to be careful, being one man alone. You never know when a jumper might show up and some of those fellows can be as deadly as rattlesnakes. A group of Chinese were slaughtered not far from here. So he tried to be careful. He said it was awkward to work wearing his gun belt, but he always kept his pistol nearby, wrapped in a shirt. He wasn't what you'd describe as a hard man, but he knew the difference between right and wrong and was willing to back it up."

"But if he'd been killed for his claim, wouldn't whoever shot him be up here working it now?"

Patterson removed his Stetson, ran his fingers across the crown crease, then replaced the hat upon his thick-growing white hair.

"Well, they could be," he said. "Or maybe they've already tried it and given up. Or maybe he wasn't shot by jumpers. We just don't know, do we?"

"I feel like it's the first day of school, when don't know outweighs know by a ton."

"Loosen up your mind a little, Captain. You've been a soldier for too long. You can't think like a soldier out here. And you can bet your boots Pryor's learned that, if he's out here."

"But you can't entirely forget that you were a soldier, either. And sometimes you can forget that you haven't forgotten."

Patterson laughed. "Is that as complicated as it sounds?"

They walked alongside the stream whose clear waters were taking small animated leaps over the rocks, where Barley Newton had stood crouched by the hour and by the day, panning for flecks of color.

Donald Honig

"There's a pathetic nobility to it all," Patterson said, looking down at their shadows crossing the moving waters. "Unlike most of your impractical dreamers, they at least labor for what they crave. But Barley was no impractical dreamer. I'd say he was a very practical man; he knew what his chances were up here. He was an extremely clearheaded sort of man."

"What you're saying," Maynard said, "is he wasn't a man to see ghosts."

"What I'm saying is that if you want to walk in his boots you'd better know just what kind of man he was."

"Is that what I'm doing, Patterson—trying to walk in his boots?"

"Well, you wanted to come up here. It's as if you wanted to prove to yourself that he really existed. Well, he did, and most of the time this is where it was."

Maybe, Maynard thought. Maybe that was indeed what he was doing, trying to get a sense of the existence of Barley Newton, the man who may or may not have seen a ghost or an uncanny resemblance of the actual man or the man himself and whose sighting of whatever it had been had brought him—him being Maynard—all the way out here. Barley himself had been real enough, because this was where he'd labored with the faith and conviction of the true believer. And here, in the lean-to they came upon, was where he had taken the faith to sleep with him and released it to wander within the naive enchantments of dream.

The lean-to had been built to accommodate a single man, with burlap bags for a floor, a straw pallet for sleeping; it was a modest point of departure for those immense dreams that could sweep the universe in a single night. The higher rear wall faced the ridges. Maynard could see daylight through some of the log chinks. There was also some daylight coming through the single-pitch roof, which meant Barley didn't have to listen to know when it was raining.

"He actually didn't like it up here," Patterson said as they stood outside of the simple structure. "Said it got lonely.

That's why when he'd come into town he'd stay an extra day or two, to fill up with talk and company, was how he put it."

"And see ghosts," Maynard said.

"You still don't want to accept it."

"As long as I'm out here, I'll accept it. But with reasonable skepticism."

They saw the shadows first, falling from the ridge above, the men and their mules imprinted on the hard Montana earth, motionless at first and then moving, as if brushed by a wind.

"Oh, Christ," Patterson said under his breath.

With none of the instruments of instituted society around to mislead or deceive, there was little chance of misreading menace for nonchalant amiability. The two gray-white mules picked their way down the incline in single file, their trail-hardened hooves dislodging a few stones that rolled for small distances and then stopped, minute sounds orchestrating the slow sullen approach. They were small men, wearing torn, oversized coats and dust-powdered bowler hats that looked like trophies on their small heads. Each was sitting his saddle above splayed legs that hung out at angles and quivered with each step forward. Each had a rifle across his pommel. Their small beard-stubbled faces were impassive, as if they had seen nothing and might be riding toward a horizon.

"I don't like this," Patterson said quietly.

"Do you know them?" Maynard asked, watching what seemed like an interminable descent from the ridge and listening to the occasional rattling stone and then the arrival at flat ground about a hundred feet away, where the pair aligned side by side as if waiting to be bugled into a charge.

"Yes and no," Patterson said. "No, I don't know them, but yes, they're probably jumpers and mean trouble."

"How much trouble?" Maynard asked, speaking in a normal voice to Patterson's apprehensive whispering.

"Well, I suppose they could have picked us off from overhead."

"Not everybody can shoot that well."

"Then take your choice," Patterson said. "Try and bluff them off or let them have what they want."

"We can't give them what we don't own, and I hate giving them what's not theirs," Maynard said, watching the two mule-sitting strangers, his mind already formulating what might be the best move and what the best odds on it, how severe the penalty of guessing wrong.

They were moving forward now, the mules gradually separating, one coming straight forward, the other beginning what appeared to be a circular approach.

"What do you want?" Patterson called out.

"You're on our claim," the forward-moving one said, sounding as if he might be taking some pinched pleasure in saying it.

"It's not your claim," Patterson said.

"We say elsewise," the forward-moving one said.

"Can you prove it?" Patterson asked.

There was no response. The mule kept moving forward. This one would be first, Maynard thought, by eye measuring the distance—less than fifty feet now. This one first, then move quickly left while the other one would be lifting his rifle, and then stop and fire, at which moment he would know if his first shot had gone home effectively.

"Start running," Maynard said quietly to Patterson.

"What—"

"I won't say it again."

It was the combination—the edged tension in Maynard's voice and the continued approach of those men and their slow outrageously passive mules—that struck Patterson and he wheeled and took flight, running with long strides that rocked him from side to side.

Maynard whipped free his gun and fired once at the forward rider and then swung quickly aside and fired at the second, his shot missing as the man hoisted and shouldered his rifle and stiffened his back as he sought to take aim, but Maynard's next shot drove in chest high and the man fell back, dropping the rifle as the impervious mule continued marching and seemed to walk right out from under him. Maynard spun around again, into a half crouch, and watched the first rider swaying out into midair as if to extend his hand toward something and then falling with what seemed sheer weightlessness as men in dreams fall, but not clear, hung by a single stirrup to the mule, which, like its partner, continued forward, toward Maynard, as if to drag up and present to him the thing he had shot.

When the perspiring Patterson returned he stood with his hands on his hips, still panting from his sudden exertions.

"Jesus," he said, "I didn't think I'd see either of us alive again. By God," he said, his voice exultant, "that was shooting."

"I think it was justified," Maynard said. He was still holding the pistol in his hand.

"Justified? By God, those bastards were about to gun us down like dogs."

"I believe that."

"You could tell by the way they were coming on, one swinging out wide like that. That was planned. Goddamn murdering claim jumpers. No telling how many honest men they buried. Listen, I ran only because you told me to."

"That was your only chance, if I missed," Maynard said, putting away the pistol now.

"Miss? You?" a still-exultant Patterson said. "I'll bet never."

"If you say so," Maynard said, trying to remember the last time he had fired a sidearm. He believed it was during some informal target shooting a year or so ago, out at the Anacostia flats during an outing with some young ladies and fellow officers.

The mules were standing still now, one with its late rider still hanging from its side. The other man was lying flat on the ground, legs angled far apart.

"They're dead, I take it," Patterson said.

"Very."

"Very dead," Patterson said. "You couldn't publish that. No editor would let it pass. But you can't say it any better. Very dead. By God, Thomas, you're a sharp edge in a round world."

ELEVEN

Maynard soon acquired two things in Baddock, one of them a reputation as a very lethal man, and although such reputations were not uncommon in mining towns, they were like intriguing appellations when ascribed to what seemed unlikely men, and the stranger Thomas Maynard, in his mild affability, was regarded as decidedly unlikely. He had, in defense of his own life and that of an unarmed friend, shot and killed two claim jumpers (it soon developed that the two dead men were known in the area as exactly that and suspected of worse), which in that part of the country was not considered killing men as much as it was helping to control a pestilence.

The second thing he acquired was an abandoned cabin on the fringe of town that Patterson steered him to. It had been built by an early arrival to Baddock who had long since pulled up stakes and left, and then later used by Barley Newton during his brief visits to town. And Maynard acquired a third thing, too—Barley's horse, a brown-and-black-mottled Appaloosa that Patterson, as Barley's close friend and therefore trustee of sorts, had been stabling since his friend's death and now loaned to Maynard for as long as the latter needed it.

The cabin was about a half mile outside of town, standing some hundred yards back from the stage road. Its builder had laid down a plank floor, but by now there was sage and greasewood growing up through it like invidious instruments of reclamation. The roof was tight enough, though its supporting uprights looked unsteady, and when a strong wind blew not all of it went around the structure, sending drafts through apertures in the walls. There were table, chairs, cook-stove, and a bed of puzzling size until Patterson explained that it had been put down first and the cabin built around it.

"Good enough for as long as you'll be here," he said. He had brought over in the trap a box of utensils, tin cups and plates, some candles, a kerosene lamp.

"Which won't be long, I hope," Maynard said.

"You wouldn't want to winter here, though I believe the first fellow did once. Of course he had plenty of blankets, a rented woman, and the fever. Of all of it, I'd imagine it was the fever that kept him warmest."

"You really believe in that disease, don't you?" Maynard asked.

"It's one of those things that you can't believe in until you've caught it or sat around with those who have. It's like a fire in them. Don't sell it short, Maynard. And look out, because it's known to be contagious."

"I'll be gone long before the first snowfall," Maynard said, sitting down on one of the chairs. "Won't even be a memory."

"Oh, you'll be a memory all right," Patterson said, taking the other chair, which wobbled a bit under the slow impact of his weight. "You were quite the topic of talk at the Honest Eagle this afternoon. They wanted to know about you."

"Who wanted to know?"

"Some of the nabobs—if you recall the word. You piqued some interest by what you did up at the claim."

"What kind of interest?" Maynard asked.

"They wanted to know all about you."

"Who wanted to know?"

"Let's see," Patterson said, crossing his legs as he leaned back and touched his chin for a moment. "There was Turner, the stage line man. And some of those I've already told you about: Abbot, O'Connor—he's the lawyer—Pearson . . ."

"The banker."

"That's right. Good memory, Thomas."

"Well, they've been on my mind, haven't they?"

"They're the town bluebloods, so to speak. The ones who've staked a claim in the town's future. Look, this is not going to be a territory forever, Tom; Montana's coming into the Union sooner or later, and when it does these fellows want to be on the front doorstep. They've got a very serious interest in establishing law and order, which means zero tolerance for claim jumpers, road agents, and any other highly unethical sorts who walk around with squinting eyes and quick trigger fingers."

"It's got nothing to do with me," Maynard said. "You know what I'm out here for. And for all you know, one of your town pillars could be the man I'm after."

"If he is, then he's a fully resurrected, reputable, and forward-looking citizen."

"Only under Montana skies. Elsewhere he's still marked down as a deserter."

"Be that as it may," Patterson said. "But the fact remains, you're the center of interest at the moment. They wanted to know all about the stranger who'd rubbed away a pair of vermin while standing up for his rights. And, incidentally, I omitted my share of the action, which consisted of running away. No matter the reasons for it, it never looks good."

Maynard smiled. "History will record the story exactly as you told it."

"Anyway, since I seem to be just about the only one around who knows you, I was asked a lot of questions, but be sure there were more questions than answers. They seemed intrigued by the fact that you were very quick and sure with a gun."

"No more, probably, than a lot of men around here."

"The difference being," Patterson said, pointing out a finger, "that you happened to be standing up for what was right. What back in the States is a mere quality is out here a virtue."

"All I did was defend myself."

"More than yourself, Maynard—a principle. And not only did you act righteously but successfully. Unfortunately, a lot of men who tried that are now populating the cemetery, like your friend Edson. You're a man who defended himself and lived to tell the tale."

"I lived," Maynard said; "you told the tale."

"A tale that intrigued them deeply, believe me."

"Did you tell them I wasn't planning on staying here very long?"

"No, I didn't tell them that. I sat there as the very presence of ignorance and awe, telling them nothing but what I saw. I didn't know where you came from, why you were here, or how long you intended to stay. In a more polite society that might make you nondescript or even a misfit of sorts. But not here. Here, you're the stranger who's on the side of law and order, and the less they know about you the more intriguing you become. This is brand-new country out here, Maynard, and among other things, they're creating myths. It's a by-product of the whole pattern of existence. I wouldn't be surprised if they aren't thinking of offering you the sheriff's badge."

"Jesus Christ, Patterson," Maynard said, shifting about in the chair, "I hope you set them straight on *that.*"

Patterson smiled down at the plank floor, where the sun was limning the four-square window pattern.

"I set them straight on nothing," he said. "I'm not supposed to know anything about you, remember. Anyway, nobody actually mentioned the word *sheriff,* but they were playing around the edges of it."

"They've got a sheriff."

"I got the impression that it wasn't going to be for very much longer. 'We need more vigor in the sheriff's office,' is a sentiment that was being clearly implied."

"Dammit, Patterson, I don't know what kind of yarn you gave them, but I'm no damned gunfighter."

Patterson stared across for several moments of frank appraisal.

"You went through four years of war, Thomas," he said, "so you can be anything, even something you don't know about yet."

Maynard didn't immediately answer that. He supposed that any man who had spent years enduring the concentrated shocks of combat was later susceptible to candid introspection, self-revelation. He had experienced many of the imperial set pieces of the Civil War, when legions had under risen flags and banners marched to battle in brigades and regiments according to devised strategies, when he had been nothing more than another slim reed of cloth and buttons. But there had been other times, when leading small detachments on probes or reconnoiters, when he had been more aware of his own humanity; those times when they had run into small, unexpected, brief skirmishes, so many times that he had finally come away wondering if he was not seeker but provoker. When the itineraries of his mind tended to be directed by the epiphanies of the self-communer, he was led to wonder if it had been Thomas Maynard who had provoked these episodes, if a man was damned by certain innate capacities and responses that communicated through thin air and stirred the blood of those who would prey.

Irately, he now said to Patterson, "Goddammit, I'm a captain in the United States Army. That's who I am."

"Lest we forget," Patterson said, "a man on special assignment, and if you want to have luck in that assignment, then let them think whatever they want. You don't have to compromise yourself one jot."

There was, Maynard allowed grudgingly, some logic to it, and maybe some advantage.

"And where," he asked, "was Lucas Bell during this discussion?"

"Mr. Bell was his usual self. Silent, watchful, and absorbing every word. A man who can sit still and yet give the impression of prowling in a lair."

Maynard grunted, seeing with his inner eye that veiled, secret-cold face with its private mockeries.

"These men are going to want to talk to you," Patterson said.

"I'm in favor of that."

"Yes, I would imagine. You never know where you might turn up an ex-major of the Union Army."

"If he's here."

"I don't have to caution you to tread carefully," Patterson said. "Finding a man who doesn't want to be found—or even looking for him—can be inimical to one's health."

"Yes," Maynard said. "*Sic transit* Barley Newton," he added, recalling General Northwood's use of the Latin.

Patterson sighed philosophically.

"It's a bizarre society out here," he said. "You'd think you'd have to cross an ocean to get to it, it's so damned different. Gold brings them out, trims their civilized edges, and takes that most honorable thing, ambition, and filters into it greed, desperation, obsession. It swings men away from just about everything they've ever known or been, and out of it eventually comes a stability common to all. God, who knows: maybe at bottom it's all very rational."

"Gold standard," Maynard said, "can be a most ambiguous phrase."

TWELVE

"So now people know you," Theo said. "That can be bad luck in a town like this."

"Nobody really knows me," Maynard said.

She laughed, as if he had said the most ingenuous thing.

"Of course not," she said, "but that doesn't matter; it's what they *think* that matters, and they *think* they know you. And because they really *don't* know you, then each one is going to see you in their own way. So you remain as mysterious as ever, but the difference is that nobody realizes it. That's why it's best never to become famous; that way you'll never be misunderstood."

"I don't know how much being famous in Baddock counts for."

"It counts for a lot," she said, "when you're in Baddock."

They were riding in the twice-borrowed trap, once by Patterson from his sometime employer and now by Maynard from Patterson. She was wearing a long black dress, the kind you saw on the wives of Nebraska sodbusters, only of finer material, and a fringed buckskin jacket against the slight chill. She had unpinned her hair—it was her "evening style," she said—and let it fall thick and free over her shoulders.

He had spent several hours with her last night at the Paradise West, bucking in and out of her, and then holding her in his arms for long, wordless spans of time, converting moments into emotion and indifferent to where this was happening, in a bordello in the midst of a gold-struck town of dirt streets and ramshackle buildings, knowing only that what was growing into him was older and more primal and more fulfilling than gold itself. As a man long detached from family and home ground, he was not one to look too deeply beyond what he saw and certainly not what he felt. Too many others had found the warmth and stability that he sometimes reluctantly admitted he envied not to make him vulnerable to any glint or glance of it.

There had been Lucy Mae, the most beautiful courtesan in Washington, known to some as the Solace of Congress for her many eminent liaisons. She lived in a small but elegantly appointed house on Massachusetts Avenue and was highly selective of clientele. Maynard, a mere captain, had gained entrance through her notorious oaken doors because she had seen him at a New Year's Eve party at the Willard and been taken by his strong good looks, his reputation as Civil War daredevil, and by what she described to someone as "the feral in his eye." An invitation had been discreetly passed along and one evening he appeared.

She knew he was charmed by her and she would chide him about it. Was it the enchantment of her four-poster with its gold lamé roof, she asked, where the power of great power had expended itself, or was it she? He avoided direct answer and kept returning to keep a three-nights-a-week appointment, to each of which he looked ahead with increasing fervor. But finally she had to know. It was the curiosity of a proud woman, one who kept tight rein on her own emotional fevers. Was he within the web or hovering on the outside?

"Captain Tom," she asked him one night, "are you taken with me?"

"I think we're best taken together," he said.

"Why have you never married?"

"I'm just a poor soldier boy, Lucy Mae," he said, being careful.

"But with a well-lighted career ahead, so I hear. And remember, I only converse with the high and mighty."

"You aren't now."

"I think a man who's heading for the top is much more interesting than one who's already there, don't you?"

"I wouldn't know," he said.

"Since most of Washington knows where I lie down," she said, "it's important to me to know where I stand. Presume a situation, of equal balance on both sides."

"Situation?"

"Of the heart. Two people in love. Can you imagine it?"

"Easily," he said.

"It's a beautiful thing, isn't it?" she said, adding, "And, believe it or not, a very rare thing. So it should be protected, shouldn't it?"

"By all means."

"Thomas, would you ever consider marriage with a common whore?"

"Common?"

"Uncommon, actually," she said. (They were in bed. She was running her finger lightly back and forth across his mustache, he would remember.) "If she promised to reform, of course."

"She would need help at that," he said.

"Of course."

"It isn't light work. The reformation of an uncommon whore is a great, great responsibility. Not every man is up to it, and only one allowed to be."

"Some have tried, of course," she said. "And failed."

"It's a situation," he said, "where one woman can succeed where many men have failed. Perhaps the only such situation."

"Will you give it some thought?"

He did, and in fact stayed away from her while he did. He wasn't sure what she really wanted, less sure of himself. There was a marvelous temptation in it, though he knew it would be impossible to marry a woman like that and remain in Washington (and probably impossible to remain in the army either). But what he did do—and later, when he had time to recollect—was realize that he *had* considered it, at least in the abstract, that instead of rejecting the notion out of hand as preposterous, had given thought to possibility and ramification. He had invited it into his mind as imaginable, then rejected it. It wasn't Lucy Mae and what she did that mattered, it was marriage that he did not at that point want, and whether she had been toying with him or not was irrelevant, like something subordinated to a larger, more important question. But he never had the chance to tell her (or find out), because he soon heard that she had wrapped up and gone to Rhode Island to marry the straitlaced son of a wealthy Providence merchant.

"However," Theo said now as they rode along the stage road, "I don't think you care one small pebble what people think of you."

"I'm not without some self-respect," he said.

"It has nothing to do with that; it has to do with independence. You seem like that sort of man to me. Independent."

"I might be."

"Don't you know yourself? Or do you see yourself through other people's eyes?"

He laughed. "Sometimes," he said, thinking of how many times he had tried to see himself through General Northwood's eyes.

"Were you in the war?" she asked.

He thought about it; what he didn't want was answer leading to question leading to answer and so on.

"No," he said.

"So, having missed it, you decided to come out here to find your adventures."

"What about yourself? I can think of a thousand reasons for a man to be out here but none for a woman."

"That almost makes you a gentleman," she said.

He had been surprised when she agreed to come out with him; he'd been certain she wouldn't, maybe even couldn't. Just a ride out along the prairie, he told her, trying to make it as innocuous as he intended to be.

"I'm glad you came out," he said.

"I was flattered," she said, "to be asked by the hero of the hour."

"As long as it's only for the hour."

"Aren't you enjoying your fame?"

"It's not an enjoyable sort of fame," he said. "I killed two men."

"Most men would be swaggering around with their thumbs in their belts." When he said nothing, she added, "But you're not them, are you? You're not most men."

They paused at a stream that was several feet deep and perhaps ten across, the clear sun-sharp water channeling down from high above.

"This stream has a tale to tell," she said.

"Will it tell?" he asked, holding the reins loosely in hand.

"A stream never talks, it giggles, and this one has something to giggle about. Some time ago, when Lucas was heading into Baddock, he stopped here. It was hot summer and they'd been traveling hard for some time."

"They?" he asked.

"He was with a woman. Very prim and proper, so it's been told. He stole her from somewhere."

"Stole her," Maynard said, not asking, simply repeating it aloud for its incongruity.

"Not with stealth or by force of arms; he used his charm. I suppose he passed through some town where she was somebody's wife, maybe even somebody's mother, but when he left that town she went with him. If you think she was foolish then you must think the whole game of man and woman, at every detail, is foolish, back to Adam and Eve, although I doubt those particular two were in love since there was nobody else around to make the difference."

"I haven't said anything," the mildly amused Maynard said, watching the stream waters splash and tumble.

"When they reached this stream," she went on, "they were tired and covered with dust and looked exactly like what they were—two people who had traveled a long way in hot weather. So they stopped here and dismounted. Then Lucas told her to strip off, right down to the skin. This to a woman who slipped into bed in a nightdress and then pulled it up under the covers in order to provide her man and preserve her modesty at one and the same time. Can you imagine this woman being told to strip off right in the middle of God's sunshine? She refused, of course, until he advised her it might be done for her instead, and none too gently. So she did, weeping and woeful. And he did the same."

"To what point?" Maynard asked.

"To bathe," she said. "To refresh and then change into clean clothes. Because Lucas Bell refused to ride into a town he meant to occupy looking anything less than a suave gentleman, and he wanted his woman to look scrubbed and stylish. 'The impression is set at the first,' he said. But it must have been a sight—the two of them here, naked as pups, soaping up and soaking their cans in the water and then toweling down and then dressing up to the nines."

"To enter Baddock," Maynard said.

"Exactly," she said. "San Francisco wouldn't have cared or noticed, but Baddock would. And did."

Maynard thought about it; not of the two naked people who had washed away their trail grime here but of what must have been the processional ride along Main Street, the impeccable Bell with his impassive face, and the woman, who . . . Maynard didn't know.

"She must have been an attractive woman," he said.

Theo shrugged. "So they say."

"What happened to her?"

She smiled at him, hooking her arm through his. "I really don't know," she said.

Maynard kissed her lightly on the cheek. Then he turned and stared at the stream, watching it come winding through its dirt-sided banks, the water running with what seemed an alacrity, as though pitching along with a springtide spirit.

Then he turned around to take a reading of the surrounding landscape; it stood in two divisions of solitude on either side of the road, an arrested portrait of young cottonwoods and patches of sage and those ubiquitous rocks large and larger that seemed like the unneeded excesses of mountain building, and which from within themselves and out of eons of anchored stillness seemed to create silence within silence the way ice turned cold colder.

Then he looked back to the stream, with one finger under the brim pushing his hat slightly up from his forehead.

"I don't want to suggest," he said, "that we're in any way dirty or dusty or smelly . . ."

She threw back her head and laughed.

"Here, Thomas?" she asked, looking at him, the mirth still in her face. "Now?"

"The place has already been anointed."

"So it has."

"If Bell can peel here, so can I."

"If you'll help a lady down from her carriage . . ."

He got off the trap and offered his hands and brought her to the ground. Then, each watching the other with delighting mischief, began stripping down, garment for garment, tossing each discarded piece of apparel back up onto the seat of the trap until they each stood in the blue-skied sunshine like epitomes of stainless purity. He had never seen a woman out to this in the open air and had to marvel at the statuesque form with its strong legs and full thighs and voluptuously incurving hips and primly matted center, hung with red-tipped heavy-bottomed breasts, and all of it ripened to the moment with the undaunted smile of a challenge accepted and met.

He took her hand and they walked alongside the stream to where deep patches of moss grew and here they stretched themselves out.

"Lord, Thomas," she whispered as she received him, "but you're a full meal."

Never inhibited, he felt more expansively liberated than
ever before in his life, felt terrifically sanctioned, as if all of
creation from the great canopy of sky and thick piles of
mountain down to the pure virtues of the running stream
were in complicity with him.

When it was over they embraced tightly for long minutes,
then lay back on their green paradise, gradually recomposing
themselves. Then he rose and with his hand led her into the
stream's cool bracing waters where they crouched and
splashed at each other like children. Then, abruptly, she
began laughing.

"God," she cried, "you forget to tether it!"

The water glistening in his tossed-about black hair and
running from him in bright droplets, Maynard shot to his feet
and looked where the horse and trap had stood. He leaped
from the stream and ran along the bank and then he saw it,
horse and trap wandered out along the prairie, no larger to
his eye than his thumb was to his hand.

"Jesus Christ!" he shouted.

"Bring it back, Thomas!" she shouted, fully risen in the
stream, hands cupped around mouth, shaking with laughter.

Running then, as fast as he could, barefoot, barechested,
bare everything, even though the horse was hardly moving
now, tugging the trap another few yards and then dawdling
as it lowered its long neck to the ground. Running carefully,
to avoid the sharp edges that littered the road, and running
with a spectacular sense of exhilaration, as if all of this was
wondrous proof of something. Running with an incredulous
smile, chest out, arms pumping, the water drops still clinging
to him feeling like they were turning to ice. Running as if to
temper and pacify the soaring founts of joy he felt.

THIRTEEN

"Ah," Patterson said, "there you are. I've been looking for you all day."

"Then I'm glad you didn't find me," Maynard said.

He had just tied his horse to the rail outside of the Honest Eagle and stepped up onto the boardwalk when Patterson hailed him. When someone opened the door and emerged from the saloon they could hear the piano playing, meaning that night in Lucas Bell's place was beginning its long hectic ramble to daylight.

"And I wasn't the only one," Patterson said. "The town fathers were looking for you too. Rode out to your cabin and back, in fact. Each time I saw one of them, he'd ask, 'Well, has he turned up yet?' "

"Who was asking?"

"The same ones who were interested before: Turner, Pearson, Abbot, O'Connor."

"What did they want?"

"To talk to you. And don't ask me what about; I'm not sure I want to know anyway."

"You're a newspaperman," Maynard said. "How come you don't want to know?"

"As far as that goes," Patterson said, "I'm a former newspaperman. But obviously it has something to do with the stage that came in shot up this morning."

"Another one?"

"I can tell you, Tom, the anger around here is burning deeper and deeper."

"It's got nothing to do with me," Maynard said.

"Are you going in there?" Patterson asked, nodding toward the Honest Eagle.

"I was thinking of it."

"Well, let's go somewhere else. I have to talk to you."

Patterson didn't wait, instead turning around and beginning to walk. Maynard glanced at the door of the saloon, then followed.

They walked through a group of a half dozen long-bearded miners in town for a binge, then stepped down into the street, stopped to allow a wagon to pass, then crossed to the next boardwalk, passing the general store, outside of which a hatless man was sitting on a flour barrel, smoking a pipe. They came to the office of the Baddock *Newspaper,* where Patterson unlocked the door and Maynard followed him inside.

"Privacy," Patterson said, turning up a kerosene lamp. "The old boy's gone home for the night. He sometimes likes to pretend there's a heavy workload but he just sits here and drinks whiskey, to avoid going home. He's got a wife big as a buffalo but not as docile. But I guess he was under orders tonight. What are you drinking? There's some decent rye. My supply, not his."

Patterson put two glasses on a table and poured them full, then removed his hat and sat down opposite Maynard, placing the hat on the table. The round-backed chairs they sat in were particularly hard and uncomfortable.

"He puts out a decent edition here," Patterson said after tasting the whiskey, "when he's able to. I do a bit of writing, try to wrangle some advertising, come in sometimes to help sling type. The old boy is a little in awe because I once worked for the *Herald.* But he does all right. Started out in a calf shed."

The office was a single large room, ink-smelling and everywhere ink-spattered, from walls to floor to desk tops. Several tables held type cases, another a two-handed ink brayer and toggle joint. An old Washington hand press stood in a corner.

A woodstove with a slender tin chimney rising through the ceiling was fixed in the center of the room.

"Sometimes," Patterson said, "you get a combustible alloy when you mix gold with type metal, but the old boy steers away from controversy, unlike some of your frontier editors, who go in for high-horse moralism and civic crusading."

"This is not what you wanted to talk about," Maynard said, sitting back, holding his glass at his belt buckle.

"No," Patterson said. "I'll tell you what it is. The driver of that stage and two passengers were wounded. They were jumped about ten miles outside of town but he wouldn't stop, just whipped the horses and kept going, with the road agents hot after them. There were about a half dozen men inside the coach, who weren't in the mood to be robbed, and they were shooting back out the windows. The stage went skidding up and down around the trail. I would've given something to have been a bird flying over. But there was hell to pay when they finally rolled in. Turner near had an apoplectic fit, ranting about anarchy and what-have-you. It got so hot that finally Dunlop said he'd ride out and see what he could see; but they talked him down from it, telling him he'd only get himself killed and we'd have no sheriff, which somebody said is the very condition we are now suffering under. I'll tell you, Tom, it got very tense."

"I sympathize," Maynard said, "but it has nothing to do with me."

"No, of course not, I know that. I'm just giving you a little background as to what your letter went through."

"My letter?"

"Mine, actually. Addressed to me, but really for you. From Northwood. It was in the mail sack on that stage. If those bastards had stopped it they might well have taken the sack and then thrown it away and that letter would be lying in some gulch or canyon somewhere."

"Where is it?"

"In my room. I'll show it to you later, but I can summarize it for you. It seems they've dug up a bit more information about your Major Pryor, and not very flattering either. From what Northwood found out, Pryor was not an officer who lived by his own rules. It seems they were able to turn up a soldier who served with him and who had some interesting things to say."

"Who turned him up?" Maynard asked.

"A fellow from the Statistics Office, whatever that might be."

"Samuel Mark. He'd served with Pryor. I spoke to him just before I left."

"Well, you must have piqued his interest, because he went out on his own and found this soldier—former soldier, actually—who had a story to tell, and tell it he did, to your friend and then to Northwood himself. Pryor may have had a book of rules that was skin tight, but it sagged somewhat when he applied it to himself. He was known to shoot deserters and to severely punish looters, right?"

"Get to the story, Simon," Maynard said.

"Pryor and a corporal were riding in an area not far from their encampment—in Virginia—when they came upon this large, very elegant house. According to the corporal, they stopped outside of it and Pryor just sat there looking at it for a long time. Then he dismounted and—with the corporal trailing behind—opened the gate and went up the path and right into the house. Nobody was there; nobody, that is, until they got upstairs and found an old woman lying in bed. What she had to say about a couple of Yankee soldiers in her house is lost to record, but when Pryor spotted a gold inlaid jewel box on a table and went over to it, I'll bet she said plenty."

"He robbed her?" Maynard asked.

"Robbed her? Drink your whiskey and listen. He shot her. She was starting to get out of bed and he drew his sidearm and shot her dead. Then he muttered something like, 'They send their sons and husbands out to slaughter us, and now they try to ridicule us.' "

" 'Ridicule'? " a puzzled Maynard asked.

Patterson shrugged. "And then he turned to the corporal and said something about justification."

"And the corporal," Maynard said, "whose face must have turned white, no doubt said, 'Yes, sir.' "

"Never having been a corporal in the presence of a berserk major holding a smoking pistol, I defer to your larger experience."

"Then?"

"Well, I suppose acting on the principle that no cold-blooded murder should be allowed to pass into the shade in vain, he helped himself to the jewels, and out they went."

"Patterson . . ."

"I know."

"No officer can expect to commit such an act in front of a subordinate and expect to get by with it. If not an official report, then gossip."

"The plague of an idle army, isn't it ever so, Maynard? Well, I'm sure the idea passed through Pryor's mind. He told the corporal to forget what he saw, that it was an order. But no order can be that magical, can it, Thomas?" Patterson laughed harshly. "Such forgetting would be a feast for remembrance and dissemination."

"All right. And then?"

"I would imagine that Major Pryor began realizing that he might as well have ordered the sea waters to turn vertical."

"How soon after the incident did he disappear?"

"Two days. A lone soldier was found dead beyond the perimeter, his face shot to pudding. He was wearing Pryor's uniform, with Pryor's papers and personal items in his pockets. Maybe even picked out and murdered by Pryor for the purpose, for all we know. And then the major headed, well, for wherever he headed."

"And arrived in Baddock."

"Where to his horror he one day passes Barley Newton on the street."

"And is recognized."

"And knows it," Patterson said.

"Listen, wasn't there an official report filed?"

"Apparently not. I would imagine that once Pryor was marked dead, what was the point? Leave it lie where it was. I guess the story drifted through the tents and finally wore itself out. Once the last campaign began, who cared? Christ, Maynard, you were in it for four years and I traveled alongside it for most of that time. This episode is a grain of sand among the boulders, when you come down to it."

"It's the grain we know about," Maynard said abstractedly.

"How do you account for him doing such a thing?"

Maynard smiled uneasily as his mind filled with possibilities.

"He was a man of good record," Patterson said.

"Maybe it was just his time for him to lose his head, that's all."

"It seems he got it right back, though, doesn't it? It's not going to be so smooth, Tom, you can see that now. He's done one murder, maybe two, and maybe three. If he sniffs you out . . ."

"Well, right now we're at equality: I don't know who he is and he doesn't know who I am."

"But your advantage: he doesn't know you're looking for him."

"Which is why Northwood wrote to you," Maynard said.

"Exactly. He's a cagey old boy. He knows how wide open it is out here, how things can go astray."

"Write back to him," Maynard said. "Ask him not to send any more letters. Explain the hazard. Refer to me as 'your friend.' Don't mention my name. But for God's sake, be diplomatic."

"Of course," Patterson said with a smile. "He is, after all, a brigadier general."

"My brigadier general," Maynard said.

FOURTEEN

Now, for some perverse reason that Maynard chose to leave unexamined, Major Andrew Pryor became of greater interest to him, as if coming more clearly through a mist, and if still unknown, then at least more known. Perhaps it was Maynard the true soldier thinking: desertion was ever a grossly unpalatable and unforgivable offense, whereas murder, with its long history of human complexity, was capable of bursting or beguiling its way through any restraint. To Maynard, a murderer always had a reason, no matter how benighted or distorted; a deserter could offer nothing.

He thought these things as he sat outside his cabin door that night, smoking his pipe, looking occasionally up at the sky where vast prairie-sized clouds had shut away the stars. The mountaintops were at one with the sky, so that it was hard to tell where one began and the other stopped. A cool wind, like raveling and unraveling sheets of air, came from somewhere, across the flat ground or running down the mountainsides, off to another somewhere.

Despite the night, wind, silence, Maynard did not feel lonely, nor had he ever under these circumstances. It may have been a firmness of mind, though he preferred to think of it as the strength of being a soldier at service, because no matter where he was, how alone, the serving soldier was a link of the invisible chain that made a man feel never unaccompanied, even if only by the idea of his own fidelity.

He tried to imagine Andrew Pryor picking his way out of the Union Army and coming west, what guises were assumed, sto-

ries told, stops made. He wondered if a man six years removed
from his offenses still listened for sounds in the night and sought
to interpret the ambiguities of silence. If Pryor had been feeling any sense of complacence after the passage of time, then it
had certainly been jolted into some commotion by the sudden
appearance of Barley Newton, which could have resurrected not
just the fear of discovery but the idea of guilt. Maynard wondered if after six years of security a man could begin to believe
in his innocence, that not punishment but lack of it was the
purifying agent. If so, then Pryor might be feeling a heated anger
and resentment now, enough to feel righteous and persecuted.

After checking his horse in the small shambles of a stable
behind the cabin, Maynard went inside and got into bed. Tired
of trying to trespass across the mind of Major Pryor, he began
thinking of a more enticing subject, Theodora Diamond. What
had happened alongside the stream, followed by that wildly
exhilarating run after the horse and trap, were now memories
above all memories, with radiance enough to throw a warmth
throughout his body. (They were bright enough memories to blot
out any thought of what she might be doing right now behind
the walls of Lucas Bell's Paradise West.) She wouldn't have done
that with just anybody, he thought. No sir. Not even a woman
of the world was going to wriggle herself down to the skin in
broad daylight just for the hell of it, nor with just anybody. No
sir. And the laughter that had come out of her sounded so fresh
he'd wager she hadn't felt like that in years. By God, he
thought, what a hell of a thing: Tom Maynard, the soldier who
had for years lived with the idea that he might die at any
moment and who had always accommodated the reality and
never feared it, now felt a genuine sweetness of life that he realized he must have always been wary of lest it be taken from him.

They talked in Washington and elsewhere of the mighty
American West, where the ground was new and ripe for discovery, where a man could renew himself and find all the
things that had never really been lost.

Yes sir, he thought. A man could.

*   *   *

The following morning Maynard was taking his breakfast in the small restaurant known as The Chinaman's, the place having been established by someone now long gone from Baddock, who had never explained the name, and was now run by a Confederate Army veteran named Haybacker.

Haybacker was this morning expounding to his lone customer upon the summer climate of his native Mississippi, to which wistful commentary Maynard was paying little attention, when suddenly a man ran past the window, boots clumping loud and fast on the boardwalk, followed by another, and then by two young boys, all running purposefully in the single direction.

"Don't tell me again," Haybacker said, walking his long, angular, almost ascetic-looking frame to the doorway, where he stood with his hands on his hips and his elbows pointed sharply out.

"What's again?" Maynard asked, sipping the last of his coffee.

"Yes sir, it looks it," Haybacker said, head turned toward where the men and then the boys had run. Then his trim-bearded face was peering back over his shoulder at Maynard. "That's the stage in from Virginia City and there's a crowd standing around it in the street. What does it tell you?"

By the time Maynard reached the stagecoach, which had drawn up in front of the Territorial office, there were about twenty men standing around it, on the boardwalk and in the street, with the driver up on the seat telling a familiar story.

"Three of 'em," he said to the assemblage. "About fifteen miles out, where the trail elbows around the twin rocks and starts climbing. Two of them jumped out from behind the rocks on one side and the other and the third one was sitting his horse right at the crest. All of them with rifles. I was just slowing for the climb and they had us dead to rights. Don't ask me what they looked like," the driver said to a question that had been called up to him. "You already know that.

They looked like the ones that were there yesterday and they looked like the ones who'll be there tomorrow."

The loss, it developed, had been substantial. In addition to the personal losses suffered by the passengers—money, rings, watches—the stage had been carrying several thousand dollars in gold bullion the company was shipping to Denver.

Turner, superintendent of the Territorial Stage Line's local division, said, "Boys, I suggest we convene in Lloyd's. We have some talking to do."

Lloyd's was the nearest saloon and the largest in town, with a long polished bar with brass foot rail and spittoons set down at five-foot intervals and a wall-length mirror behind the bar, breakage of which, Lloyd had warned, would be considered a capital offense. The floor was scattered with fresh sawdust every day.

When the dozen or so men surged through the door they momentarily startled the card players sitting under smoky wreaths at the tables, while the men along the bar—not that many at that hour of the morning—watched with shot glasses held breastbone high between thumb and forefinger.

"There's more," the driver said after downing a shot of whiskey with a quick gulp. "A few miles further along, after we'd been cleaned out, we came across some poor sod who'd been bushwhacked on his way into town. Pockets turned inside out. A miner, from the look of him. Shot in the back."

"Probably the same crew of bastards," Turner said. He was standing in the middle of them. He was big and bulky, wide-shouldered, gray-haired, with a gray mustache and beard that seemed to be bristling with anger. "There's a day's work for you—robbery and murder."

The effusion of voice with which they had entered had reached a crescendo and then began to diminish, leveling down from indiscriminate and public indignation to sullen private conversations. Turner jammed his thumbs inside his belt and hoisted his trousers more securely up around his strong man's broad hard belly and glared from face to face.

"It's your stage line, Turner," someone said. "Do something about it."

"My stage line, bullshit," Turner said. "It's our *town*. We live here. We've all got a stake in this place. It's like we're under siege here. If this sort of thing keeps up we'll be written off and nobody will want to come here and we'll just dry up. Just because of a handful of bastards." He brought his fist emphatically down on the bar, like a physical exclamation mark.

"Here, Mr. Turner," the bartender said quietly, pushing a pacifying drink across the bar to him. Turner ignored it.

"Mr. Turner is right," a man called Abbot said in a calmly measured voice. He was trimly built, perhaps forty years in age, clean-shaven, his face earnest under a black Stetson.

Standing among the crowd, Maynard studied him with inquiring eye, as he would each speaker as the talk brought forth one man after another. Within all the gathering, his were thoughts and speculations in isolation, unconnected to stopped stages or dead miners.

"You all know me," Abbot said. He was neatly turned out in a short black linen coat, brown silk vest, black trousers, polished boots. He was one of the few among them not wearing a gun belt. "I've invested time and money and a good deal of effort in this town. A lot of us have. Mr. Turner is right; we can't let it be taken away from us. These crimes are getting out of hand."

"Getting?" Turner asked, reaching for his drink now. "They've *got*." He swallowed his drink, then put a sour face on it.

Maynard felt someone brush against him. He turned to see Simon Patterson, standing arms folded, almost conspicuously innocuous of face, staring, as Maynard was, from one speaker to the next.

"They hit those stages any damn time they feel like, seems," someone said.

Turner passed him a disdainful look. "Is that a fact?" he said sarcastically.

"Had you ever seen them before?" someone asked the driver.

"How the hell am I to know that?" the driver asked. "I've driven in California and I've driven in Colorado and now up here, and I'll tell you one thing for free: a road agent with a mask and a long coat is a road agent, no matter where he's standing or what time of day it is."

"Well, it stands to reason." This was O'Connor, who had ridden into Baddock several years before with a wagonload of furniture and crates of wide-spined legal tomes and set up practice, and soon most of the town's legal business was being transacted through his Main Street office. Generally a man of impeccable formality, he had obviously come hurrying from his office, hatless, vest and suit coat undone. He had a narrow black mustache and a short spade beard that gave his rather fine-boned face a distinctive look and reminded Maynard of daguerreotypes of certain young statesmen of the late Confederacy, except that O'Connor was not young—in his forties perhaps—and from the geography of his precise and self-assured tones surely not south of Mason-Dixon. And this too: when he spoke no one else did; there were no interruptions or interjections, just that quiet, occasional nodding of men who had made up their minds to agree before hearing.

"If he," O'Connor said, pointing to the driver, "had recognized any of those holdup men, or given indication of so doing, he wouldn't be standing here now. Remember, gentlemen, what we have operating along those trails aren't just plunderers but murderers as well. Lord only knows how many poor souls have been murdered for their sacks and are moldering up in the mountains. And I'll tell you something else, boys—the longer they're allowed to operate unhindered the bolder they're going to get. Eventually we're going to be living here by their forbearance, unless something is done to cut them off."

"We don't know who they are, O'Connor, or where they're holing up," Turner said from where he was leaning on the bar on crossed arms, watching it all in the backbar mirror. He said it not as a point of contention but wearily. "We don't know how many they are, whether it's one gang or more. Jesus, they could ride into town anytime they like— and probably do—and have a few drinks and a card game and slap us on the back and we'd never know."

"They seem to know every twist of the trail," the driver said sullenly.

"Of course they do," Turner said, staring at his own unhappy image now, as if trying to offer it some consolation. "It's their place of business. Lloyd knows his bar, Abbot knows his stores, O'Connor knows his office. We all know the place we work, don't we?"

"I always figured road agents were part of the job," the driver said, "like lame horses and broken axles and rain storms and flooded streams . . ."

"And drunken stationmasters," Turner said quietly, as if to himself.

"But," the driver went on, "this is like a plague. A goddamned plague."

"We've got to come up with a plan of action," another said.

Patterson sidled closer to Maynard and softly said, "Pearson. The banker."

Maynard seemed to heave himself taller as he folded his arms and tilted his head just aside and studied the man. By height, age, bearing, Pearson could have been a certain former Union Army major (or, more prosaically, he could have been exactly who he was). He had thinning dark hair, was clean-shaven, with small shrewd eyes, an implacably set underlip, and a voice of deep bass timbre that could sternly have sent men into battle. His only separation from his almost stereotypical banker's image was his gaudy checked suit that stood out among the buckskins and flannels and austere blacks around him, his trousers tucked into the tops of high-sheen leather boots.

"That's very well said, Mr. Pearson," Turner said, his voice flat, almost without interest.

"You could put a gun up with the driver," Pearson said.

"I could. But not every driver finds that comforting."

"He's right," O'Connor said. "This doesn't sound like a gang that would be shy about picking off a shotgun rider."

"And maybe clipping the driver by mistake," Turner said.

"Or not by mistake." That was the driver, sullenly.

Lloyd, the saloonkeeper, announced his sympathy and then reminded them that this was a saloon and not the town hall and asked how many glasses he was standing up. They pressed in to call drinks and there were some moments of silence while civic indignation was quenched with whiskey.

"We're not going to let them cow us," Pearson said, resuming the discussion. "Goddammit, we're honest men but we're not weaklings."

"We've got a sheriff," someone said. "Paying him good money."

Abbot lit a cheroot and clenched it between his teeth as he spoke.

"John Dunlop is a good man," he said, "but he's only one man and his charter doesn't extend to prowling around the mountains looking for road agents."

"Neither does his wind," someone muttered, to muted laughter.

"And it wouldn't be his lucky day if he found them anyway," O'Connor said.

"It's his job, nobody else's," someone said.

"Look," O'Connor said, "as Abbot says, John Dunlop is a good man. But we knew when we hired him that he had his limitations."

Someone gave a short, mean laugh.

"But within those limitations," O'Connor went on, "he gets the job done. When there's some dustup in town he's right there seeing to it. You all know that."

"He's getting too old for that too," someone said.

Lloyd, with more customers than he'd ever had at that hour of the morning, asked for fill-ups. He had a few takers as coins were bounced onto the bar.

"They're not going to stop hitting those coaches," Pearson said, "until they're forced to."

"That's right, Mr. Pearson," Turner said, rapping his knuckles on the bar for another drink. "And until that happens, there's no damned reason for them to stop. They've got plenty of men panning flakes up in the gulches for them to steal and a company shipping boxes of bullion right into their hands, free of charge. Maybe I ought to put a gun on those vehicles after all. Anybody interested?"

The comment drew an uneasy silence. They could hear cards being shuffled and chips rattling at a table where the game had gone steadily ahead with insulated detachment.

"I'll pay top dollar," Turner said.

"That gang hasn't been tried yet," he was told; "so you don't know what top dollar might be."

"You mean," Turner said, "the job's worth more if you get shot at."

"If you get shot at," was the response, "the job ain't worth a bucket of mule piss." There was an undertone of laughter.

"Then before long," Turner said, addressing himself in the mirror, "everybody in Baddock is going to be working for them, one way or another." Then he said, "I'll tell you what we ought to do. We ought to raise a dozen or so good men and go up there after them ourselves. That's what we ought to do. And don't anybody give me any crap about those being my stages; a lot of you ride them at one time or another, when you're looking for a little work up in the camps or when you're coming back. When those stages get stopped, then it's your ass in the boiling water."

"I'll vouch for that," one man said in a surly voice. Several months before, he had sold out his claim and boarded a stage with four hundred dollars secured in a buckskin purse that was strapped to his chest. On the way in they were stopped at a narrow cut in the mountain by a pair of holdup men, who carried off, among other things, the buckskin purse.

"Hell," someone said, "you could ride around up there for weeks and never come close to them. They find out we're up there, they'll hole up somewhere until we're gone."

"Or," said another, "they could ride in and hole up right here."

"That's true," another said waggishly. "Living right upstairs," he added, pointing a finger upward to the rooms that Lloyd let.

Lloyd glared at him. "Why don't you try farting?" the saloonkeeper said. "It might clear out your mind."

"And anyway," someone said to Turner, "what you're suggesting is we take the law into our own hands."

"I'm talking about taking our security into our own hands," Turner said.

"What do you propose we do with them when we bring them in, Turner?" O'Connor asked.

"Who says bring them in? I'm sure there are some pretty sturdy trees up in those mountains."

"You'd go outside of the law," O'Connor said, not reproachfully but as if taking it under adjudication. "Summary execution, without trial."

"We've already undergone the trials," Turner muttered. "You're talking like a lawyer, O'Connor."

"Which I am."

"They did it in California," Turner said.

"I know about California," O'Connor said. He began buttoning his vest as he spoke, and then his jacket, as though, consciously or otherwise, intending to make a formal debate of this. "And don't think those vigilance committees didn't get out of hand after a while. You don't want to start something you might not be able to control."

"It depends on how the thing is organized," Pearson said. "I'm not advocating it, but it seems to me that if you start with good men you'll end with good men."

"It's a dangerous trail to go down, is all I'm saying," O'Connor said.

"So instead," Turner said, "we pussyfoot around and let ourselves be knocked about by a handful of men wearing masks." Then he raised a mollifying hand. "All right," he said. "You want to do it legal? Then we'll get the sheriff to deputize the lot of us. How does that sit?"

Pearson looked at O'Connor. "That's a consideration," the banker said.

"Except," the lawyer said, "for the danger involved."

"We've got some good men here," Abbot said, looking around. His glance lingered on Maynard for a moment. "Some proven men," the merchant said.

"I'm still not sure that's the answer," O'Connor said. "We don't know the trails as well as they do. And we still don't know how many of them there are. We could find ourselves being picked off one by one."

"The gentleman is right."

The voice, insinuating itself upon them, spoke from the fringe of the gathering. It was not just that it came from what sounded like a distance removed, away from the discussion's inner circle, lending to itself a quality at once intrusive and presumptive; it was in the intonation, assured, faintly mocking, like a blanket judgment on everything that had been said, on all of them, their opinions and their postures, their anger and their solutions. It implied other possibilities.

They made way as Lucas Bell came forward. He leaned casually against the bar on one arm, lifting one booted foot to the rail, as if positioning himself as he sensed they expected him to. A cold smile was fixed on his lightly closed lips; the men found it slyly derisive, though not offensive, since it suggested that something was known that they were as yet uninformed of.

Patterson leaned close to Maynard. "Most, most unusual," he whispered.

Unusual because it had been Bell's way to remain aloof

from the concerns of the community. Polite, even gracious when spoken to, he seldom initiated conversation. The mannered quietness seemed to have been born into him, the same as eye color and bone structure. When he smiled it was like something written on his face from without rather than an expression of inner warmth or congeniality, smiles that were almost instantly voided by the chill blue alertness that never left the centers of his eyes. It was this, all of it, that made them stand attentive now.

"What do you know about it, Bell?" Turner finally asked.

"I know fool talk when I hear it," Bell said.

Involuntarily, Maynard felt himself taking several small steps forward, closer.

"Just whose fool talk are you referring to?" Turner asked. "There's been a lot of it."

"Yours."

The men waited.

"All right," Turner said with an obvious mustering of indulgence. "Every man's got a right to speak. Let's hear it, Mr. Bell." There was a faint line of sarcasm under the *mister*.

"You go up into those mountains with a dozen men, or two dozen men, and you'll bring most of them back bellydown across their saddles."

"I know," Turner said. "I've heard that suggested."

"You didn't sound convinced." The cold smile came and went so fast it was like a twitch.

"I'd take the lead horse," Turner said. "That ought to be understood."

"Courage doesn't equal smart," Bell said. "Seldom does. Anyway, there wouldn't be a lead horse, not with that gang watching you from God knows how many different angles."

Leaning heavily on the bar, Turner glanced across one broad, hunched-up shoulder, then back into the mirror. "All right, Mr. Bell, then tell us what you have to suggest." He seemed to be making some effort to sound like an impartial moderator.

"That you send one man up after them."

"One?" Abbot asked, his teeth appearing around his smoking cheroot. "One?" he asked again, with incredulous emphasis, as if wanting to make certain he had heard correctly. "Against at least three and maybe more?"

"One good man," Bell said, still resting against the bar in his original position.

"Against a gang that will shoot him down like a dog the moment they see him," Turner said.

"If they see him, Mr. Turner," Bell said. "And if he's any good, they won't. Not if he values his life."

"He wouldn't be going up there in the first place," Turner said, "if he valued his life."

"That would be his decision," Bell said, "and no concern of yours."

He wants to go, Maynard suddenly thought, studying Bell, whose eyes locked on his own in a moment of brief communion that Maynard did not understand. *That's what this is about. That's what he's going to tell them.*

"I don't know of any such man," Turner said. "Do you?"

"You haven't asked for a volunteer yet," Bell said.

"I wouldn't waste my breath. I don't think there's a man in the Territory would take that job for a sack of gold."

"Hold on, Turner," Pearson said. "Mr. Bell's not a man for idle talk. Maybe he knows someone."

"As a matter of fact, Mr. Pearson," Bell said, "I do."

Now Turner picked up his drink and with a great display of uninterest began sipping, letting them know he had removed himself from the discussion.

"Who would that be?" O'Connor asked, just the merest smile painting the skepticism into his voice.

Again the sounds of riffled cards and dropping chips became audible, very distinctly, because for the moment there was nothing else, not even from outside. *Tell them,* Maynard thought, watching Bell. *Go ahead. Tell them.*

Bell's face became momentarily, and uncharacteristically,

expressive, as if he'd been brought to the threshold of concession and relinquishment.

"I don't think it would be very sporting of me," he said, "to suggest an enterprise so audacious and then expect someone else to undertake it."

"You'd go?" Abbot asked, not skeptically but warily, sounding like a man waiting to be convinced.

"As I said, Mr. Abbot, courage doesn't necessarily equal smart."

"No," Abbot said, watching Bell now with near-predatory interest. "More times than not it equals foolishness."

"Just a minute," Pearson said. "If Bell has this idea, and thinks he can carry through with it, then we ought to hear him out."

"Before he changes his mind," someone said drolly, which comment drew from Bell an unpleasant smile.

"Might be something to it," another said. "One man could get the drop on them better than ten, if he knows what he's at."

"You're a pretty good gambler, Bell," Abbot said, "but you'll be at the short end of long odds."

"Seems that's when he's best," someone said with a disgruntled laugh.

"What's your stake in it, Bell?" O'Connor asked.

"My stake, gentlemen, is the same as everyone's and more than most. I'm running a business in this town and I mean to stay here and prosper. I won't be able to do that if the stages arrive with penniless passengers and the miners are afraid to come down here and spend. I'll have to pack up and go elsewhere, and elsewhere might not be as good as here. It's as plain as that."

"But to go alone . . ." O'Connor said.

"It's a fool's errand," Bell said, "but one fool is always better than two or more—there's the advantage of less foolishness."

"It's an admirable thing to attempt," Pearson said soberly.

"*Noble* to attempt," Abbot corrected, "admirable to achieve."

"I don't want to dampen the accolades," O'Connor said, "but what's your price?"

"We'll settle that when I get back."

"What's your plan?" Abbot asked. "Do you have one?"

"Yes," Bell said. "To bring them back dead."

FIFTEEN

"I think that between us," Patterson said later, "we've had a decent amount of experience in certain areas—like dealing with men of authority in the military. I spent several of my prime years, when I was supposed to be most alert of mind and acute of sense, observing and analyzing officers. I regarded myself as a man of more than passable judgment. And you, Thomas," Patterson went on as they crossed the street, hurrying to get out of the way of a wagonload of timber that didn't seem about to slow down for them, "you've been even closer to them, all ranks and sizes, in peace and war, glory and disgrace, and all the other combinations that military men bare their souls to. So tell me: what did you see in there?"

"There were a lot of things to consider," Maynard said as they stepped up onto the boardwalk.

"I'm not talking about road agents or murdered miners or vigilante committees or what we can both agree is the curious behavior of Lucas Bell."

"I know what you're talking about," Maynard said. "What you're saying, or implying, is that responsible military service leaves behind an insignia like invisible stars. Well, I don't know what army you were observing, Simon, but the officers of my army—in peace and war—were of all demeanors and bearings; there was nothing singular to the breed, no marking that you knew would make them jump out at you years later."

"But a certain glint of authority, a self-assurance," Patterson said as they entered The Chinaman's restaurant and took a table and ordered coffee. "Listen," Patterson said after the coffee had been served, in less than immaculate cups, which they appraised dubiously but drank from without comment, "no matter what, no former battlefield major is going to stand silently through that kind of talk. If nothing else, we've *got* to believe that, otherwise you might as well pack up and head home right now."

"A lot of voices were raised," Maynard said. They were alone in the place, except for Haybacker, the Mississippi "Chinaman," who now went outside and with a damp rag began rubbing at his window. Maynard, facing out, watched him, the cup of steaming coffee raised in both hands to chin level but barely touched.

"Forget Turner," Patterson said. He kept sipping at his coffee, leaning forward to it, as if his chin had to clear a fence to get at it. "He's too old."

"Too bad," Maynard said idly, watching Haybacker, who stepped back now for a critical examination of the window. "He was the one who seemed intent on organizing things."

"Too old," Patterson said again, "and anyway he's been out west at one place or another for too many years. So you've got Abbot, Pearson, and O'Connor. They're the only 'nabobs' who fit."

"O'Connor seemed too cautious."

"Well, he was seeing something that was tactically unsound."

"When would our man have become a lawyer?"

"Anybody of any intelligence can become a lawyer, as well as a lot of dolts. He shows up in a town like this and says he's a lawyer. I don't know of anyone who's asked him to prove it, or who's questioned his work. Look, Pryor was an educated man, and he had years to pick up the law, if he wanted to."

"Abbot was pushing for action," Maynard said. "So was Pearson. Said we had to come up with 'a plan of action.' What do you know about them?"

"Respectable enough, since they've been here. Before that,

who knows? You have to be careful about asking, and with what we know now, as close to nonasking as possible."

"As a newspaperman, you could claim certain latitude."

"True; but it puts a lot of slack in your curiosity when you know you might be talking to or asking about a potential murderer. Remember, Thomas, I gave up the war, I gave up my job, I gave up the whole goddamned dance and bow of polite society to come out here and settle my nerves." Patterson closed his eyes for several moments, as if the speech had evoked memory and then passion and then a hard clash of each, and drank some coffee. Maynard, his cup still raised up in front of him untouched, watched his friend with some sympathy, momentarily stilled by the evocation of not memories but rather memory of them.

"All right," he said when Patterson was looking at him again. "Have you found out *any*thing?"

"Listen," Patterson said, "this isn't your normal small town; there's no old codger sitting next to the stove in the general store who remembers when there was no road, no school, no church, and when everybody's grandfather was barefoot and red-cheeked. I've been here less than two years myself and those three gentlemen were here when I arrived. Each a respectable pillar, then and now. Abbot was in business and on the look-see for more; O'Connor was in practice, and Pearson was running the bank. What you see now is what you saw then."

"Family men, any of them?"

"No, or not as far as Baddock is concerned anyway. And nobody knows where any of them came from—back East, is all—but that's hardly worth a raised eyebrow around here because so many men seem to have jumped over the mountain from nowhere, and because so many of them have histories they don't want to talk about there's an understanding about those things. I'm sorry, Thomas; there's just not a hell of a lot to tell."

"Honest businessmen," Maynard said, placing his untouched

cup of coffee down on the table, watching Haybacker, who was
now simply standing outside watching the street, the damp rag
hanging from his hand like an unheeded flag of surrender. "But
none of them seemed reluctant about going after that gang, did
they?"

"Doesn't make them former army officers."

"We're not trying to carve a statue, Simon, just unveil
one."

Patterson sighed. "I'd be a lot happier if he wasn't a murderer."

"Pearson and Abbot were the most aggressive, weren't
they? About going after the gang, I mean. 'Admirable thing
to attempt.' That was Pearson. And then Abbot touching it
up a little bit: 'Noble to attempt, admirable to achieve.'
O'Connor was less sanguine, wasn't he?"

"Lawyerly," Patterson said.

"Or maybe he just didn't want to push too far into it. Not
just a lawyer but a cautious man, for a reason."

Patterson sat reflectively for several moments, staring
down into his half-finished cup of coffee, looking as if he had
just decided he didn't like it after all.

"Tom," he said, "do you think that Pryor might feel he's
clear by now? It's been six years, and he's living in an environment where the normal rules of law don't really apply.
That can permeate a man after a while and get him to stop
looking back over his shoulder."

"No, because there are too many closed-mouthed men
around here to remind him. And even if he thought it was all
safely behind him, remember, he had the shock of seeing
Barley and of being recognized, or believing he'd been recognized, which in his mind would have been as good as the
same."

They sat quietly for a while, Maynard watching Haybacker standing outside turning his head this way and that,
as if looking for something to settle his attention on.

"What does anyone know about Lucas Bell?" Maynard

asked. Patterson deduced from the quietly released note of interest that the question was not entirely spontaneous, probably not spontaneous at all, but an eddy of curiosity finally given voice.

"If there's a prototype of the unknown man in Baddock," Patterson said, "it's him. You know more about the interior of a cloud that passes on a midnight dark than you do about him."

"And yet there he is, for all to see."

"Showing only what he wants to be seen, Tom."

"He perks one's interest," Maynard said musingly.

Patterson sensed a concurrent thought of Theodora Diamond, but chose not to remark upon it.

"He's got grudging respect," Patterson said. "He's a gambler, but they say he runs an honest table."

"And an honest house of ill repute," Maynard said tersely, more for his own pondering, Patterson felt. Maynard looked at him briefly, then turned away, as if afraid the thoughts he was connecting might be read.

"You'll find a Lucas Bell in all of these towns, I suspect."

"Nobody knows where he's from?"

Patterson shook his head. Then he said, "You don't think he could be a candidate, do you?"

"What do you think?"

"Doesn't seem the type at all. I can't imagine Lucas Bell ever taking orders from anyone, and even majors have to take them now and then. Nor can I see him whipping up the froth it takes to lead men across a field. Nor do majors volunteer to undertake suicidal enterprises all by themselves."

"What do you think of his proposal? It doesn't make sense, does it?"

"No, it doesn't. Frankly, I was stunned. I think everybody was."

"The man is a professional gambler, Simon, a man who always has to have the odds with him. Why should he offer to do something like this, when it's all stacked against him?"

"Thomas, don't ask me. It's hard enough to figure a man that you know; but when you don't know him, don't even try. I got the impression he was mocking them."

"Yes, I felt that," Maynard said. "But to what point? At best he'll make a fool of himself, and at worst he'll get himself killed."

"Count not on either, my friend," Patterson said with deliberate pomposity. "I may not know Lucas Bell, but I know him well enough to assure you that."

"He could go and camp out for a few days, then come back saying he saw nothing and earn himself a bit of cheap glory."

"Not Bell," Patterson said. "He goes into a game to win. Anyway, I think this has all been well calculated, Tom. He chose the moment and the audience for it, didn't he?"

"Tell me what you know about him," Maynard said. "Everything."

SIXTEEN

No one in Baddock knew very much about Lucas Bell (or even if that was his name; names were known to wear out in a hurry in that part of the country); but that was more usual than not, since there was no reason, nor was it necessary, to know anything more about a man other than what he wanted you to, which usually was enough to suffice. Men appeared and then disappeared, to try their luck in the gulches, or simply left town, compelled or impelled by whatever it was that might have brought them there in the first place. Sometimes they didn't stay long enough to leave behind a name to be forgotten by. But it was all right. Few wondered; none cared. Everyone was more or less alike—when you were possessed by a single passion strong enough to have brought you across a continent that was what you believed, what you almost had to believe.

The enchantments of the future lay partially in coming to a place that had not the least semblance of a past, a place so far uncursed by failure or disappointment. There was no common experience here, no visible or traceable continuity of human striving, no meaningful commingling of lives and blending of dreams, no mellowed rack of memories with which to define and catalog, no binding sense of annealed emotion: no reason to mourn and grieve or rejoice or share in any of it: at best there was migrated and reapplied tradition, to embrace or discard.

They were separated by the single cause that had brought them there and so which in its way also united them: gold.

Strength was still far in the vanguard, beating the path for profundity (which it had been wont to do throughout history), in its heated obsession carpentering the rudimentary outlines of a civilization that was shadowing irresistibly forward, like an ocean extending its grip on land by gulp, leap, surge, and sweep; and at the same time, unwittingly, with the same strokes and unbridled energy, shaping the myths and the legends that would come sooner rather than later, because the very appetite for gold was probably aiming the town more toward extinction than growth. They were building civic skeletons, creating ghosts and phantoms for later generations to evoke and muse upon.

Not even the most single-minded obsession was impenetrable, however, and it would have been impossible for Bell's arrival in Baddock to have gone unnoticed, and not because there was anything particularly noteworthy or remarkable about another cool and self-possessed gambler coming to sit with lethal patience in the social hub of an impromptu Western town, positioning himself where he knew the laboring dreamers with their little leather-stringed pouches of gold dust would inevitably and compulsively come. The gamblers were totally acceptable; they provided one of the community's three diversions—whiskey and the brothels were the others—and if a man was aboveboard no one faulted him or begrudged him his profession.

What caught their attention was what he did immediately after settling in. He bought for almost nothing one of the town's first buildings, a crudely raised, avidly patronized, and now abandoned saloon that stood in empty solitude at the edge of town (at one time it had virtually been the town). His first act upon taking possession of the small building was to burn it down. Then he cleared away the charred timbers, and after that tore up the floorboards and then by careful sifting through the ground was able to recover the gold dust that had fallen through during various transactions. In all he recovered nearly two thousand dollars' worth.

They had to admire the man's initiative and resourcefulness. They also liked his style. Although reserved and sometimes almost formal in demeanor, he could effect a most engaging manner when he chose to. He was as graceful when he lost as he was modest when he won. He would not take advantage of the rank amateur or the man in his cups. When the game was over, usually at the dawn hour, when whatever torrents born of the night had finally ebbed and the chairs around the oval green-cloth-covered table had emptied, he would go to the bar and order a shot of whiskey (his first and only taste of the night). At these times he stood quiet and solitary, sipping the whiskey, studying with detached irony his reflection in the backbar mirror ("Probably," one man remarked humorlessly one night, watching him, "trying to figure out for himself who the hell he is"), politely turning aside all attempts at conversation.

He was able to evoke himself with such ambiance that it soon became understood that he was not to be casually approached, that he was not a man to be taken by the arm or told a ribald story. The ambiance was evident, though they could not describe it. It was condescension, so subtle and cordial that they missed what it was, only that it was there, something. Most of the affronts suffered by them in their lives had been crudely direct; this was different, too light to offend but enough to cause unease. And, too, his concentration at the table was so anchored as to make him present and remote at the same time. It was as if he had effectively zoned and circumscribed parts of himself: his voice terse and businesslike, the smiles he allowed for their sour jokes mechanically polite, while the fingers with which he ran the cards were the smoothest and most well informed they had ever seen.

When he left the saloon at those dawn hours, Bell crossed the street through the moist air to the hotel and went upstairs to his room. He would not reappear until midafternoon, when he came downstairs to the dining room for a solitary meal. And then he went back upstairs to his room; and again it was something they did not understand, like the condescension. They knew there was a lot going on beneath that surface, but not even twelve unbroken hours at a card table got them the merest glimpse of it.

Occasionally, perhaps once every two weeks, he took his horse from the stable and rode alone out of town. Whoever saw his leisurely departure would watch, until distance had reduced him to a speck, until the watchers, suddenly self-conscious in their preoccupation, turned away and cleared their throats. He would be gone for two days, usually, and then was back at the Honest Eagle (which he took possession of one night when the owner's luck died wretchedly at his own table), his face set in its passionless mask, as if he had already foreseen and dealt with every thought and idea that might have claimed his attention from then till dawn, renewing his cycle of hours and their single concentration.

But even though he was a singular presence, no one would have taken more than curious notice of his arrival if it had not been for the woman. They rode into Baddock from the southeast one hot summer morning, through the thick moist mud, their horses' hooves squishing, though they themselves were impeccably dressed and groomed, in spite of the hot sun almost disdainfully fresh. It was the woman who first caught the attention of the onlookers; there were not that many women in town then, outside of the bordello, and when they did arrive it was usually by stagecoach. The onlookers remembered that the woman's face under a black bonnet was grave and vague, her sidled glances circumspectly seeing nothing that interested her. A black cape across her shoulders made her look like a wanderer from some procession. There was about her an apparent weariness that suggested she was sitting that horse unhappily and probably for far too long, and that she was doing so now with inert and leaden obedience, with an internal relinquishment that left her close to oblivious.

The man was different. He was obviously at his destination. He was not a prospector, that much they could tell from the beginning; nor was he going to be a storekeeper, nor a homesteader (in spite of the woman). Some guessed he might be a lawyer, but most sensed the gambler and therefore wondered about the woman, since most gamblers they had known—the good ones anyway, and there was that air about him—tended toward celibacy in their strictly structured and migrating lives.

The man and woman stopped in front of the hotel and she remained sitting while he dismounted and secured the horses. Then he turned and planted his boots in the mud and lifted her down from the horse and with an ease that implied greater strength than might have been supposed by his trim frame swung her around onto the boardwalk. Then he stepped up and gave her his arm—so formally it looked rehearsed—and walked through the hotel's double door, whereupon the onlookers turned to one another with raised eyebrows.

Soon after he had bought and burned down the abandoned saloon and then recovered its lost gold dust, Bell appeared in the Honest Eagle, but only to stand at the bar and sip whiskey and observe the action at the tables, more than anything else studying faces. He stayed until past midnight. He returned the following night and did the same thing. On the third night he took an open chair and sat down with that air of arrival that had been implicit from the beginning.

He won seven hundred dollars that night, his skill keeping the tension high and the players sullenly alert. He intrigued them—he seemed aware of that and to be working at it as much as anything else—and after a while they were consciously trying to keep their eyes from meeting his: he could stare across at them as if he knew their dates of death. "He'd better come back," one man said sourly after the gambler had left. "You'd better hope he doesn't," another said with a laugh. "Cleaned you up, didn't he?" one who had only

watched said. "How could you tell from over at the bar?" he
was unpleasantly asked. "I could tell," the observer said,
"because he was the only one who sat with his shoulders
straight up all night long."

He came back. They knew he would. As long as men were
washing gold out of the gulches and seeking relaxation from
their labors, a man with his nerve and proficiency would be
there, an adjunctive presence to every scene of thriving and
diversion, coeval of the labor and the dream, like further rat-
ification.

But while Bell was conspicuously present every night, and
occasionally in the afternoons as well when circumstances
warranted, no one saw the woman. She simply never left the
hotel. A girl who cleaned there could not help but comment
upon the strange behavior of Mrs. Bell (for that was how
they were registered in the oversized clothbound ledger).
Mrs. Bell never left her room, the girl said, even had her
meals sent up, and when not lying dreamily on the bed sat in
a chair and quietly wept. She would smile wanly at the girl
but never speak. But there was a lot of eccentric and untoward behavior in Baddock and a silent woman who wept and
who never took sunlight, who never imposed or impinged
anywhere, was of fleeting interest. If anything, her behavior
only served to confirm the judgment they had formed out of
their own experience and raw common sense: a gambler's
woman had to be peculiar and unaccountable.

And then one particularly quiet night, with a soft rain running through the Montana darkness, when the piano player's
fingers were idling and the line at the bar was thin and the
delicate click of chips was almost the only sound heard, there
was a gunshot in the night, clear enough but muffled; a single
shot, unthreatening, almost formal, like an evening cannon.
The men at the bar looked around. Bell's eyes rose from the
fan of cards in his hand to the night outside, but only for a
fraction of a moment, remaining motionless under the hanging lamp and the perennially hovering web of smoke. The

rain was invisible and silent, but you knew it was out there from the wet bootprints on the floor.

Then he called a raise, pushed forward his chips. He took another card, bet, called. He sighed—from him so unusual a sound it was noticeable. Then he showed his cards and reached out and curved his hand around the pot and drew it toward him. Then he stood up and asked them to excuse him.

He left the saloon and walked across the street in the rain to the hotel, his boots sounding like they were gulping at the muddy Main Street, his eyes raised toward an upstairs window. He mounted the front steps and went inside. One of the Lamont brothers—the thin one—was running down the stairs in a state of great agitation. He stopped when he saw Bell.

"I was just coming to get you," he said.

"Thank you," Bell said.

"I'm afraid she's gone and—"

"I know," Bell said.

SEVENTEEN

As if out of respect or appreciation or in some amorphous way to make common cause with him, they crowded into the Honest Eagle to drink after Bell had made his predawn departure.

"He stopped in for a warmer before he left," one of the men who was running the place in the proprietor's absence said.

"What did he have to say?" asked Pearson. If the banker was a drinking man, it was seldom in public; but here he was now, lined up at the bar with the others.

"Nothing," said Bell's man, known only as the Frenchman. He was unusually tall—maybe six and a half feet—and swarthy, with an old knife wound scarred along his cheek like a vivid warning, a "beware" sign. He had snarled black hair that fell to his shoulders. Part of the fascination of Lucas Bell was the way the Frenchman and the several others who worked here and across the street at the bordello obediently took their orders from him.

"Did he take a guess at how long he might be at it?" This was Abbot, the merchant, another infrequent patron of the Honest Eagle, but here now.

"Lucas never guesses at anything," the Frenchman said. He was standing behind the bar, hands spread out on the surface.

"I just hope he knows what he's at," Pearson said.

"I would imagine he does," Maynard said. He was not surprised that Bell had actually gone, only that the gambler had slipped away without any fanfare.

"Is there a tote board on it?" someone asked lightly.

"We'll offer one," the Frenchman said humorlessly, "if you want to bet against him."

"No thanks," the man said. "I've learned not to bet that way."

When Pearson and Abbot retired to a table together with their drinks, Maynard joined them.

"I'd say Mr. Bell is very courageous," Pearson said, his implacable underlip giving the words a stern emphasis.

"As bold as any I've ever heard of," Maynard said.

"You took a fairly bold stand yourself, Maynard," Abbot said.

"I hardly had time to think about it."

"Just as well," Abbot said. "Hesitation in a situation is usually fatal."

"I remember hearing tales of men in the war," Maynard said, pausing to sip some whiskey, "who did things on the hurry that they could not remember later having done."

"There's nothing to remember," Abbot said, "when the hand outraces the mind."

"Fear is a hell of an engine," Pearson said. "In any context."

"Fear?" Abbot asked skeptically. "Or is it obligation motivated by instinct?"

"I would imagine," Maynard said, "that under the conditions of battle there is no such thing as the irrational act." He waited. When there was no response, he went on. "I've met men whose minds were broken by the war."

"They conceded as much?" Pearson asked.

"They saw no shame in it," Maynard said.

"What shape did this take?" Abbot asked.

"Endless brooding, senseless muttering, empty gazing."

"Depression," Pearson said. "Or too many hard memories. And were these broken minds put back together?"

"Oh yes," Maynard said. "Sometimes to make a different man."

"A truer one?" Abbot asked. "Or more false?"

"That's not to say," Maynard said. "I would imagine war can cut a man down from true to false, or up from false to true."

"Then he ends up being what he didn't know he was in the first place," Pearson said. "I see no change there."

"Except for the surprise to himself," Maynard said.

"You're fresh off of killing two men yourself, Maynard," Abbot said, "has it made you any different, do you think?"

"I don't know; it's too recent."

Abbot laughed. "Then you're going to have to gauge yourself carefully from now on. Keep an eye inside yourself. I've heard of soldiers, who once they got a taste of it never lost it. Though I would imagine that's the nature of war."

"Then it's a converting nature," Pearson said with a brief smile.

"You mean unnatural to man?" Maynard asked.

"Yes," Pearson said, "in spite of its history."

"What of mankind's history?" Abbot asked.

"I'm not so learned," Pearson said. "I'm merely a banker."

"Were you in the war?" Maynard asked.

"No. And you?"

"No."

"So we can all speak authoritatively on the subject," Abbot said with levity.

"You weren't in either then?" Maynard asked.

"In spirit only," Abbot said.

"Are you sorry?" Maynard asked.

"How can a man be sorry about missing something he has no firsthand knowledge of? I'm afraid the imagination—mine anyway—doesn't reach that far."

"I haven't met that many ex-soldiers out here to begin with," Pearson said.

"Some might not choose to say," Maynard said, trying to make it sound idle.

"There seem to be more rebels around than Union," Pearson said. "Unless the Union boys just don't want to own up."

"Why shouldn't they?" Maynard asked. "They won."

"Losers can be harder on themselves," Pearson said. "The winning side has a shorter memory; they want to forget about it as soon as they can. For the losing side—I imagine—the war is never over."

"Forgive and forget, I say." That was Abbot.

"Ideally, yes," Pearson said. "Except that the loser can't forget the winner nor forgive himself."

"That's burden enough to crush a mule," Abbot said.

"A strong man can stand any burden," Maynard said, trying to hook something with a banality.

"To that," Abbot said, "I would answer that it's impossible to judge a man, since you can only do that by knowing all the things about him that you can't possibly know."

"That makes us a race of strangers," Maynard said, smiling.

"Not so strange," Abbot said. "To know that you don't know someone is to know an awful lot. I'm being general, of course."

"I've heard it said," Pearson said, "that a man's fate is measured to his capacity to endure it."

"That sounds like it came out of a pulpit," Abbot said dismissively. "Look, gentlemen, since every man is his own riddle you can't say that this or that is the final word, not on a man or on anything he does. The only known sameness among men is that they die. That's the only thing you can count on."

"And then all the secrets will out, I suppose," Maynard said, putting a smile on it.

"Not if a man has been careful," Pearson said soberly.

"Or he has no secrets worth knowing," Abbot said.

"That would be a tedious individual," Pearson said. "Can you imagine a man living in defense against anything that would make him interesting?"

"Well," Maynard said, "I knew some who were completely the opposite, fellows who hitched into the army in eighteen sixty-one just for the excitement of it."

"And probably found more than they bargained for," Abbot said.

"Some of them found more than they lived to tell about," Maynard said.

"What does a man do, I wonder," Pearson said, "when the excitement shuts down? I would imagine that sudden calm might be a shock to certain men." Then he said, "Maybe that's your type; maybe they fall to claim jumping and holding up stagecoaches."

"Well," Abbot said, "whoever they are, they'd be well advised to stop. As strange as it may sound, there's no more dangerous place for an outlaw to practice his trade than a place where there's no effective law. A book of jurisprudence improvised to address a specific situation is a book of doom."

"Well, let's hope that can be avoided," Pearson said. "Let's drink to Bell's success."

"How do you see it?" Maynard asked when the glasses were down.

"I have no forecast on that," Abbot said. "On the face of it, it's madness. But who can tell?"

"I try never to judge a man's wisdom or foolery," Pearson said.

"Very remiss for a banker, Pearson," Abbot said with a wink at Maynard.

"I wasn't referring to financial transactions," Pearson said almost reprovingly.

"I trust not," Abbot said, "otherwise I'd say I hope your safes are sounder than your appraisals of men."

"You can take comfort on both accounts," Pearson said.

"And on my own account as well, I hope," Abbot said, again with a wink for Maynard.

So what did he gain from that? Maynard asked himself when he left the Honest Eagle and walked along the boardwalk, pausing to light a cheroot, then went on, holding the cheroot in place with his hand as he drew on it. The day was bright and cool, the mountains standing under a cloudless blue sky. He paused at the end of the sidewalk and leaned against a support post,

watching the wagon and horseback traffic in the street, the cheroot between his teeth now, the smoke slanting up to his hat
brim. Across the street, in front of a saloon, a man was sitting
with his head dropped behind his drawn-up knees. A woman
passing with a small boy in hand pretended not to see him,
though the boy spun about strenuously to look.

Well, Maynard thought, you let out as many questions as
you discreetly could, and found out what? That neither man
had been in the war? Well, Pryor (if he was sitting there)
would not have said otherwise, would have a practiced story
by now, and shot and smoke would not be part of it. Each
man had been somewhat analytical and philosophical on the
subject. Was a major being general? Pryor had yearned for
promotion, Maynard recalled being told. *"I'm being general,
of course."* Abbot had said that. Droll wit for his own self-
amusement? There was too much float and distance to their
comments. Nothing hard, no nailed-in insight to suggest the
real business of the battlefield.

By their lives in Baddock each was an honest man who had
built success for himself, but what was that to one drop of
suspicion, which could make denial sound like affirmation,
innocence smell of guilt, and litter the empty sunlight with
shadows?

He stepped down and walked across the cross street,
mounted the next boardwalk, and again lolled against a post,
the cheroot between his teeth. You really should know an ex--
major when you see one, laddie, he thought. You used to
watch them carefully enough, the majors and all the other
seniors, since you were hoping to step up when they made
room. You used to watch their eyes when they issued orders,
paying attention not just to what they were saying but that
straight line of voice with which they spoke, which knew that
no question or dispute was coming back. You wanted to
catch all the nuances for when they became your own to use.
You became a good sergeant that way, and then a good lieutenant, and now a damned good captain, better than a lot of

sculpted West Pointers who had been groomed for it, with uniforms measured for them rather than the other way around, as it was for you.

Major Andrew Pryor, Maynard told himself, was a man whose mind had somewhere along the way broken. But not irredeemably so. It had rebuilt itself and was probably strong again, thanks to justification and self-forgiveness (if that latter had actually been needed). One of them—Abbot—had spoken of "the nature of war," and Pearson had referred to its "converting nature." So war itself could have been the offender, the major its blameless victim. When a man drew all of his information about himself from himself self-understanding came with a mother's kindly voice. You were going to get his reconstructed version of himself, meaning the potential for dangerous sway was still there. If a helpless old woman wanted to struggle for her valuables, then you shot her and later extended the boundaries of what was permissible (or excusable); and if you then perhaps had to shoot a soldier in defense of those boundaries, well, the principle was already established. And if Barley Newton suddenly appeared years later it was as threat as well as memory, throwing into you the shock that those boundaries had (by light of your new, honorable existence) been artificially created. But that didn't stop you.

Maynard had a last draw on the cheroot and then threw it into the street. Then he walked to the end of the boardwalk, to the last building, which housed the apothecary and upstairs from it the two rooms where Bell had installed Theo, thus investing her with a certain status. Maynard couldn't help but wonder about the implications of that, though what was apparent to him was no doubt also apparent to Bell—Theo was special. But what else? Special to the Paradise West? Or simply special to Bell? (But how likely could that be, with his allowing her to work there, subject to the grime and stench of any unbathed mountain rat who had the price of a toss?)

He began ascending the outside flight of stairs that clung

to the building's blank side wall, his hand touching the splintery railing at intervals. When he reached the top he rapped on the door.

"Hello, Thomas," she said when she opened the door.

"I'm sorry; did I wake you?" he asked, noting her not fully alert eyes, her unattended hair. She was wearing a dark blue robe that was too large for her, that looked to be engulfing her.

"Come in," she said, walking back into the room as he entered and closed the door behind him.

There were just the two small rooms, the sitting room, which they were in, and the bedroom. Someone had hauled a thick-legged crushed velvet sofa up that flight of stairs and set it in here, along with a few wooden chairs and an oval table (it looked like it might have been brought up from the Honest Eagle) and a small chest of drawers.

He wanted to ask her if she'd worked late last night, but what the hell kind of question would that have been?

"Sit yourself down," she said. "Do you want a drink?"

He eased himself onto one of the chairs. From where he was sitting he had an angled view of the bedroom, seeing three-quarters of a bed with tangled covers, and a chair stacked with what was probably last night's clothing discard.

"I've had a drink," he said as she sat on the sofa, her arms folded across herself as if they were helping to keep the robe shut.

"So what do you want then?" she asked.

He didn't know what he wanted, actually.

Then she shook her head, as if to strike her previous words, or at least their unintended import, shutting her eyes for a moment.

"I'm sorry, Tom," she said. "I've hardly had any sleep. In fact, I don't think I had any. I got into bed before midnight, hoping to sleep it away, but I just lay there."

"Sleep what away?" he asked.

"The idea of it, of him going out there alone."

"I see."

"God knows what can happen."

"He'll be all right. That seems to be the consensus."

He wanted to ask her why she was so concerned, but he reckoned he had better not.

"There are a lot of strange people in those mountains," she said. "Look what almost happened to you."

"He seems a capable man."

"That means nothing up there."

She was right about that, he thought. A quick hand and a good eye meant little if somebody was sighting on you from behind some rocks.

"It was his decision," he said. "His alone."

"I know," she said, taking small consolation.

"Did you try to talk him out of it?"

"Why should he listen to me?"

Maynard didn't know why.

"But he always knows what he's doing," she said, sounding now as if some other side of her was speaking. "He'll be back fine, you'll see. Lucas is beyond destruction. I know that. A woman knows. A woman can know a man better than any man can know him. Because we're not allowed to do anything but watch, you see. If you've ever spent just five minutes watching, you know how much you can learn. Well, try doing it for a lifetime. Oh, he'll be back all right."

"Everyone hopes so."

"Not everyone. There are plenty of them around here who don't like him, because he's better than they are, smarter."

"You seem to know a lot about him," he said.

"Enough."

"Enough for your satisfaction maybe," he said, "but is it enough for your own good?"

"Why do you say that?" she asked, with some wary interest, he felt.

"Maybe that woman who rode in here with him originally felt the same way, until she blew her brains out."

"She wasn't for him, that's all," she said shaking her head, as if explaining some ludicrously simple proposition. "He told me about her. Her problem was she came from some- where."

"And brought it with her," he said; "or at least some of it."

"That's right."

"What have you brought with you, Theo?"

She laughed. "What have you brought with you, Thomas?"

"I haven't fully unpacked yet. Have you?"

"Where are you from, Thomas?"

"Back East."

"Why are you here? You're not panning for gold, you're not looking for work."

"Maybe I haven't asked myself that yet."

"Maybe you should. People grow old in a hurry out here."

"Right now," he said, "I'm too young to grow old any- where, and just old enough to stay young for a long time."

"Where back East?" she asked.

"Upstate New York."

"You're a long way from home."

"And how far from home are you?" he asked.

"I am home," she said.

"Here?"

"Right here."

"Why here?" he asked.

"Because that's where I am."

"You're being facile," he said; "saying something just because it sounds right."

She had been sitting forward; now she leaned back in the sofa and enclosed herself more tightly in her arms and smiled coquettishly.

"You can be very mischievous," she said.

"I don't mean to."

"Then you're being quite serious."

"In an around-about way."

"And what are you around and what are you about? I still don't know."

He laughed; it was to cover his unease. There was a lot he wanted to tell her and a lot that he couldn't; his fear was that the telling of the one might lead to the escape of the other.

"Thomas," she asked coyly, "have you come up here for a slide?"

"I'm a gentleman paying a call on a lady." He almost said *his* lady.

"That still doesn't answer."

"I had only the one answer."

"Because if that's what you want, it isn't here for you. Not until he's back. It isn't for anyone until he's back. I'm sitting right here."

"You sound like a sea captain's wife, scanning the horizon. Suppose the masts never appear, Theo? What then?"

"Then we have a new story, don't we? But he'll be back. Unlike most, he has something to come back to."

He chose not to ask what that might be. Instead, he said, "Then I take it you won't be employed down the street either, until he's back."

"Does that disappoint you?" she asked.

He smiled. "Quite the contrary."

She rose and crossed the room to him and bent and kissed him affectionately but softly on the mouth. He raised his arms and encircled her around the waist, closing his eyes as he leaned his face against her, inhaling his fullness of feeling.

"I wonder where he is now," he heard her say.

EIGHTEEN

Bell followed the stage road for several hours, watching the new day birth itself behind the mountains, the new day brightening with a freshness so comfortable he might have been wearing it upon him like a cloak. Maynard's cabin was one of the places he passed on his way out, and as long as it was ahead of him or alongside, he kept his eyes on it, thinking of the man inside. When he passed it he stopped thinking of Maynard.

When he reached the foothills he picked up one of the cross trails that became a switchback as it worked its perverse and sinewy way up into the mountains. Riding slowly, his back and shoulders in harmony with the horse's motion, he passed in and out of ravines, pressed through thickets of stunted pine, saw patches of wildflowers in sudden bursts of yellows and reds and purples, feeling a subtle cooling in the air.

At the edge of a screen of alders, at the crest of a ridge, he paused to let his horse breathe. The noon-high sun slanted an equestrian shadow of great magnitude across the rocks and gravel below, momentarily like a conquering stain in drape across the earthen contours. A flock of ravens in search of carrion flew overhead with malign, discordant squawking, catching his attention. Flying in close formation, looking like a fabric shredding against the blue sky, they dipped and banked low and then whirled off behind a stand of pine on a further ridge and disappeared. He leaned forward and slapped his piebald's neck affectionately a few times.

He put a cigar between his teeth and lit it, gazing off into the distance as he fanned out the match. In the bright still air the smoke turned as languorously as in a sealed room. Some men might have been intimidated by the vastness here of earth and sky, by the implications of man's puniness and inconsequence. For Bell, however, a man's brief shadow was the verge of the path out to opportunity, and opportunity was best taken in conjunction with vast scope, where what was grandiose of mind found its match.

He looked far out, to where Baddock was a series of carpentered dots within the bowl of land among the mountains. They were talking about him there, he knew, and wondering about him, and some of them—he smiled at the thought— had by now no doubt established the odds against his return.

He was dressed in what for him was uncharacteristic informality. Gone were the frock coat and the white shirt and string tie and the silk vest and the broadcloth trousers; in their stead a buckskin-fringed coat, flannel shirt, rough trousers, and on his head a flat-crowned broad-brimmed Stetson. A Winchester carbine was strapped to his back and he was wearing a short-barrel .45 Peacemaker, as opposed to the flashier ivory-handled pistol that sometimes decorated his hip and was just that—decoration—for he knew that under no circumstances, virtually, would he ever have to draw at a card table. It would be in extremely poor taste for a professional gambler to kill a man at the table. If there was good reason for it, then it could hold until a more appropriate time and place, and even then it would not be he performing the job but one of the sharp-edged men who worked for him, whose presence in the Honest Eagle precluded much of this happening to begin with. So the weapon now in his embossed holster was the deadly one, the killing one, more easily handled and trustworthy, its cutaway trigger guard giving him an extra fraction of a second of advantage.

He turned from his contemplation of the far distance and slid his hand into the horse's mane, watching his fingers in the long, fine hairs. When he withdrew his hand he held it out in front of him, fingers slightly splayed. He thought he detected just the merest unsteadiness. *Since when?* he wondered. Too much sitting in one place. Not enough fresh air. In a country like this it was unwise to spend so much time indoors; there was an effect. This wasn't like San Francisco, say, where you could breathe smoke and stale whiskey breath for weeks on end and never know there was anything different. Here, the outdoors, the polished air, the wind, rain, everything, was constantly shaping and reshaping—landscape and people, too—was so powerfully transcendent it became hazardous to remain inattentive to it.

Gently he shook the reins and the horse began to climb again, picking its way through the rocks, pulling its conquering shadow higher and higher. Bell watched the trail, which sometimes was not a trail at all but simply a place where his horse would walk, like some begrudging and resentful earthscar that would lead him out into thin air if it could.

He stopped when he saw the narrow pillar of smoke rising into the air beyond the ridge like a faint spiral of penciling against the sky. His first thought when he saw the smoke was that he had not eaten since late last night, in the hotel dining room, with some of Baddock's first citizens sitting at the table with him, watching him intently, as if for some signal or indication that he was not going to go through with it, that after sober reflection he had come to his senses and was now simply trying to find a way of telling them that. They could not believe he was really concentrating on his steak and potatoes and then later those drafts of black coffee, all of which he consumed while seldom setting his eyes on any of them, as impassively unmindful of them as though he were sitting alone. They assumed that the inordinate amount of time he was taking with his meal was deliberate, calculated, that either he was hoping they would try to talk him out of it or else that he was stalling, waiting for the precise moment to tell them he had thought it through and decided not to go ahead with it. No reason would have been necessary either; no one would have reproached him for changing his mind. Even as he patted his lips with the cloth napkin they were expecting it, the repudiation of his own gratuitous proposal. But he surprised them (and maybe even offended some, who were privately envious of whatever it was that had enabled him to offer himself for such service) when he got up, bade them farewell, and walked outside into the night to get ready, leaving them mystified and even with a vague sense of resentment.

The cabin, built and abandoned by some prospectors who had grown weary of washing dirt only to find more dirt, stood in a place that was like an open vault in the side of the mountain, under a jutting rocky ridge lined with willow and aspen. The roof was slanted to slide the snow and from a distance one could see how badly out of rank many of the logs were. The cabin had been raised not by carpenters but gold seekers—men who didn't want to spend time at anything but getting rich—hoping to leave it shortly for a gingerbread mansion in Denver or San Francisco or whatever place had been shaped and defined by the idea of gold. A small corral stood out front, three horses idly inside the railings. A doe was stretched by its hind legs on the cabin's outer wall.

Moving soundlessly, Bell crossed a stream, dropping the stub of his cigar into the running waters and expectorating tobacco shreds from the tip of his tongue, eyes fixed upon the cabin's open door. Once he saw a man cross the interior carrying a frying pan, but that was the only movement. When he reached the corral he dismounted and tied his horse to the upper rail, eliciting some mild curiosity from the horses within. He unstrapped the carbine from his back, crooked it in his arm, and walked toward the cabin, as silently as floating. He could smell the cooking meat now, the boiling coffee. It reminded him of how hungry he was, made him irritable.

"Don't move," he said, filling the doorway, holding the rifle steady in the crook of his arm, covering the three men who were crouched facing the fire. They whirled, three sur-

prised and outraged faces, made the more fierce and incensed
for the three short black beards that seemed to bristle with
hostility.

"You sons of bitches," Bell said quietly.

"Lucas!" one said.

"What the hell you doing up here, man?" another said,
showing in his beard a slow, pleased, gap-toothed grin. He
was wearing a derby, tilted over one ear, was shirtless, the
upper portion of his long johns buttoned to his throat.

Bell studied them expressionlessly, then lowered the rifle.

"Sons of bitches," he said again, walking into the cabin. It
was one, plank-floored room. A table and chairs stood to one
side, three pallets to another, flat on the floor. A crackling fire
was making a cut of spitted venison sweat and drip. Coats
and hats were hung to pegs on one wall. There was a single
window, with an X of boards nailed over its smeared glass.
The cabin was permeated by a stale rank odor that was not so
much men as it was the absence of women.

The three men stood up, watching Bell with varying
degrees of self-conscious amusement.

"I could have opened up the three of you," Bell said. "Why
wasn't somebody posted?"

"I just walked in, the minute before you came," the one
with the derby said. "I swear, Lucas."

Bell contemplated him with an icy smile.

"Nobody comes up here, Lucas."

"I just did," Bell said.

"We weren't expecting you, Lucas," one of them said. "At
least not for a while yet."

Bell sat down at the table, his back to the log wall. He
tilted the Winchester against the wall, then removed his hat
and placed it on the table.

"Is anything the matter, Lucas?" he was asked.

"Where?"

"In town."

"Why should anything be the matter?"

"There shouldn't."

"Well then, there isn't," Bell said. "Is that ready?" he asked, nodding toward the venison.

"Just about."

"Then let's have some."

While one sawed at the meat with a knife, the other two joined Bell at the table.

"Plenty of game up here, Lucas," one of them said. "See that honey outside? Josh shot her this morning."

"Did he?" Bell said, looking across the table at Josh, who was wearing the derby. Bell's voice sounded more ironic than complimentary. It was those sly changes of tone, always unexpected, that kept them alert when he spoke, as if they were codes to what he might really be saying. "But I hear you fellows achieved even better game than that."

The two at the table guffawed and the one at the fire turned and grinned.

"Heard about it, huh?" Josh asked. "Well, pardon me, suh," he said, giving the derby a quick 360-degree turn around his head.

"Somebody in town mentioned it," Bell said.

"I'll wager they more than goddamned mentioned it," Josh said with loud, foolish enthusiasm.

"I hope he was worth it," Bell said.

"He was heavy with dust," another said. His name was Tyler. He was thin, sallow-faced, wearing a Confederate Army slouch hat, the brim dipped forward almost to the bridge of his hooked nose, lending a sinister look to his small, narrow eyes. "He was worth it, Lucas."

"You had to shoot him?" Bell asked.

Tyler shrugged, as if the question was too slight to answer.

"A man carrying that much gold dust," Josh said, "traveling alone in a place like that—deserves to be shot."

"Just like he was begging for it," Tyler said.

"They're easy up here, Lucas," Josh said. "Hell, they don't even ride a shotgun on those stages."

"That might change," Bell said.

"What are they saying about us, Lucas?" the one at the fire asked. His name was Spillner. He was the oldest of the three. His beard, which grew around his face but hardly below it, was threaded with tiny gray clusters, though the gray hadn't reached yet into his thick black hair. He had a bit more bulk than the others, a strong man slowly turning toward middle age.

Spillner had a large chunk of steaming meat soaked in its own juices on a tin plate now and was ladling some beans alongside it, doing it carefully, as if neatness mattered. Then he streamed some coffee from a short-handled pot into a tin cup and brought plate and cup to Bell and set them down. Bell reached out for some utensils lying nearby—a rusted knife and fork, which he regarded dubiously for a moment and then rubbed at with his fingertips—and began to eat. The others watched him, each sitting on a reversed chair, arms and chin rested on the backs, watching him eat even as the men in Baddock had done last night, watching the slow meticulous slicing of the meat, the fastidious shifting of fork from left hand to right.

"Huh?" Spillner asked.

"What?" Bell asked, shifting a mouthful of meat to say it.

"What are they saying about us?"

"They're looking forward to decorating their tree limbs with you."

The men laughed, Spillner's sound more of a snicker.

"And if it had been them riding up here instead of me," Bell went on, pausing to sip some coffee, "you boys would be saying your prayers now. If you know any."

"We ain't ready for that just yet," Spillner said.

"They're not going to wait on you being ready, Spilly," Bell said. "Just don't get overconfident. It wasn't by much more than a prayer that you got out of Nevada."

"Different breed of goat over there," Josh said.

"The goats around here are hardening up," Bell said.

"So what are we supposed to do?" Tyler asked.

"Be warned, be careful," Bell said.

"That's what you come up here for, to tell us that?" Tyler asked.

"If Lucas thinks it's worth telling," Josh said, "then it's worth hearing."

"All right," Tyler said. "But I'm not worried." With the slouch hat pulled so close to his eyes he seemed to be saying only half of what he was thinking.

"Well," Josh said, "if they get *too* intended we can always slide off to Colorado." He picked up a fork, stabbed a few beans from Bell's plate, caught a glance from Bell, and put the fork down.

"No," Bell said. "I don't want to leave this place just yet. They're just getting started down there. You have no idea what they're pulling out of these mountains."

"When can we go into town, Lucas?" Josh asked. "We're gettin' the itch."

"Do you think it's wise?" Bell asked.

"Nobody'll know us."

"They don't have a line on any of us yet, do they?" Spillner asked.

"I don't think so. But you never can tell. Angry men develop a sharper eye. They'll hang you and hold the trial later."

"Nobody's hanging us," Tyler said, surly. "And anyway, we can't winter up here. That's for shit sure."

"That's right," Josh said. "Once it starts snowin' the passes will fill up. Then what?"

Bell finished his meal, drained his cup, then sat back.

"So business has been good, has it?" he said.

"You know that as well as we do," Spillner said.

"Yes, I do know. In fact, I've been thinking of bringing in some new men."

"What for?" Tyler asked, frowning.

"What do you think? There are more and more stages coming through, and some of them pretty ripe with bullion, and more diggers riding around with fat pockets. And anyway, you fellows are starting to run the risk of being recognized; you're out on the trails a hell of a lot."

"Who are you bringing in?" Tyler asked, still frowning.

"You'll see," Bell said. Then, "Where've you got your pickings?"

"Buried behind the shithouse," Josh said. "It's piling up, Lucas. Greenbacks, dust, bullion, rings, watches. Jesus, we'd like to put it to use."

"You will," Bell said. He unbuttoned his coat; they could see now the handle of the Peacemaker.

"You come set, hey, Lucas?" Josh said.

"I hear these mountains can be dangerous," Bell said.

"Don't listen to those rumors," Josh said, laughing.

"What've you been doing down there?" Spillner asked.

"Playing cards. Seeing to business."

"How's your luck running?" Tyler asked.

Josh laughed. "Lucas never loses. You ought to know that."

"What are the women like?" Spillner asked.

"Amiable."

"You should have brought one up with you, man," Josh said.

"It's been a while, Lucas," Spillner said.

"Are you still pushed that way?" Bell asked with a flicker of smile.

Spillner's teeth showed unpleasantly in his beard.

"They'll make trouble for you, Spilly," Bell said.

"That's right," Josh said. "They're not all as polite as Lucas's was."

"You have to be lucky," Bell said.

"You should never have brought her," Spillner said, his voice tentative, as if to leave himself room to withdraw from the subject if he had to.

"It was her idea," Bell said.

"That's right," Josh said to Spillner. "It was her idea."

"Should've sent her back," Spillner said.

"She wouldn't go back," Tyler said. "Wouldn't stay, wouldn't go. Wouldn't anything. Like a mule stuck in mud."

"You should've seen it coming," Spillner said.

"She had a lot of inner turmoil," Bell said. "But now she's at rest," he added with sardonic piety.

"You'd better look to the day," Spillner said, "when her husband comes riding in."

"If her husband was capable of coming after her," Bell said, "she never would have left him. And let's leave it at that."

"That's right," Josh said. "It ain't religious to talk about her."

"Anyway," Tyler said, "let's get to business. Are they planning anything with those stages?"

"There was some talk of putting guns on," Bell said, "but I didn't hear about any takers."

"We're gonna get rich up here," Josh said.

"Not if you keep missing the ripe ones," Bell said. "I've seen some really loaded stages pulling in."

"They keep rigging the schedules to different times, Lucas," Josh said.

"You said you'd be getting hold of those schedules," Spillner said.

"They're not so easy to come by," Bell said. "The only one apart from the line people who has them is the sheriff."

"Did you bring whiskey, Lucas?" Josh asked.

"It's in my saddlebags."

"Well, then . . ." Josh said with a grin, getting up.

"Then what about the sheriff?" Spillner asked.

"He's just about played out," Bell said. "They'll have themselves another one before long. Then we'll see."

Josh was standing as if waiting for dispensation.

"Go ahead," Bell told him.

"It would make life a whole lot easier," Tyler said, "having those schedules."

"Be patient," Bell said. He watched Josh pass through the doorway, the derby skimming under the top of the door frame.

"I wasn't born to be patient," Tyler said.

"Then you're in danger of dying in a hurry," Bell said with a pleasant smile. He pulled his hand back from the table, the slow, casual gesture coming to a halt at his hip.

They watched what he was doing, following the movement with their eyes, not curious, but simply as the eye will follow a moving thing when the mind is preoccupied. So neither of them made a gesture either retaliatory or evasive, or said anything, or probably even thought anything, though when the Peacemaker came up in Bell's hand Spillner did frown, because he was the older, the shrewder, with more hard-bought experience, and because of the two he was by nature the more cynical and mistrustful and hence more dangerous; and so he died with at least a flash of vindication for his lifetime of sullenly accumulated percipience.

Bell took Spillner with the first shot, drilling the irately startled face just under the eye. Spillner, still holding the back of the chair, took it over with him as his head jerked up and he flew back. And even before Spillner had hit the floor the Peacemaker's barrel shifted several degrees to point at Tyler's severely incredulous face with its near-hidden eyes brightening fiercely at the brim of the slouch hat. The pistol discharged again, blowing Tyler to the floor with a scorched round disk in the center of his forehead, the emptied chair tipping and slowly following him down, as if summoned by the one upraised and stiffly quivering hand.

Bell quickly holstered the pistol, picked up the Winchester, and went to the door.

"Hey!" Josh said, turned in his tracks, a few steps from Bell's horse. "What the hell—"

Bell lifted the rifle and sighted along the barrel.

"Hey!" Josh cried again, half turned where he stood. He raised one arm out face high and spanned his fingers wide as if trying to cover the Winchester's leveled muzzle.

The discharge tore into his chest, the impact throwing his hat off, upending him as if he had been standing on a snatched-away rug. He struck the ground violently, heaved over once, and died facedown. His derby rolled off on its edge in a little circle and then came down on the ground like a lid.

NINETEEN

Maynard knew it was around five o'clock in the morning. He knew it even before he opened his eyes and he knew it even before he saw through the cabin window the frailest infiltration—more of an insinuation, really—of gray into the darkness. He knew it as a soldier who has gone through monumental multiday battles knows of dawn's imminence no matter how profound his sleep.

He sat up in his blankets, leaning back on one arm, not yet clear of sleep's leaden anchor. Then he swung the blankets back like a man waving a cape and got out of bed and walked barefoot across the floor, feeling the chill in the darkness, the unspent sleep sullen in his face. He felt like a wraith in his own cabin, summoned, as if he could turn around and see himself still asleep in the bed.

He could hear the sounds even before he got to the window—horses softly walking (or at least moving: it was quiet enough for motion to be its own noiseless vibratory sound), a metallic jingle so soft as to be magical; whereas at sunset it might have signaled departure, now it hinted arrival. A dying moon in the northeast was letting just enough light to lend the sheerest of dimensions to the compacted unity outside, enough for him to see the four horses strung out in single file along the stage road like a moving fence, walking as though they were not for sight but memory alone.

He flattened his hands on the window's low sill and leaned slightly forward. The lead horse appeared the most substantial, where he believed he could see a rider, the other three following in procession so quiet it was as if their hooves were barely in touch with the ground. He watched until they were gone. Then he eased around and returned to the bed and fell back to sleep.

He didn't remember any of it until he rode into town late in the morning. He tied up outside of The Chinaman's and went in and ordered breakfast. The place was empty except for Haybacker.

"So," Haybacker said when he set the tin plate of eggs and bacon in front of his lone customer, "what do you think of it all?"

"I never think before breakfast," Maynard said.

"So be it," Haybacker said, walking away.

Maynard sat with his back to the window, to the street, to Baddock, to everything, completely turned in on himself. What was in his mind now, what had been there all morning, had probably slipped in sometime during sleep because when he awoke to a cabin bright with Montana sunshine his mind was already at fullness of thought. Theo, in face, body, voice, and Theo in abstraction, in star-point imagery, pervading him with the most refining subtleties, at times so vivid she was like a blood-bearing extension of himself.

He had not been this way about a woman for a long time—maybe never, from the feel of it. He was occupied to full length through the corridors of his mind as well as surrounded of heart. The man who had braved Confederate gun and cannon, who could associate his name with Gettysburg and Cold Harbor, was being undone and made frail by a woman.

One thing he had resolved: he would not return to the Paradise West. He could not stand the thought of her being there, and he would, in fact, start thinking about how to get her out of the place, and not by preaching the evils of it, either. Of all such women he had known, she was the most unlikely. She'd had some bad luck, that was all. And when a woman had a run of that in a country like this, well, it seemed they took the easiest turn. Bell certainly knew her qualities. What he sees in her so do I, Maynard thought, the difference being I would not permit her to warm the sheets with anybody who had the price of it.

When he was finished eating he walked outside, where he quickly remembered why he was there in the first place. It was the sight of O'Connor heading toward his office, a somewhat pleased expression on his spade-bearded face. The lawyer was smartly dressed, topped off by a narrow-crowned fedora, a distinctive piece of headgear in Baddock. When he saw Maynard he stopped and broke into a smile.

"So," he said as he waited for Maynard to close the distance between them.

"Good morning, Mr. O'Connor," Maynard said, stopping.

"It looks like you're no longer the reigning hero, eh? But I guess you don't mind, modest fellow that you are."

"Heroes come and go, don't they?" Maynard asked, wanting to add "Major" to the remark, as if with a single thrust to get it over with.

"With remarkable celerity sometimes," O'Connor said. Then he paused, studying Maynard. "You *have* heard what happened, I take it? If not, you're the only one in town who hasn't."

"I just rode in and had breakfast."

"Well then. You haven't heard the biggest news to hit these parts since the ground started to glitter. He's back. Job done. Job incredibly done."

"Bell?"

"Did what he said he would and hauled back the proof. Rode in just at dawn with three horses behind him, each with a dead road agent draped over like a sack of flour."

Maynard was twice struck—by the news and by what he now remembered seeing earlier from his cabin window, what hadn't been a dream, not a caravan of ghosts, but a reality.

"If you'd have been living in town," O'Connor said, "I

assure you you wouldn't have slept through it. Whoever was around began hurrahing until they woke up everybody. It was like the end of the war all over again. And in its way this was something just as special."

"Worthy of decoration," Maynard said.

O'Connor laughed. "Well said, Maynard. It's already been seen to. He's been decorated with the sheriff's badge. By acclamation. I'd say it's a bright day for Baddock. Look at that," the lawyer said, pointing skyward. "Never been brighter."

Maynard found Patterson at a desk in the office of the Baddock *Newspaper*. The shirtsleeved journalist was running a quill pen back and forth across a sheet of foolscap. He turned and spoke across his shoulder. "Give me another moment, Thomas."

Maynard waited outside. Christ, he thought, now what? He hadn't understood it from the beginning, and now he was being told to believe something when there was even less understanding for it. Lucas Bell, known as a gambler and otherwise unknown, pursues a most inexplicable course and returns a hero and through a burst of civic gratitude is appointed sheriff (and accepts, which might have been the most surprising aspect of the whole thing). It could only happen in a town that hadn't existed a few years ago and might well vanish back to nothingness at any given moment. Bell and his abrupt eminence was like a seed out of mythology, where something happened or might have or ought to have or was believed to have and then left itself behind with just enough verisimilitude to grow into whatever proportion imagination designed or a rudimentary culture required, trusting the future to supply such narrative embellishment as was needed for eternal levitation.

Patterson came out of the office pulling his jacket on.

"Made me feel like a newspaperman again," he said. "First time in years."

"Are you going to tell me," Maynard asked, "or do I have to wait for the first edition?"

"You mean to say you don't know?"

"Just the bones of it."

"Well, there's not more than that. So it called for a flourish or two," Patterson said with a whimsical smile, and began quoting: " 'Lucas Bell has outdone Julius Caesar. Caesar came, saw, and conquered. Well, Bell came, saw, conquered, and returned. Triumphantly.' " Patterson shrugged. "What the hell," he said. "If you have a pen in your hand, might as well use it. Have you had breakfast?"

"Yes."

"All right, then you can come watch me eat."

They crossed the street to the bakery, where you could get hot buttered bread and the only decent coffee in town. A taut-faced and severely thin woman served them, then disappeared behind a curtain into an interior room. Maynard had coffee, watching Patterson bite away at the bread and wash it down and talk, sometimes with a full mouth.

"I heard the noise at about six A.M.," Patterson said, "and looked out the window and saw them running around the street. I hadn't heard any shooting, and around here you generally don't get any excitement without some gunfire. So I got dressed and went downstairs and all I had to do was follow the noise, right on up to the Honest Eagle. Well, there it was, the damnedest sight. Three horses tied up at the rail, each of them with a dead man slung over the saddle."

"Like a sack of flour," Maynard said tonelessly.

Patterson paused for a moment, gave Maynard a curious look, then went on. "Three of them, Thomas. And nasty-looking customers, too. You wouldn't have wanted to meet them in church, much less alone up in the mountains. I went inside to talk to Bell, when I could get near him. In my capacity as reporter. He wasn't saying much."

"Modesty," Maynard said.

"Could be. Or maybe he was just worn out. All he'd say was he'd found them, confronted them, and did what he had to do. By that time everybody was there, with your nabobs leading the way. They told Bell they wanted to make him sheriff, right there on the spot."

"Where was Dunlop?"

"Standing there. The forgotten man of the moment. Didn't say a word. Bell demurred, said he didn't want to be sheriff. But they said he had to be, that he was needed. Cheers all around. It was done by proclamation and acclamation. He finally said all right, but only for six months or until they found somebody suitable. That was when old Dunlop came forward and took off his badge and laid it on the bar and walked out. That part of it was kind of sad."

"None of it sounds right to me," Maynard said.

"But it happened, Thomas. And I'll tell you something else. I went around to the undertaker later and he told me that each of those men had been shot in front, that Bell must've gone right at them."

"Doesn't make sense—men like that."

"You're forgetting, friend—I saw *you* drop two. So it isn't so unlikely."

"Still—"

"I'll tell you more, in case you're having any pernicious doubts: He also brought back a sackful of booty. Bags of coins and gold dust and rings and watches he found in their possession. Whoever can come in and give a description of their goods can get them back."

"And the rest goes to widows and orphans," Maynard said.

"You're being cynical," Patterson said. "Maybe too much."

And maybe he was right, Maynard thought. There had been that not entirely unwelcome possibility that maybe Bell would not come back. He hadn't wished for it—he was firm on that, he told himself with maybe too much self-persuasion—but the possibility had been clearly in thought.

"Was Theo there?" he asked.

"She was," Patterson said. "Heard the racket and came downstairs."

"What did she do?"

"Nothing. Just stood there and watched."

"Admiringly, I suppose."

"I wasn't giving it that much attention."

"Did he talk to her?"

"Not while I was there." Patterson finished the last of his bread, swallowed some coffee, then peered down into the cup, which he held in both hands. "Look, Tom," he said tentatively, "I don't want to interfere . . ." He waited, expecting to be cut off. When he heard nothing, he went on. "You still have a job of work to do out here."

"I know that."

"It should be the first thing in your mind, nothing else."

"It is the first thing," Maynard said; "it's just not the best thing, that's all."

"To you it's an assignment from on high, but to me it's something more. Barley was a good friend, and if your major was the one who ran the lead into him I'd like to see him pay for it. But with this other business pushing things aside in your head . . ." Again Patterson waited, still looking down into the cup; from a distance he might have appeared rueful. Then his eyes came up and he smiled like a man freshly awakened from a pleasing dream. "Ah, hell," he said, "it's none of my business. We've all passed through it, haven't we? There's no sound advice for it and no known cure."

"I can stand the no cure," Maynard said; "it's the advice that wears me down."

When he left Patterson, Maynard felt the impulse to do the decent thing. He crossed the street, stepped up onto the boardwalk, and entered the sheriff's office. John Dunlop was standing behind the desk, the back of his flannel shirt turned toward the door. He was reaching up and untacking an American flag from the wall, leaving behind a wide square slightly lighter than the rest of the wall. He was hatless, showing an impressive growth of gray hair. When he turned around and saw Maynard standing there the doleful expression around his gray drooping mustache never changed.

"Mr. Maynard," he said.

"Don't really know you, Mr. Dunlop," Maynard said, "and we've hardly spoken, but all the same . . ." He extended his hand across the desk and Dunlop shook it briefly. "I want to wish you luck."

"Thank you," Dunlop said. He folded the flag neatly several times over until it was a small square, then put it down on the desk. "Just taking what belongs to me," he said.

"I think they'll be sorry," Maynard said.

"Do you?" Dunlop asked, appraising him shrewdly for a moment. "Well, it's not for me to say. Anyway, I won't be here to see it."

"Where are you heading?"

"I've got a brother who keeps a business in St. Louis. Sells haberdashery. He'll take me on."

"Going to seem tame."

"I just might grow to like it," Dunlop said, sounding as if he had been giving the possibility some thought. He opened some of the desk drawers and removed papers and envelopes and placed them on top of the desk. Then he unbuckled his gun belt and placed it and the holstered gun on the desk too. "I've been a sheriff here and there for a long time," he said, his eyes lingering on the gun for a moment. "And I've seen some sheriffs leave the job in a pine box. So maybe I'm lucky."

"I'd say this town has been lucky to have had you."

"Do you think so?" Then, with more sobriety than Maynard anticipated, the older man said, "Thank you, Maynard."

Embarrassed by the emotion of the response, Maynard nodded his head and looked away for a moment.

"You don't become a sheriff just because they put a badge on you," Dunlop said. "There's a bit more to it. An approach that you have to learn, for your sake and everybody else's." He looked around the office as if the lessons he had learned were invisibly present. "You have to know whether a fellow's standing with both feet over the line or just one, or is standing right at the line. There are times when your mind's got to be quicker than your hand."

"And the other way around," Maynard said.

"Most decidedly," Dunlop said, looking back to him. "And how do you come by that? Not by putting on a badge. It's knowing how to think like a sheriff. Day and night and when you're asleep too." He sat down slowly in the swivel chair behind the desk and folded his hands over his large middle. He looked older than a few days ago, wearier, more worn. "Or maybe," he said, "I'm just too damned old now to remember what being young is like. Maybe he can do it."

"Seems a capable man," Maynard said.

"Think so?" Dunlop said, the merest air of skepticism in his voice. "It's not done by scaring people, by popping your badge wherever you go, but by getting their respect."

"And Bell?"

"Too much of a watcher."

"What does that mean?"

"Watched me too much when I went by."

"He seems to do that with everyone," Maynard said.

"I think I was special for him."

"He never broke the law here, did he?"

"Not here."

"But somewhere?" Maynard said.

What passed for a smile expanded Dunlop's lips by a fraction.

"Not for me to say."

"But you think so."

"You're taking an interest, Mr. Maynard."

"I find him an intriguing man."

"As he no doubt finds you."

"You think?" Maynard asked.

"I know what you did up in the mountains, Maynard. I won't judge it; I wasn't there. Simon Patterson spoke for you and his word is good. But I'd steer clear of the new sheriff, if I were you."

"I'm no threat to him."

"He's the kind of man who looks for midnight in the sunshine."

"Do you know much about him?" Maynard asked.

Dunlop shook his head.

"What about some of the other pillars of respectability around here?" Maynard asked.

Dunlop smiled slowly; it made his already sad face turn sadder.

"You're pretty close to giving yourself away, Maynard."

"I don't know what you're talking about, Sheriff," Maynard said blandly.

"Who are you looking for?"

Maynard said nothing.

"You're not a law man," Dunlop said. "You would've come to me on the first day. But all right. You won't tell me. It doesn't concern me anymore anyhow. But I'll give you a penny's worth: I don't to my own knowledge know of anyone here who's on the run, particularly among the local pillars. But that's your business."

"I haven't said it was."

"Of course not. This whole conversation was never said. You can rest on that. As I say, it doesn't concern me anymore."

"When are you off then?"

"Tomorrow morning's stage."

"I hope you're not stopped along the trail," Maynard said lightly.

"Why, I thought Mr. Bell's cleared all that up."

"But you're not so sure."

Dunlop smiled enigmatically. "Yet to be seen, Mr. Maynard," he said.

TWENTY

Maybe the adulation had been too sudden, for no sooner had Bell been badged than certain doubting comments concerning the installation were being heard. How, it was asked, could a man running a gambling saloon—where it was imperative an eye be kept on things—also fulfill the often time-consuming and sometimes wide-ranging obligations of his new office? There was some concern voiced about the Honest Eagle's becoming the de facto sheriff's office.

There was also some discreet clearing of throats about the propriety of the sheriff running a house of ill repute. But Bell quickly disarmed these concerns by announcing he was relinquishing his interest in the Paradise West and allowing it to be taken over by "others." The "others" happened to be, of course, the men who were already working for him in the Honest Eagle, but the town accepted the formality as a gesture of goodwill.

In fact, Bell became a ubiquitous presence as sheriff, strolling about town, a slender, observant figure, cool but cordial. He made it a point to spend little time in his own establishment and from the moment he put on the badge never sat down at one of his own card tables. Some people said he was making a genuine effort to respond to his new responsibilities and praised him; others withheld judgment.

What impressed even the cynics was how the new sheriff's mere appearance at a scene of brewing trouble could instantly defuse it. Even the small bands of roughnecks who occasionally rode in, who had made John Dunlop make a wide turn around them, deferred to Sheriff Bell. Some people attributed this to the fact of Bell's own employees at the Honest Eagle and Paradise West, each of whom had arrived in Baddock soon after he did and who were obviously loyal to him, and who had already demonstrated a willingness to stand hard ground in the face of trouble. It was indeed the fact of these men that made the town fathers refuse his request for deputies, though Bell claimed that one or two were needed.

"You've already got some of the hardest men in town who'll back you," O'Connor said when Bell came to the lawyer with his request.

"I can't ask men to throw in with me when they're not being paid for it," Bell said. "They might think twice about the morality or legality of taking some drastic action, even on my behalf."

O'Connor suppressed the smile he felt at such questions ever entering the minds of the men Bell had surrounded himself with.

"We'll take it under advisement," he said.

"There's got to be somebody in charge when I have to leave town on sheriff's business."

This "sheriff's business" was part of Bell's stated policy upon assuming office. The policy was very simple: to bring law and order to Baddock and its environs. Not only would he see to its implementation in town, but he would also be going out to handle what he described as the town's "most damning problem," the road agents. He had merely "trimmed some branches" on his recent foray, he said. The bullion-laden stages rolling through the mountain trails were still too tempting. He meant to investigate every stage robbery and attempt to track the holdup men.

To this latter end, he said, he intended to take "preventive steps." These entailed his occasionally riding out to meet an incoming stage, to "show the badge" and escort it in, as John Dunlop had done. The idea received the enthusiastic endorse-

ment of Turner, who, as he had done with Dunlop, handed
over the schedules.

The idea of a woman, Maynard was thinking, was so ingre-
dient filled it could erode whatever lay around it. It had certainly diverted some of his attention away from finding
Major Pryor, and there was no other reason for his being (or
staying) in the Montana Territory, especially with autumn
beginning to color the trees and reports of snow in the higher
elevations. He had to press his mind in the direction of his
responsibility and give it something more than his second-
best considerations.

He had always seen himself—particularly since making
lieutenant and then captain—as distinctively the soldier, as
though he had been hewn by nature with glints of marble in
his being. It was an inner light that persuaded the face to an
explicit manifestation, for today and for ever. He knew this
because, ostensibly homeless, he was everywhere at home,
wherever he made his march or rolled his blanket, anywhere
in the whole full world, beneath any star, upon any ground.
Forever a soldier, to any eye, even when it was done and he
was shawled before the last hearth fires.

But now he was questioning even that, that single eternal
unity of soldierliness. Maybe it wasn't so indelibly unique
after all, its mark of singularity any more enduring than that
of the farmer or tradesman. If a former major—and hero of
war—could vanish without vestige (even to my own eye, he
thought) into a gold-town merchant or lawyer or banker,
then maybe there wasn't anything so grand about it to begin
with.

Almost as if by manual effort, he focused his thoughts
upon O'Connor, Abbot, Pearson, each of them a Baddock
"nabob," one of them almost certainly the man Barley Newton had recognized. He contrived to speak with each, fabri-
cating a legal matter for O'Connor, a banking question for
Pearson, and in making a purchase at Abbot's general store

engaged him in protracted conversation. But what information he pried advanced nothing. He could find a major in
none of them; or worse, in each, for there were similarities of
personal strength and self-assurance, the things Maynard
associated with a Union Army commander.

But in one of these men, Maynard was convinced, something was at rest, but poised. Certain heroes of the field could
be deeply at peace with themselves as men, and not because
they had conquered others but themselves. But no matter
how deeply at rest, nor how idyllic the serenity, at the core lay
a keen stillness prepared to echo sharply back if the right
shout was heard.

Maynard was sitting outside his cabin on a bright fresh-
sired morning, smoking his pipe, chair tilted up against the
log wall, watching the lone rider moving from the direction
of town in an easy gallop along the stage road. When he recognized Lucas Bell, he tipped the chair slowly forward to the
ground, put the pipe between his teeth, placed his hands on
his knees, and watched.

Always neatly dressed, but never to the point where it
hinted of vanity or undue self-inspection before a mirror, Bell
was now wearing a rough black woolen coat with the collar
raised like a tiny fence around his neck, his trousers stuffed
into mud-stained boots, a flat-crowned black hat. Where in
his smoother apparel he sometimes exuded a subtly villain-
ous air, now he seemed just another man at life with the hard
beauty of the Montana Territory.

He cut away from the road, approaching Maynard at a
canter.

"Doesn't look right to me," Bell said as he neared, smiling
with a geniality that caught Maynard's attention; the man
seemed various at smiling, the same expression capable of
concealing, disarming, misleading, or, as now, presenting a
friend.

Maynard chose not to ask what didn't look right. Bell had
stopped, was sitting his horse some ten or fifteen feet away.

"I think you're a man too active by nature to be sitting idly," Bell said. "Just doesn't look right." Apparently the smile had been designed for the comment; now it went away.

"A man sitting still," Maynard said, "can be dangerously active."

"So you're hunkered out here to do your thinking, is that it?" Bell said. With a smooth limber movement he swung from the saddle and came lightly to the ground, watched by Maynard with an insouciance that suggested that even had Bell fallen on his face there would have been no movement toward assistance. Maynard's steady eye, clenched pipe, and now folded arms gave him an adamant posture. "Well, you may be right in what you say," Bell said. He was wearing his gun belt and pistol outside of his coat, but the star, if that was pinned on, was under. "I daresay the probing mind has moved more things than the hurling body. What do you think?" Bell smiled again, briefly, as if inviting Maynard to give some powerful example of thought.

Maynard unfolded his arms, pulled the pipe from between his teeth, and appeared to relax.

"What can I do for you, Sheriff?" he asked.

"You can bring out a chair, so a man can sit down."

"You're welcome inside."

"Thank you, but no. It's too pure a day to be spent out of. I prefer your idea—a sit out in the sun."

Maynard went inside for the chair. He felt annoyed from several sides: he didn't particularly feel like having a visitor and particularly this one, who had a track with Theo that he both envied and deplored; and he didn't like the idea of hauling a chair outside for him. And there was something else: when he glanced around at the decidedly crude, almost monastically furnished cabin he was embarrassed at the thought of Bell seeing it, and this, too, piqued him, this caring what Bell might or might not think.

"This was Barley Newton's place, wasn't it?" Bell said from outside.

"That's right," Maynard said, picking up the chair. He paused. "Did you know him?"

"I knew him."

"Well?"

"What?"

"Did you know him well?" Maynard asked, still standing motionlessly, holding the chair.

"Not especially. Did you?"

"Never met him."

"You're living in his cabin."

"It was standing empty," Maynard said, emerging with the chair now. He put it down about six feet opposite his own.

"Then it was for claim, I guess," Bell said, taking the back of the chair in hand for a moment as if to test its sturdiness. "This is now the seat of law and order in Baddock," he said, sitting down and crossing his legs, separating the skirts of his coat over his knee. His smooth face smiled again, this time as if to say that he was comfortable. Maynard resumed his seat against the wall, knocking his cold pipe empty against a chair leg and then holding it in his hand.

"He was shot, wasn't he?" Maynard asked.

"Barley? Yes."

"Does anyone know why?"

Bell smiled quirkily. His eyes were of palest blue, with a softness not of expression but of organic texture. There was no expression.

"I don't think anyone asked," he said. "A dispute, I would imagine."

"Was he a disputatious man?"

"I don't think so. These things happen. In a place like this, where people appear suddenly, some of them as if out of nowhere, a disappearance just as sudden doesn't cause much comment."

"Even if they've been murdered?"

"Murder is different out here," Bell said, almost offhandedly.

"That's a hell of an attitude for a sheriff."

"I was giving you society's point of view, not the sheriff's."

"Nobody tried to figure out who shot Barley?"

"John Dunlop did, of course. But all he had was a dead body lying in the street and no witnesses. You seem interested."

"I'm living in his cabin."

"So you are," Bell said. "Do you intend staying on?"

"Well, Sheriff, at the moment I have no answer to that. What about you?"

"Out here we're all creatures of fate. Who knows for how long before Baddock plays itself out? There could be—probably will be—another strike somewhere, and then that becomes the place."

"And there you'll go."

Bell laughed. "We're all victims and, God willing, beneficiaries."

"Of what?"

"Somebody else's wild dream, which I'll never belittle, because it feeds me. Beware of the gold fever, Maynard. But I don't think you have it. You seem too steady. But just think of the poor bastard who does, who hauls himself up into those mountains with his sacks of bacon and flour and coffee and bottles of whiskey, and of course his pick, shovel, pan, magnifying glass, rifle, and nothing but horse or mule for companionship, disappearing from the world for months at a time."

"Could you do that?"

"It's not for me," Bell said. "But bless them all, I say; they're running a stream of glitter that eventually crosses my bar and stops at my tables. No, I couldn't do what they're doing, but they've got my admiration. They never get lonely or disappointed—the dream won't let them. They probably even forget there's a world below the mountains or that they ever had a life before, because there's always that thing just up ahead. They'll even abandon ground that's been good to them, simply because there's another mountain on ahead that might be better, or because they just have to *know* if it is or isn't."

Maynard was listening carefully, watching him.

"It sounds lunatic," Bell said. "But it isn't. It's spiritual, in a way. Maybe it's being up so high you can reach out and touch the clouds. You get up high enough and sometimes the clouds just come floating by; things you've always had to lift up your eyes to see. Suddenly you're breathing them."

"And there you'll always be," Maynard said. "In one form or another."

"With the bigger and the better, always. Partner to the dream."

"Silent partner."

"Silent is always best," Bell said, showing a slow smile, communicating something that was meant only to be guessed at. "But you see, Maynard, sometimes there's more to it than they can ever hope to know about, though they wouldn't care a damn if they did. You see, sometimes the prospector in his blind foolish faith becomes a pioneer of the path of empire, a road maker, a moving outpost of civilization."

"And sometimes they die right there," Maynard said.

"Oh yes," Bell said, nodding. "Tired and worn out, but I daresay never beaten. But hell, it must be a gentle way to go, with your dream still right there to the end."

"Except when they've taken a couple of bullets in the back."

"Yes," Bell said, "and robbed of the money they were coming to spend in my place. Frankly, Maynard, that's why I accepted the badge. I've got a financial stake in law and order around here. I can take care of my own place; anybody who starts blowing his bugle there will find himself drinking his soup through his forehead. But if these robberies keep on it's going to affect my livelihood."

"And everyone else's."

"There's been talk of a citizens' committee."

"So I understand."

"We can't let that root get above ground," Bell said. "That's death to a town. People hear about it and it's like a plague. Vigilantes spell trouble any way you look at it."

"Sometimes honest men have to take the law into their own hands," Maynard said.

"Then they cease being honest men. Once you start hanging people without a fair trial, you have anarchy. When everybody is the law, nobody is."

"But it seems to me, Sheriff, where there's no answer to murder there's no law to question."

Bell smiled wryly. "Are you being philosophical?"

"Only if there's philosophy in a fact."

"Well, those facts are going to change, otherwise this town is going to eat itself up, inside out and outside in."

"I wish you luck," Maynard said noncommittally, wondering where this was going. He had something else he wanted to discuss with Lucas Bell but wasn't sure how to get to it without too much personal exposure. Not helping any was the disturbing feeling that he might have formed a biased and inadequate judgment of the man. Bell had spoken of the dreams of prospectors beating a path into the future, of bigger strikes, towns, growth, where he, Bell, would follow with his own expanding ambitions and become part of. Bell may have been a man of less than perfect scruples, but the source of any ambition was a heat-generating purity, no matter how it might be channeled. (For a man who lived and worked in Washington, D.C., it was no strange thing; Maynard knew how it moved certain things and shook others, attracting people to its fervor.) Maybe that was what Theo saw in Bell and maybe knew that it was rare enough and thus compelling, no matter its form. *As opposed to the eternal credo of the soldier: to serve, to take orders, to wait, responding only when it was to someone else's ambition.*

"I need more than luck," Bell said. "I need some help. Look, Maynard, I need some deputies. They won't give me any; it's probably because they don't care for the strain of men I have around me. But I think they'd accept you. You're well respected."

"Because I killed two men."

"That's the way judgments are made out here."

"Not the most flattering," Maynard said.

"The niceties haven't arrived yet. Baddock is still too fresh a bump on the earth for that. But I need a man to cover the town when I'm away."

"Where will you be going?"

"Out there," Bell said, pointing toward the mountains. "That's where the trouble is. That's where it's got to be stopped. A stage was hit last night."

"I hadn't heard."

"Loaded with bullion from one of the mines. Maybe six, eight thousand worth. They killed the driver this time. One of the passengers was able to bring it in."

"So you're heading out there again?"

Bell lifted his hands for a moment. "I've taken it on."

"You're out of your mind, Bell. You got by with it once."

"I'll take my chances. But I'm going to need somebody down here while I'm gone."

"I'm not available," Maynard said. He wanted to make it sound definitive, and he did.

"I won't ask why," Bell said, a new, curious interest entering his face, followed by the merest wisp of conspiratorial smile. "What are you doing out here anyway?"

"It's the place to be. The Montana Territory."

"But you're just watching it."

"It's a beautiful place."

"Beautiful can be dangerous," Bell said. "Like a woman."

Ah, you bastard, Maynard thought, offering a complacent smile.

"You're looking for somebody, aren't you?" Bell asked.

"What makes you think so?"

"You make me think so. You do nothing, but seem very active at it. That's a disturbing quality, Maynard."

Bell's horse shifted its weight, let a softly rolling blowing sound and lowered its face studiously to the ground and began cropping at the short brown grass.

"Where are you from?" Bell asked.

"East," Maynard said. "And you?"

"Pretty much."

"Were you in the war?"

Bell laughed. "If I say yes, you'll want to know on which side and that could launch into a great political debate. And a man of the law should be above that."

"Then we could discuss tactics and strategy."

"Assuming I knew anything of either. But if you want to deliver yourself of some opinions, I'll be happy to listen."

"It's hard to imagine a gambler going off to war," Maynard said.

"Why? More survive than not. The odds are good."

"But the risks are total."

"You seem to know about it," Bell said.

"It just takes listening to know."

"And you're a man who listens."

Bell shifted about in the chair. He's going to leave in a moment, Maynard thought. Maybe he's waiting to be asked; maybe that's what he came for, to find out.

"Is she back at the Paradise?" he asked.

"Now and again," Bell said. "When she's of a mind."

"Let her go, Bell."

"To where?"

"Just away."

Bell laughed, as if there was no consequence to the matter. "She's free to do as she wants," he said. "Free as a bird. Belongs to no man."

"She works for you," Maynard said.

"Call it work. Anyway, she came here and enrolled herself."

"I thought you might—"

"I'm not really in the business of pandering," Bell said. "Frankly, I find it sordid. But inevitably somebody was going to offer the supply and I thought it might just as well be me."

"But you can walk away from it anytime you want."

"And you think she can't? You think she's trapped? Listen, Maynard, there's a fever to that sort of thing too, but she doesn't have it. The person might be the occupation, but the occupation doesn't always describe the person."

"There's the danger of becoming what you don't think you are."

"There's only the danger of acquiring a label, which you can peel off whenever you like. Pour milk into a whiskey bottle and what have you got? Whiskey? No. Milk."

"With an odor, perhaps."

"You seem to be a moral man, Maynard, which probably colors your understanding of things," Bell said. "But this isn't a question of morality, is it? She's a prize, isn't she?" he said with an appreciative smile. "Fine-looking woman, with a brain, and a flame all throughout. You don't know how many men have offered to marry her right out of that bed."

"Then you ought to get her out of there."

"She doesn't check in as often as you think. Spends most of her time up in her rooms."

"For Christ's sake, Bell, the last one blew her brains out."

"The last one was a creek run dry; this one's a river at torrent. Don't worry about her."

"Where does she come from?" Maynard asked. "What's her story?"

Bell shrugged. "I don't know," he said. "I imagine she has one. Everybody does. Even you."

TWENTY-ONE

Two days later a stagecoach coming through one of the high-altitude passes was stopped and robbed. A passenger who objected to being parted from his valuables was shot dead on the spot. The following day some men riding down from a mining camp found the bodies of two prospectors who had been shot and left with their pockets turned inside out.

It was not unfamiliar news, but this time Maynard noted a difference in the reaction on Main Street. Turner, for one, usually so vehement when one of his stages was hit, said very little but merely retreated to his office. Unstirred by angry outbursts from any of the town's leaders, the gathered crowd merely muttered sullenly and broke apart, going off in twos and threes to philosophize over one bar or another.

"It looks like they're getting used to it," Maynard said. He was standing in front of the newspaper office with Patterson, watching them.

"Or not," Patterson said. "You can brew more out of silence than you can out of a Fourth of July speech."

"I didn't see Bell."

"They say he rode out early yesterday morning."

"Where to?"

"Back up into the mountains, to do some tracking."

"That makes no sense," Maynard said.

"It did last time."

"What I mean is, it shouldn't make any sense to him. A full-time, professional law man wouldn't do that, why should a temporary? What's he stand to gain?"

"Thomas," Patterson said, "sometimes when I wake up in the morning I don't even understand the face I see in the mirror. Do you want me to explain Lucas Bell?"

Pearson emerged from the bank carrying a tin pail of water by its loop handle. At the edge of the boardwalk he took the pail in both hands and streaked the water out into the street, then stared morosely for several moments. When he saw Maynard and Patterson he walked toward them.

"Another bad day, hey, Pearson?" Patterson said.

"Not a good one," the banker said, holding the empty pail by the loop handle. His face was set with an anger that made it sterner than usual. His black silk vest was buttoned tightly across his white shirt. He studied Maynard with a peculiar severity for several moments, then looked away.

"At this rate," Patterson said, "they'll be able to start their own bank up in the mountains."

"That's not funny, Patterson," Pearson said. "I'll tell you what I'm concerned about. I'm concerned about one day those bastards getting cocky enough to ride in here and try my bank on for size."

"Always a possibility," Patterson said.

"Well, if they do," Pearson said, "they'll find a warm reception."

"That can be risky," Maynard said.

"You think I'm afraid of taking a risk?" Pearson said. Again he studied Maynard, again with that odd severity of expression.

"Not if you've taken them before," Maynard said.

"That's right," Pearson said. He turned and walked off, the pail swinging with empty nods in his hand as he returned to the bank.

"I figured," Patterson said when the banker was gone, "you were going to ask him if it was at Antietam or Gettysburg."

"Where the hell would he have taken risks? He's a goddamned banker."

"Talking in heat."

"Are you going to write a story about what happened?"

"I told the old boy to just slot in what I wrote last time. Just change the date."

"You're getting cynical, Patterson."

"No, sir," Patterson said. "I just have the feeling there may be a better story brewing in the teapot."

There was indeed a better story and Maynard learned about it that evening. He had just scraped the last of his ham and beans from his tin plate when he heard a horse ride up and then his name called.

Maynard stood in the doorway, drinking a cup of coffee.

"What are you doing out here?" he asked. He had recognized the voice as Patterson's, who had reined in about twenty feet away. There was a late moon tonight, the sky alive with stars that hurled from one end of the seen world to the other.

"I've been asked to ride you along," Patterson said.

"Where to?"

"It could be very interesting, Thomas."

There was only one place Maynard wanted to go and he in fact had already twice started for it, the first time getting as far as his door and the second as far as his horse, each time turning around and going back and sitting down with his hat and coat on, damning himself for wanting to go and damning himself for not going. There was almost a third time, when he considered the possibility that perhaps she was hoping he would show up, that whenever the door opened she was hoping to see him. But the third time he never even got up from the chair, because he had resolved he wasn't going to see her in that place again and that his abstention or disapproval or offended affection—however she saw it—would convey itself strongly enough to move her out of there once and for all.

But now he was out, riding alongside Patterson, their horses at moderate gallop across the prairie to the southwest, the town lights dimming away behind them. A night wind, flourishing with hints of winter, blew at them in the darkness from all directions, as though they were riding through a convocation of gusty spirits. Patterson had not confided very much, but Maynard had an intuitive understanding of what it might be, having taken note of the sullen mood on Main Street earlier in the day.

They caught onto a seldom-used road that had been ground into existence in Baddock's early days by supply wagons but had later been bypassed by the stage road. Several miles on was an abandoned store standing amid a grove of trees, whose original builder had guessed at the main road into town and guessed wrong.

When they rode up to the store, Maynard saw seven or eight horses tied to the hitch rail outside. There was a wind-swaying bargeboard hanging from the sloping roof with an inexpertly cut GEN. STORE barely visible in it. The light inside was unsteady, suggesting guttering candles.

"Who's in there?" Maynard asked when they'd dismounted and were lacing their horses to the rail. A strong wind blew against their backs, scattering sand audibly against the store and creaking the bargeboard several times.

"You'll see," Patterson said. He had been uncharacteristically quiet through most of the ride, almost somber, and Maynard had gone with it. If it was what he thought it was, then he didn't want to hear about it from Patterson.

"You're in it?" Maynard asked.

"Not really."

The board porch in front of the old store was almost level with the ground, so close to it, in fact, that their boot heels on it barely reported. Patterson opened the door and Maynard followed him in.

The light from a pair of candles set on tin plates in the middle of the floor created a sinister aura, which was heightened further by the silence among the men who were assembled there, with a sense within that silence of conversation that had been quiet and tersely to the point and had just this moment fallen still. The former store, now just a large room, had nothing in it of previous occupancy except a long counter, upon which some of the men were sitting, booted feet dangling. Others were squatting near the candles, a few standing, the yellow malign light flickering up to and away from their faces.

Maynard recognized some of them—Pearson, Abbot, Turner, O'Connor (the latter's presence something of a surprise), and others whose faces he knew and one or two who were strangers to him, or at least in this dim light were. Patterson had waited behind while he entered and closed the door now. Maynard walked toward the candles, then stopped.

Maynard was greeted by Pearson. The banker wasn't wearing the gaudy checked suit he often appeared in but was instead, like the rest of them, in trail clothes, with a gun on his hip. He was one of those standing and Maynard had a sense, from his posture and from the fact that most of the others were sitting on the counter or squatting, that the banker had been leading what discussion there had been.

"You know what this is about, don't you?" he asked Maynard.

"I can guess," Maynard said. "But I'd rather hear."

The answer came not from Pearson but Turner. The stage line man was squatting near the candles, looking bulky and uncomfortable, and with his long beard in the candlelight giving the intense appearance of some Biblical prophet. Lifting his head as he spoke, appraising Maynard with eyes that seemed aflame, he said, "We've formed up, finally." Then he turned back to the light and muttered, "And about damned time, too."

"Formed up what?" Maynard asked.

"You know what," someone on the counter said, voice low, insinuating.

"We've been pushed hard enough and long enough." That was Abbot. He was standing furthest from the light so that he looked wrapped in layer upon layer of shadow. "Our tolerance has been misconceived as weakness, and now we're going to correct the misconception."

"You too, O'Connor?" Maynard asked, turning to the lawyer, who was among the men sitting on the counter.

"You see me here," O'Connor said.

"A man of the law?"

"I practice law; I also understand it. I try to live within it and help others to do the same. But where law barely exists, or where it exists for some and not others, then the whole concept becomes a farce. You're trying to carry buckets of water that have holes in them."

"You can die of thirst," someone said.

"Look," O'Connor said, "civil law is at the moment far away in miles and who knows how far away in time. It'll get here one day, but meanwhile we're here now. As Abbot says, we're tolerant men; if we weren't, we would have done this a long time ago. Why the hell should we suffer just because we're men of goodwill?"

"The way I look at it," Pearson said, "we're undertaking a civic responsibility."

"Amen," Turner said.

"If we're doing wrong," Pearson said, "we'll stand up and answer to it when the time comes."

"The hell we will," someone said, to a round of nervous chuckling.

"That's not something we're going to concern ourselves with," O'Connor said. "We're the town leaders. People look to us. We've been entrusted with authority. And now we're saying, 'This is the right thing to do. It's morally permissible. It can be done.' "

"And we're about to do it," Turner said, eyes hypnotically watching the small buds of candlelight.

"Before we go a word further," Pearson said to Maynard, "we want you to understand that whatever you hear in this room tonight is to be kept in the most solemn confidence. We need your word on that, whether you join us or not."

"It seems to me," Maynard said, "you've just hired your-selves a brand new sheriff, who's shown himself to be pretty capable."

"Bell is very capable," Pearson said. "But he's only one man and no one man is going to stop the depredations."

"I hear he's out there again, trying."

"Good luck to him," Turner said, talking straight at the candle. "He was fortunate the first time; he's not going to have it his way every time. Anyway, as Pearson says, no one man is going to stop it. The only way to stop it is to put the fear of God into them."

"And there's no fear," someone said, Maynard hearing the voice floating from behind him, "like an empty circle of good hemp."

"A committee," Maynard said, "can stir up more dust than it settles."

"Not if it's responsibly organized and disciplined," Abbot said, still in the shadows. "Anyway, we're not here to justify what has already been thoroughly debated and unanimously agreed upon. The question remaining is, is Mr. Maynard with us or not, and if not, do we have his pledge of secrecy as to these proceedings?"

"Maynard?" Pearson asked.

"Who's going to lead?" Maynard asked.

"Lead?"

"It can't be untidy. Somebody's got to give it direction."

"We know the direction," Turner said acidly, still crouched at the candles as if at any moment to open his hands to them for warmth.

"I can lead," Pearson said. "If needed."

"Can you, Mr. Pearson?"

"If needed."

"Well, Maynard?" Abbot asked.

Maynard turned to Patterson. "Where are you in this?" he asked.

"I'm in," Patterson said. "As an observer."

"Jesus Christ," someone sitting on the counter said. "What the hell is he going to observe? Is this going to turn up in the newspaper?"

"Don't be stupid," Patterson said.

"The more riders we have the better," Abbot said. "He can observe whatever he wants. If he's with us, he's with us."

"Yeah," the voice from the counter said, "but will he draw if he has to?"

"If he has to," Turner said, "he'd be a damn fool not to." He laughed harshly, then drew himself to his feet, sighing, as if with the effort. "What about you, Maynard? We've talked long enough. In or out?"

Maynard shifted his weight and lowered his head for a moment, smiling tightly, thinking: *I'm a captain in the United States Army, being asked to ride with a band of vigilantes.* Hard provoked and well motivated, certainly; vigilantes nevertheless. But he was a one-man deputation out here, with no one to call on for advice, every decision his alone to take. And he still had a job of business to do and so far had not done it, nor been close to doing it. What did a soldier on his own call on, experience or common sense? Or did they become interchangeable? Or at times mutually nullifying?

You can do this and at the same time not be of it, he told himself. And even as he thought these things he knew very well that his mind was closing upon what he wanted to do, irrelevant of anything else. Still rankling was the memory of standing with his hands in the air while Edson, that naive gold-fevered young man from Philadelphia, was shot dead. The United States Army, Maynard knew, bloodline to his pride and self-respect, was his control and discipline; but the man born still had deep within him the feral prowl that had been only lassoed, not broken.

"In," he said.

"I told you," O'Connor said.

"We wanted to hear it from him, not you, lawyer," Turner said.

"All right," Pearson said. "We're ten strong, counting Mr. Neeman here."

Neeman, a slight wiry man, had been silent throughout. Sitting on the counter, his boots at higher reach from the floor than any of the others, he nodded to Maynard, who had turned to him. Maynard saw a mild expressionless face flaring with short prideless whiskers, small candlelit eyes under unusually thick brows, and above that a slouch hat utterly shapeless as if it was stuffed into a pocket when not worn. He was wearing a buttonless old Union Army coat that was held shut by a piece of rope. He could have been anywhere in age from thirty to sixty. Even with his limited experience out here, Maynard knew a mountain rat when he saw one, one of Lucas Bell's oblivious and obsessed builders of empire, one of those creatures dimmed out to civilization but yet fully a repository of its fondest dreams.

"It's because of Mr. Neeman's fortitude and resolute desire for justice," Pearson said, "that we're here."

"It's the justice," Neeman said simply, like a man who chose to use his voice sparingly.

"Nevertheless . . ." Pearson said.

"We've had enough goddamned speeches," Turner said. "Let's get to it."

"The man has grit and should be honored for it," Pearson said sternly.

"Well," Turner said, hoisting his trousers up around his large front, "you can best honor him by stringing up the bastards who murdered his friends."

The men began sliding down from the counter.

"See to the candles," Abbot said, striding out of the shadows now and heading for the door.

TWENTY-TWO

"It isn't all as spontaneous as you might think," Patterson said as they rode alongside one another. "It's been on their minds for some time. All the talk was for your sake."

"Whose idea was it for me to come in?" Maynard asked.

"Just about all of them. I argued against it."

"On what grounds?"

"That you were a stranger and had no stake here. But they wanted you in. Which is both flattering and not. Some of them think you're a reformed gunslinger and therefore just the ticket. Others said that if you were a friend of mine you had to be all right."

"Is that the unflattering part?" Maynard asked.

"It could be," Patterson said with a laugh. "Look, some of these men are pretty tough apples, but not all of them are that sure with a gun, if it comes to that. So they asked me to bring you over. I think I was surprised when you agreed to throw in with them."

"Were you?"

"I hope you're not exceeding your mandate," Patterson said. "Actually, you probably won't have to do anything; there are plenty of hands eager for the rope."

"Yours among them?"

"I put it on the scales. I don't particularly like the idea of vigilante action, but I like murderers less. I felt that if I was in even the slightest sympathy it would be hypocritical not to go along. But I'm on the fringe. They know that."

"I hate to tell you, Patterson, but in this business there is no fringe."

The strong wind had died off, as if it had been but herald to the bright moon that had ridden up from behind the mountains; a bit too bright perhaps, Maynard thought, for what they were out to do. The occasional cloud cover was too thin to do more than slightly mist the light.

They were moving at a steady jog, strung out along a trail that was breaking away from the road, Maynard and Patterson bringing up the rear, as they had contrived to do. Maynard had buttoned his coat to the neck against the chill night air, his hat pulled forward. Here and there the ground pitched, then rose, then pitched again. They clattered over some small rocks and then gravel and then splashed across a shallow stream and came out of it across the gravel and small rocks on the other side.

"Why tonight?" Maynard asked.

"It's that fellow Neeman," Patterson said, riding close, their horses almost neck to neck.

The wind rose again, though this time they heard more than felt it, as if it was brawling up in space with itself. It sounded circular, indefinite, then seemed to fly off with a roaring gust through a stand of tall pine that appeared moonlit for its passage.

"Who is he?" Maynard asked.

"Prospector. He was heading for town with two friends, coming to resupply. It seems they were planning to spend the winter up there. Well, he fell back. Stopped to take a dump. He told the other two to go on, that he'd catch up. Well, he was picking his way down some high ground and had them in sight when he saw a couple of riders come out of the trees and stop them. Robbed them and shot them down. No reason to shoot them, he said. They were just standing there with their hands in the air and one of the riders swung around behind them and shot them in the back. What Neeman did—and this took a bit of nerve, you'll agree—was follow them, at what he described as 'a respectable distance.' "

"To where?"

"To where we're going. Do you know Bone Canyon?"

"No," Maynard said.

"Well, you pass through there and the ground spreads out and there's a small ranch house. That's where he followed them."

"He's a nervy bastard."

"Those were his friends who were murdered."

"How did this get to the committee's ear?"

"Well, when he rode into Baddock he asked for the sheriff, but Bell wasn't there, so he went looking for what he deemed was an authority figure and walked into Turner's office."

"He picked the right one," Maynard said. "Will you draw if you have to?"

"I own a pistol and I'm wearing it, but primarily because I like to be in style. The man I aim at will be in little danger."

"Have you ever fired it?"

"Only to see that it worked. I couldn't hit a barn wall from the inside. Were you intrigued that Pearson offered to lead?"

"I'm withholding judgment."

"Anyway, there was no crisp delivery of orders. In fact, there were no orders given at all."

"There was one," Maynard said. " 'See to the candles,' Abbot said, as he walked right past them."

"That told you something?" Patterson asked with a quick glance across.

"Oh, I don't know," Maynard said offhandedly.

"It was 'majorly'? That's a slim reed."

"O'Connor still puzzles me. What is a lawyer doing in the middle of this?"

"You heard his explanation. But of course he could be cynical about it, going where the local power goes. Lawyers have been known to park their scruples."

They rode silently for a time, following the others, listening to hoofbeats rap the Montana earth with a fluid, punctuating beat. Now and again the trail swerved around settlements of huge boulders, the pale moonlight creating a sudden flow of shadows against them like images of black flame, and then the riders were out to open prairie again, hardening their resolution of purpose through their ceaseless onward motion and their near-wordlessness, which was like the seal of a vow or compact.

"I saw her earlier today," Patterson said after a time. He had been jouncing in his saddle, holding the reins in his gloved hands. He sounded as if he had been thinking about it for a while.

Maynard didn't have to ask who. He didn't say anything.

"On Main Street," Patterson said. "She greeted me. A nod of the head, but that was more than ever before. It was because she knew I was a friend of yours; I could tell that, from the way she looked at me. I went into the Eagle for a drink and a few minutes later she came in. She asked for Bell, was told he was away, and left."

They rode on in silence, watching the others up ahead.

"I don't think," Patterson said after several minutes, "that you should let it trouble you that she was asking for him. What you ought to do is feel good that she didn't know he'd gone off, that he didn't tell her."

Maynard appreciated the information and at the same time resented having it told.

"She looked well," Patterson said. "Handsome woman."

He'll keep nattering, Maynard thought, until I say something.

"She left in the direction of her rooms when she went out," Patterson said.

What he's saying, Maynard thought, is that she didn't go across the street to the Paradise West and take off her clothes and slide into bed and go to work.

"All right," Maynard said, putting a stop to it.

Not long after, they came to a halt and gathered together.

"The canyon's not far ahead," Pearson said. "I suggest we ride through two at a time and then wait for the rest."

"Jesus," a burly, bearded man named Duckworth said, "it's not going to be posted. It's nearly two in the morning."

"Why take any chances?" Pearson said.

Maynard looked up; the moon had skimmed far across the sky now, was higher, farther out, its light a pale, melting silver. The rocky, small-treed, toughly brushed landscape was like a thickness of shadows around them. The wind was close to the ground now, purring, not strong enough to move anything, coming and going in light nomadic tides.

"Everybody keep a sharp eye," Pearson said. "Let's not start shooting at any shadows."

"Unless the shadow is holding a gun," Duckworth said, to some uneasy amusement.

"How tricky is that canyon?" someone asked.

"Not tricky at all, according to Mr. Neeman," Pearson said.

They all looked at Neeman, who was obviously uncomfortable being the center of interest.

"It's not tricky at all," he said.

Pearson swung his horse around and began riding on, the others following.

"I think Mr. Neeman's beginning to wonder what he's started," Patterson said when they were riding again, again bringing up the rear. "The surge of civic duty is almost always crowded to the front, backed up by second thoughts."

"I like him," Maynard said.

"I feel sorry for him."

The moon was shining on the sheer white walls of Bone Canyon. The passage through, maybe a hundred feet wide, was about a quarter mile between flat rock that rose to several hundred feet in height, the bluffs topped by growths of small pine that against the moonlit sky looked poised like monks at prayer.

Following the procedure suggested by Pearson, they rode through two at a time, the sound of hoofbeats accelerating clearly as each man sought to traverse the passage as quickly as he could.

When they had all ridden through they regathered. A few of the men were having a bit of trouble holding their horses;

some old horsemen, Maynard thought, would say the animals were sensing their riders' nervous anxiety.

"It's about a half mile on from here," Pearson said. "We're going to cross some flat ground that runs up to a crest, get to a screen of trees and down below that is the ranch. Mr. Neeman says there's a small corral alongside. I suggest a couple of men get in there and take charge of the horses while the rest of us hit the house."

"We'll hit it straight on," Abbot said.

"Why don't we just shoot 'em outright instead of hangin'," someone said. "I don't like hangin'."

"Hanging is going to be the message of this committee," O'Connor said.

"I don't care if you shoot 'em, hang 'em, or boil 'em in water," Turner said. "Let's just get on with it."

They moved on again, crossing the flat ground, which was rock strewn and nested with sage. The ground began rising, gradually, toward a stand of trees. Maynard saw Neeman, riding in the lead with Pearson and Turner, point out ahead.

"Does it take you back?" Patterson asked quietly. They were riding so close together their stirruped feet occasionally came in contact.

"No," Maynard said. But it was taking him somewhere; he could tell by the constriction of excitement he could feel and that it was reacting to something inside of him that was not tension or memory either, something that a man didn't examine but simply obeyed.

When they reached the crest and had picked their way through the trees each man came forward to have a look until they formed a nearly straight line, as if on parade.

About three hundred feet of open, sloping ground lay between them and the house. It was just the one building, flat-roofed, large enough to accommodate three, maybe four rooms. It was dark. The trees picked up again several hundred feet behind, leaving the building clear on all sides, except where the small corral stood, and beyond that the collapsed ruins of what probably had been a small stable. In the moonlight they could see two horses standing in the corral, so still as to seem carven.

"Does that mean just two men inside?" Patterson asked Maynard, whispering.

"Probably," Maynard said. "But from now on you don't assume anything." He touched the handle of his pistol, as though completing some cycle that had begun with a thought.

Pearson told two men to swing around and cover the rear of the place.

"If anybody busts out that way," he said, "you know what to do. The rest of us will crash straight on in. Mr. Neeman," he said, turning to the prospector, "we won't ask you to join us. You've done your share; we'll see to the rest of it."

Neeman chose not to argue about it.

After several more moments, during which no one said anything but simply sat and watched him, Pearson began walking his horse down the slope. The others fanned out around him, some with pistols in their hands, others holding rifles diagonally across their chests.

Maynard, who had motioned Patterson toward the rear, was riding near the front now, watching the windows of the moon-draped house. The deep quiet was but minutely trespassed, by the clip of hooves against rock and the other plain inevitable sounds of mounted men moving forward, no matter how self-consciously careful. The light faded as the moon took momentary cover, then reappeared, falling like a pale breath against the windows.

When they were within fifty or so feet of the house Pearson raised his hand. When he stopped, they all did, and when he dismounted so did they, to the slightest sounds of saddles being emptied. When they gathered in a knot, Maynard said quietly, "I suggest Patterson and Neeman stand back and hold the horses. We don't want them scattering if there's anything sudden."

Pearson nodded his approval and Patterson and Neeman went around gathering the various reins in hand. The more prudent Neeman walked his charges back closer to the trees, Patterson remaining where he was.

"All right," Turner said.

Crisp and purposeful, rifle in hand, he led them forward. When he reached the door he raised one leg and then drove in his foot with force enough to throw the door aside, then stormed inside, shouting, "Any man moves a hand, he's dead," at first saying it to thin air, not knowing if anyone was in that room or even in the house, rushing in upon a frail silken moonlight. The others crowded in behind him.

The light that filtered through the windows fell upon two startled men upraised on straw pallets in the room's center, up so suddenly they hadn't been seen rising, so that they appeared to have been waiting like that, each poised back on a single arm, blanket fallen around waist; first startled and then furious, one with murderous black hair falling in long broken strands along the sides of his black-stubbled face, the other half bald, what hair he had thick above his ears as if it had slid down.

"Who the hell are you?" the bald one demanded, a cold rage clenching his face.

"Friends," Turner said, holding the rifle on him as the others drew around with pistols and rifles.

Maynard, who had raced with drawn pistol straight through to the other rooms, now returned.

"No one else," he said.

"These will do," Pearson said.

"So will these," O'Connor said. He was crouched over several hacked-open but empty bullion crates against the wall. "Christ, talk about evidence. Where is it, boys?" he asked, turning on his heels.

"Don't know what you're talking about," the bald one said churlishly. "You got no right bustin' in here." The other one said nothing, simply remained fixed, leaned back on the one arm, looking from face to face, one corner of his mouth lowered into a sneer.

THE GHOST OF MAJOR PRYOR   203

"Don't you just move at all," one of the men said, unnerved by the calculated hatred of that face.

"We're prospectors," the bald one said. "Just passing through. Bunking down for the night."

"You're supposed to get your gold out of the ground," Pearson said, "not out of somebody's crates."

"Found them here," the bald one said. "Just so."

"These too?" O'Connor asked, rising and turning to them. He was holding a small canvas bag, which he rattled several times. "Watches," he said, "and rings, and whatever else."

"We won them in a poker game," the bald one said, frowning, as if to lend credence to his assertion. The other one smiled coldly for a moment, as if to dissociate himself.

"Get up," Turner said, gesturing with the rifle.

"Who the hell are you anyway?" the bald one asked, this time with indignation.

"Up," Turner said. Now he had the rifle aimed.

"Why? What for?"

"Up," Turner said.

"Do as he says," Abbot said.

"You can go to hell," the bald one said fiercely. "All of you."

"You first," Turner said and pulled the trigger. In the confined space, and maybe, too, because it was so unexpected, the report sounded enormous, shocking.

The bald one was hurled back onto the pallet with such force and suddenness it seemed he might have been flattened into a single dimension. The charge had taken him full in the throat, flushing out a sumptuous leap of blood, much of which struck his companion, who had fallen aside at the rifle's roar.

"Jesus Christ, Turner," Pearson said.

"That was uncalled for," Abbot said severely.

Turner had shifted the rifle's aim by several degrees, his face looming savagely over the stock.

"Get up," he said.

With an angry swipe the man threw back his blanket and got

to his feet, glancing with what seemed disdain at his companion, from whose blown-apart throat the blood continued to roll. He was wearing a pair of dirt-smudged long johns—bloodstained now—that came down to his ankles. His eyes were on Turner, holding a hard mix of wariness and contempt.

"Who was he?" Pearson asked, indicating the dead man. His response was an indolent shrug.

"What's your name, mister?" O'Connor asked.

"Dust," the man said, making of it an odd, scornful sound, as if trying to imply some private humor. "My name is Dust."

"You'll be living up to it 'fore long," Duckworth said.

"Well, who gives a damn what his name is?" Turner said. "Let's get on with it."

"How many of there are you?" Pearson asked.

"Come stretch a rope with me and I'll tell you."

"Light a fire under his balls," Turner said, "and he'll tell."

"We'll have none of that," Abbot said.

"Where's the loot?" O'Connor asked. "You might as well tell us."

"In a safer place now than it was before," the man said.

"If it's here we'll find it," Pearson said. "March him out."

"Don't I get a trial?" the man asked mockingly.

"No," Turner said. "Just the verdict."

Given a shove toward the door, the man braced his shoulders and began walking.

Maynard holstered his pistol and went outside to where Patterson was standing amidst the horses, his hands full of reins.

"What the hell happened?" he asked.

"The fellow said one word too many to Turner."

"He killed him?"

"Thoroughly."

"For God's sakes."

"It makes no difference," Maynard said.

"But are they the right men? Is everybody sure?"

"They're the right men," Maynard said, touching Patterson's arm reassuringly for a moment.

"I would hate to . . ." Patterson said. Then, "How many were there?"

"Just this other one."

"They're going to hang him in his long johns?"

"There's no way you can dignify a hanging," Maynard said. "So don't worry about it."

"Did he own up?"

"Pretty much."

"What's his name?" Patterson asked. He was watching them. They were tying the man's hands behind his back as he stood erect; thin and bony he was, staring out, almost casually, as if unaware of what was happening or else was complicit in it. No one was saying anything, simply watching, Turner with his rifle on his shoulder like a sentry.

"He said his name was Dust," Maynard said.

"He was joking, I take it," Patterson said, watching, his eyes squinting at the corners as if he was trying to memorize something.

"Bravado," Maynard said. "I think Abbot might have admired it."

Patterson looked back to him. "You've settled on Abbot?"

"Not really. But in a way it's all even."

"How so?" Patterson asked, moving aside as one of the horses ventured too near.

"I don't think I care for any of them. But, under these circumstances, of course . . ."

"You can't go back to Washington *thinking* you know who it is."

"It's better than nothing."

"You can't tell that to Northwood."

"I wouldn't," Maynard said. "I'll just tell him I don't know."

"Then you'd be better off not thinking you know. You'd be better off just forgetting the whole thing. Tell him it was a washout."

"I thought I might find out something tonight."

"That's why you came along?"

Maynard shrugged.

Now the man who said his name was Dust was being marched toward the trees at the rear of the house. One of the horses had been led out of the corral and was being brought on after them. Another man, having retrieved his horse, was riding on ahead, toward the trees. When he reached the trees he began going through some gestures, and although they couldn't see it precisely, they knew he was getting the rope over a likely-looking limb.

"Christ," Patterson said tautly.

"Did you think they wouldn't?"

"It isn't that. It's the wrongness of it. I don't mean what they're doing; it's having to do it. You have to bear in mind that these are by and large honest, God-fearing men. . . ."

"Are you going to watch?" Maynard asked.

"Do you mean am I going to move closer? No."

But he was going to watch; Maynard knew that. He could tell from the way Patterson was talking—not just the words but the tone, which was giving away the mind's fixation— that he was going to watch. Maynard had seen men turn away from firing squads, but never from a hanging. There was something barbarically fascinating about thrusting a man into thin air and watching the stiff, primal struggle for the last bit of what was no longer worth having.

Because it was happening silently it seemed further away than it actually was, men moving about in the delicate moonlight, others standing as still as posts. The man who called himself Dust had been hoisted onto the horse, hands tied behind. He sat quite still and erect as the noose was adjusted and tightened, as if there was something ceremonial about it all, an honor being conferred. He looked strangely clarified by the white long johns.

Except for one who was holding the horse, the others began drawing back, fanning away to either side. Then something was being said, murmurous and indistinguishable where Maynard and Patterson were standing.

"It's almost ritualistic," Patterson said.

"He's splashed all over with his friend's blood," Maynard said.

"Is he?" Patterson asked, as if this confirmed something. "Do you think people believe in their own deaths?" he asked vaguely and not, Maynard sensed, for response. "It's an unimaginable thought," Patterson went on, not even listening to himself, it sounded like. "It would *have* to be unimaginable, don't you think? Don't you? It's the idea of time stopping."

"Maybe you'd better not watch."

"Unimaginable."

"You've seen men die, Patterson."

The sound of his name made Patterson glance at Maynard. "Yes," he said. "And each time . . ." He returned his flat, somberly amazed gaze to the scene under the tree. "He seems stoical enough."

"He's a son of a bitch," Maynard said, his voice conversational, without inflection. "An outlaw. A back-shooter. An irredeemable piece of vermin." He smiled mildly at Patterson's rapt profile. There was no indication that a word had been heard.

Maynard took the gathered reins from Patterson's slackening fingers. Patterson wet his lips. Maynard gripped the reins tightly in both hands, bracing himself, watching the men at the trees. The man holding the horse sprang back. The gunshot came a moment later as Patterson turned away and the riderless horse came bolting past them as Maynard felt the reins strain and go taut as the startled horses swayed and threw their large heads about. The death-seat horse galloped on through the moonlight, went up the slope, and stopped at the trees, where it turned in profile to the men below and simply stood there.

Behind the group of men, who were coming back now with a hurrying, bustling quickness, the man who had said his name was Dust was suspended like a white slash against the night, a thing creating its own ambiance of silence.

"Come on," Maynard said, placing his hand on Patterson's shoulder. "It's over."

TWENTY-THREE

Maynard had to admit this: other than having narrowed his list of candidates for the mysterious Major Pryor to a handful of men, he really didn't know any more today than he had on the day he arrived. When he pondered the likelihood of each man in turn, he came to the same conclusion: this had to be the one, because it certainly couldn't have been either of the other two.

It had to be Pearson because he had, after all, assumed leadership of the group and, all things considered, handled it tolerably well. It had to be Pearson because, after all, Abbot was a respectable merchant, a man who seemed to know how to acquire and build, a man of commendable if unimaginative integrity, a man of the community. And O'Connor had so far shown not a hint of the dash or élan one associated with a major of the Union Army.

But then again, it had to be Abbot, because he had shown brief flashes of leadership and had deliberately resisted taking control for the very reason that he was so capable of it. A man who had built this new life for himself certainly was not going to jeopardize it for the sake of some old aroused nostalgia for command. It had to be Abbot because, after all, Pearson was a banker and evidently an efficient one, meaning that his experience at it had to go back in years; maybe too many years.

But when considered coolly, it had to be O'Connor, simply because of the respectability of the other two, because Pearson had, after all, assumed the leadership almost by default.

And, plainly, a Union Army major would have done a better job of surveilling that house before breaking in. And if it wasn't Pearson, then it couldn't be Abbot either, because the merchant had chosen to subordinate himself to Pearson, which no battle-stained veteran officer would have done.

And so around he went with it, each time coming back to the very place where he had begun. It was a different world out here, he would have to tell General Northwood, where men came and didn't just change their names and histories but also seemed to undergo rebirth, bone-by-bone restructure, a rinsing of memory.

He would, Maynard conceded ruefully, have probably packed up and headed back by now except for the one thing that had been occupying his mind more than the identity of Major Andrew Pryor. If he could have brought himself to believe that there was a chance of her accompanying him, he would have been gone already. But of course he didn't know the answer to that, because he hadn't broached it to her, and not because of what she was doing but because of what he was afraid she might say in reply.

The irony was almost insidious: a man who had never flinched in the face of murderous Confederate infantry, who had himself led men into lines of crackling musketry and booming Napoleon smoothbores, was timid when it came to speaking certain mere words to a woman. It was as if an unwanted response could plunge deeper and more injuriously than any blade or bullet could, find the most sensitive and least protected interior; not open him like a wound but close him like a grave.

He could take her from this wild country of new lives and bring her somewhere to what would be truly a new life. No one would ever have to know anything about her except what he wanted known. She had come to Baddock from somewhere, had been something other than what she was today—something better—and could be again, because no woman ever set out to become what she had become. He did not see it as salvation, merely as an adjustment of direction, a betterment.

He owned up to it in self-deprecating dismay: *Jesus, but you're in love, laddie.* Where the hell did it come from? How did it find its way in and then where to make its drop? Well, he supposed, it wasn't something you stood guard against. It just seeped in, was all. It found you, just as the sun did when you walked outside. And once it did there was no shucking it. You woke up into it each morning. Even the morning after you'd seen a man shot and another hanged.

He sat out at his cabin all the next day and night, smoking, taking his meals, staring out at the mountains, watching the afternoon stage come in, riders go by, wagons roll. He wondered what they were thinking about in town. He wondered if it was business as usual, Abbot in his store, Pearson sitting in his bank president's office, O'Connor plotting some legal strategy, the others doing whatever it was they did. Turner had no doubt greeted the safe arrival of the stage with grim satisfaction. He wondered if there had been any loose talk across the tables at one saloon or another. He speculated about doubts and reconsiderations. But it had been a committee, of course, honest men bound together in mutual outrage, and there was always justification in that. O'Connor could tell them that where there was a gap in the law they were obligated to fill it in, otherwise the gap would widen and eventually engulf them all. What honest men united together said was law, became law, and once it did they were morally responsible to it. Improvise first, rationalize later. Well, how else did you build a new country?

A crazed major could have told himself the same thing once upon a time, Maynard thought as he sat outside his cabin and watched the mountaintops sharpen with the folding of day, the sky rendering unto them a great and patriarchal aspect, like massed vaults of all judgment and wisdom. A crazed major with years of combat hung to his bones and tumultuous in his blood, a commander of fighting men who was accustomed to obedience, could create sudden law in the face of an old woman who did not want to yield up her treasures to a stranger, could tell himself that she was an extension of the rebellion against the cause his obedient men were dying for, that she must not be allowed to stand in the way, any more than holdup men could hinder the thunderous roll of progress.

Two days after the episode near Bone Canyon, Maynard rode into town. He wasn't going to be able to remain in the Territory much longer, he knew. For one thing, snow flurries had blown down on last night's wind. He'd been warned about winter out here; it didn't come in bursts and retreats, as did winters he had known; out here it came with a lunge and wrapped you up in an embrace that held until spring. A hard winter could permanently block the trails and passes, and the best hope for stages getting through was to mount them on runners, and you traveled knowing that it wouldn't take very much bad luck for you to end up frozen to death.

Maynard tied up outside of the Honest Eagle, then went inside.

"Is Bell in?" he asked, going up to the bar, where the bartender, damp rag in hand, was swinging one gartered arm around and around upon the oaken surface.

"Sheriff's in his office," the bartender said. He stopped his activity. "Shall I set you up, Mr. Maynard?"

He had never been called by name in this place before, and now it wasn't being done casually either, he felt, as the bartender stared at him with indolent, heavily lidded eyes.

"Later," Maynard said.

He went outside, with the distinct sense of being watched all the way through the door. He walked along the boardwalk, raising his coat collar against the chill wind that had followed him into town. The sun was trying to break through a cover of gray-stained clouds. The wagon traffic was sparse on Main Street. He couldn't imagine spending a winter in a place like this, when the miners and prospectors came in to hunker down, or at least those who didn't elect to tough it out in the camps or in lonely cabins. There would be months of drinking, gambling, whoring; acceptable enough activities, he supposed, but not when there was nothing else to do.

Passing the office of the Baddock *Newspaper,* he saw Patterson sitting alone inside, slouched at a desk.

"How are you doing today?" Maynard asked, entering.

Patterson tossed a look over his shoulder and then shrugged. He was wearing a heavy plaid overcoat despite the heat shimmering out from the woodstove. A glass and open bottle were on the desk.

"I'm never going out with them again," he said, his voice flat.

"All right," Maynard said. He stood there, watching Patterson, whose eyes were set dully on the bottle. "Has there been much talk?"

"You can't expect to keep a thing like that private. Not in a town like this, anyway. Turner says fine, let it be known. That's the medicine, he says."

"Is it known who was involved?"

Patterson shrugged, closing his eyes for a moment. "I don't think so," he said. "But it will be before long. Not that it will make any difference. They'll be hailed as heroes and saviors."

"They?" Maynard asked.

"I don't count myself among them, Thomas. Spiritually and morally I was never there."

"You may not make it into the future, Simon, but you cannot vanish from the past."

"I may vanish from Baddock, though."

"Where will you go?"

"I don't know," Patterson said listlessly, staring at the bottle on the desk with eyes that seemed never to blink. "I find this whole business very distressing, Thomas. Very distressing."

"You're a man who moved through years of war."

"And I'm also a man who moved thousands of miles to try

and get away from it. The odd thing is, I was able to do that. I could feel my mind cleansing itself. You know, Tom, I walked over the field at Antietam while you could still smell the smoke. In places I had to step over rows of dead men, some of them stacked one on top of the other, just the way they'd gone down. I was able to live with that because the journalist's eye covers up for the rest of the mind. Then that cold little eye closed up and everything that had been hidden away became uncovered. It was like I was seeing it all for the first time, all of it, all at once. Anyway, I wasn't much good to anybody after that. They had to send me home. Which didn't really help a whole hell of a lot. So finally I came out here and found I was able to put it all into a framework and look at it without shivering. Out here it was all different. New lives, new dreams, new everything."

"A new Simon Patterson."

"At least one who was able to convince himself of it, which is all it takes, just like these foolish buggers are able to convince themselves they're going to strike the mother lode. Sometimes you're better off in the land of illusion."

Patterson reached out and poured himself another drink, filling the glass halfway and holding it in his hand as he slouched back in the chair, his overcoat collar bunching up around his neck.

"You're a different kind of man, Maynard," he said. "Not better, not worse. Different. You have that soldier's backbone. But look out—you could just be holding a lot of things off. Things that are capable of subverting the most solidly held defensive positions."

"Those men were killers, Simon."

"Do you think I'm mourning them?"

"I don't know who the hell you're mourning," Maynard said. "Your foolish buggers are being murdered out in the mountains."

"I know that," Patterson said, shaking his head irritably. "I shouldn't have come along. I should have known better."

He sipped some whiskey, then sighed. "Maybe I was trying to prove something to myself, but all I did was wake up some putrefied memories." He looked up at Maynard for a moment, smiling oddly. "Do you want a drink?"

"No. Have you spoken to any of the others?"

Patterson shook his head. "They don't give a damn. They're going about business as usual, with little winks and nods when they come across one another. I shouldn't disparage them. I'm not, really. If it affects me this way, then maybe they're brave men following a highly principled course."

"It doesn't take any particular grit to hang a man."

"Then maybe that's the trouble," Patterson said: "ordinary men doing it, making it an ordinary thing. But when you stop to think what it is that's passing for the ordinary . . . Jesus. I can still see that son of a bitch hanging there. Even when the sun is out bright, I still see night out there. I'm sorry, Thomas; but that's how I feel."

"I think you're forcing it into your mind."

"Maybe. But I do know I can't force it out. You ought to go home, Thomas. Pack up and go. Best thing."

"Soon."

"And the hell with everything. Tell Northwood you couldn't find your man. Tell him everybody looked alike. That a Union Army major isn't so special after all. Tell him the man we hanged was Major Pryor. Maybe he was. Who knows? Who the hell cares? It doesn't make any difference. That's the thing, Tom: nothing makes a damn bit of difference. Not when it comes down to everybody being a murderer."

"Is that how you see it?"

"Sadly, yes. Does my conscience offend you?"

"Your groveling before it does. It's quite offensive, Simon," Maynard said. "You're staking out a moral ground for yourself and leaving the rest of us outside."

"I apologize, Thomas. Believe me, I do. Don't think I haven't engaged this matter in mortal combat. Do you know what I did last night? I went across the street to the house of passion and tried to clear myself out with a good humping. It helped. Momentarily."

When there was a prolonged silence, Patterson looked up. "No," he said, "I didn't see her. But of course I didn't look behind every door. Oh, Jesus, Tom, forget it. Forget it all. Go home. You're not moral, you're not immoral. You fit in very nicely around here. Which means you'd better get the hell out."

"And you?"

"I'm going to sit here and empty this bottle. Right now I'm in charge of the office of the Baddock *Newspaper*. I used to be the top correspondent of the *New York Herald*."

"Cold-bloodedly reporting the slaughter of thousands."

"Weren't those the days?" Patterson said whimsically.

Maynard left and went farther along the boardwalk, avoiding a plank that had rotted out and swung down to the ground. Yes, he thought, what had happened was known in Baddock; he could tell that from the circumspect glances he received from whomever he passed, by horse or by foot, glances that told him they were wondering about him and if he was doing the same about them. The new air of circumspection was confirmed for him by Pearson, standing outside the bank. The banker gave him a curt nod of greeting, then turned and without a word went inside.

The conversation stopped when Maynard entered the sheriff's office. There were three of them gathered around the desk, which stood under the pale space on the wall where John Dunlop's flag had been tacked up. Two of them were leaned forward on the desk on flattened palms, the other standing with his arms folded. Maynard knew them; they worked for Bell at the Honest Eagle and, occasionally, across the street at the Paradise West. They were known, jocularly, and of course privately, as "Bell's peacekeepers," and with the local guess being that they were nastily enough disposed to be just that, there was little breaking of the peace wherever their shadows fell.

The conversation didn't just stop, as though for pause, but came to a total halt, creating a tensely self-conscious quiet.

Bell was sitting behind the desk, the badge pinned to his frock coat. He was wearing a flat-crowned gray hat with a brim edge so narrow that when he looked at you from a certain angle it looked thin enough to slice with.

"All right, boys," he said. "I'll see you all later."

Without further word the three men left, each with a glance for Maynard, who stood aside for them.

"You've come in for something, Maynard?" Bell asked, leaning back in the swivel chair with an ease and comfort Maynard found irritating.

"I wanted to talk to you again about Theo," Maynard said, standing in front of the desk.

"We've already talked about that. It's a subject I believe you've covered," Bell said with the faintest drollery.

"How long is she planning on staying here?"

"I wouldn't know."

"If she stays much longer she won't be able to get out until spring."

"I haven't heard any talk of her leaving. What about you? How long are you staying?"

"I haven't decided."

"You've got unfinished business?" Bell asked.

"I never said I had any business," Maynard said. "Finished or unfinished."

"That's right," Bell said with an inquiring gaze. "You've never said."

"Did you have any luck?"

"Luck?"

"You were out for a couple of days."

"Oh." Bell laughed. "You mean did I bring back any more trophies. No, not this time. These fellows don't exactly send up smoke signals telling you where they are. Have you given any more thought to my offer? It still stands."

"I'd rather not be a deputy," Maynard said impatiently. "Look, do you think she'd leave here?"

"You mean on her own, or if somebody asked her to?"

"Either one."

"I don't think she's ever thought about it. She seems content. But you can never tell. Why don't you ask her?"

"You don't think she'd leave, do you?"

Bell smiled. "I don't know, Maynard. I've never discussed it with her. But pull over a chair," he said, pointing. "There's something I want to talk to you about."

Maynard sat before the desk on a straight-backed wooden chair that looked like it had been culled from somebody's kitchen. He felt himself being leisurely studied for several moments by a man who was too deep into his own speculating to be anything but absolutely poised.

"You've heard what happened the other night?" Bell asked.

"You'll have to be more specific."

"It seems that some of the townsmen have formed a committee. They rode out a few nights ago and shot one man and hanged another. Do you know anything about it?"

"No," Maynard said, staring straight back into those flat, almost lifeless blue eyes, wondering if he was being believed.

"They killed what they believed were two road agents."

"Were they?"

"Well," Bell said, shifting in the chair now, "I goddamn hope so. Not that that excuses it any."

"How did you hear about it?"

"Something like that? A town like this? Christ, Maynard, what doesn't cross a bar will surely be passed across a pillow."

"In the whorehouse."

"House of leisure," Bell said with mock delicacy, smiling.

"Then you know who it was."

"No, I don't know that. But I want to. I'm going to stop it. Either that or they can have their goddamned badge back. It makes a mockery of the office. Makes me look like a fool."

"Have you spoken to anyone about it?"

"Not yet. But I'm going to put the word out. I don't need this job, Maynard, and don't really want it. I was pressed into it."

"You didn't have to accept."

"I'm beginning to regret that I did."

"Do you think you can get them to disband?"

"Well, once it's pointed out to them that winter's coming on and this town fills up with all sorts of hard-assed types, and that they'll be without a sheriff, maybe they'll get the point."

"It's a good argument," Maynard said.

"This town would become wide open. Hell, I can look out for my own interests, but everybody else will be on their own. And if they think they can form up a committee to operate inside of a town, they've got another think coming. People don't like waking up in the morning and finding somebody hanging in their front yard."

Bell came forward to the desk and rested on his arms.

"I think I can make them see reason," he said.

"If they're reasonable men."

"I hear there were six, maybe eight of them. You sure you don't know anything about it?"

Maynard stared back.

"In confidence, Maynard," Bell said.

"If I knew," Maynard said, "I wouldn't tell you."

Bell seemed to ponder it for several moments, then leaned back again, smiling. "And I wanted you as my deputy," he said in a lightly chiding voice. "You know, Maynard, a man who runs a gambling establishment has to know a lot about people, about human nature. It's a very delicate operation. People get foolish, desperate, dangerous. You've got to be able to read all of that, for their sake and your own. A man walks into my place, in five minutes I've got him sized up. I know what he's after and I know how he's going to handle it if he doesn't get it, and I know how I'm going to handle him. But I'm not sure about you."

"I don't gamble," Maynard said, "so I don't call for any handling."

"There are other ways of gambling, away from the card table. You see, whenever I try to size you up, I get the feeling you're doing the same with me."

"Why would I do that?"

"I don't know why," Bell said. "Maybe you shouldn't."

"Maybe I'm not."

"It's safer for me if I think you are."

"Safer?"

"In a manner of speaking."

He was right of course, Maynard thought. He—Maynard—had been thinking very hard about Bell, about what could be inside that man as to lay so firm a control upon her. The man could unquestionably be enticing, no doubt with seductive currents under that often protective exterior. Maybe it was the contrasts in him, the varieties of humor and purpose, a man who could never be anticipated. And of course he had his magnitude of ambition, which he could no doubt depict for her with enough fervor to color the thin air and populate the imagination with self-transfiguring personae.

"Well, anyway," Bell said, "I'll find out who they are. It's just a matter of time."

"What will you do?"

"My sworn duty."

"Which is?"

"To enforce the law, and vigilante activity is outside of the law."

"They might not want to see it that way."

"There's only the one way. The town wants law, they'll have to back me up."

"You'd better get your backing first," Maynard said.

"True enough, but not until I know who the hell I'm talking to. If it comes down to it, where do you stand?"

"Alone."

Bell smiled slowly. "Always alone, Maynard?"

"So far."

"Is it so far, so good? Or just so far?"

"It's so far, so near," Maynard said.

Bell's smile faded off. "I'll bear it in mind," he said.

TWENTY-FOUR

After leaving Bell, Maynard climbed the steps of the outside flight of stairs attached to the apothecary's building. He knocked on the door and waited. He didn't really know what he was going to say to her; maybe she would say something to get it going. That chill damp wind blowing down from the mountains was beginning to thin his time in Baddock. He knocked on the door again; the lack of response was starting to make him feel superfluous. You always expected a knock on the door to be answered. When it wasn't, the only thing for you to do was to decide how long to stand there; not a very compelling business. He stood for several minutes, feeling emptier and emptier, then walked back down the stairs.

He spent the rest of the day in town, having a meal and then sitting alone at a table at the Honest Eagle sipping whiskey, feeling himself coming under occasional surveillance by Bell's people, which increasingly annoyed him, and it was the annoyance that kept him sitting there, like a deliberate provocation.

From where he sat he could see across the street to the entrance of the Paradise West, noting that business was sporadic. He couldn't help noticing, too, the difference with which men went in and out compared to the circumspect, sometimes furtive entrances and exits of similar clientele in Washington. Here, they thumped in and out with unreserved stride. It was indeed a society almost totally without guideline, free of severity or stricture, where even lynch parties could be convened under the aegis of law and order, where law and order had to adjust to the environment until its gradual and inevitable seepage became commanding.

There was no point, he felt, in communicating with General Northwood and waiting to hear back. He would simply return to Washington and appear in the general's office and report. The general would be understanding. *All right, Tom. I'm sure you did your best.* Maynard could hear it. He didn't like the sound of it.

It was after dark when he returned to his cabin. He had taken on a bit more whiskey than he realized and was wobbly in the saddle, felt more like he was being carried than riding, his horse moving so slowly as to suggest it was embarrassed by its burden.

After seeing the horse into the stable he walked to the cabin with the poised unsteadiness of a man trying to resist his lack of sobriety with dignity. The moon was up solid and bright but at the moment dimmed down by a quilt cover of processional clouds. He entered the cabin, closed the door behind him, and hung the latch and allowed a deep sigh of vague dejection. He had not taken more than two steps when he sensed someone there and an alertness sparked through the hung webs of his mind. He was in the act of striding and turning, his hand dropping intuitively to his gun holster, when he was struck, not by a weapon or a blow but by the force of someone in full lunge against him. The abrupt and sudden collision knocked him tumbling sideways to the floor, and then whoever it was had fallen upon him with a gasp. With an angry effort, he heaved himself out from under and got to his feet and sprang back, clenched fists up. He heard a scrambling and then there was another collision, an awkward stumbling together and again he was pitched off balance, falling back and striking a wall shelf, dislodging several tin plates that crashed to the floor with foolish, metallic noise. Throwing one arm around his attacker, Maynard was about to bring down his fist when he realized what he was holding, feeling under his fingers. He held back the intended blow, hearing panting mischievous laughter.

"Damn you," he said in furious whispered exasperation. "I might have . . ."

Now he found the kerosene lamp and lit it. In the flaring shadows raised by the light he saw her standing near the wall, the smile on her face as mischievous as the laughter had sounded.

"You're damned lucky," he said. "If I hadn't felt tit under that coat I would've knocked your head in."

"I couldn't resist," she said.

"How long have you been here?"

"An hour or two."

"How did you get out here?"

"I walked."

"Jesus, Theo, I was in town all day. I knocked on your door."

"Was that you? Thomas, I wish I had known."

"Why didn't you answer?"

"Because I didn't know who it was. The people you don't want to see are always the hardest to get rid of."

She was bareheaded, her dark hair caught behind in a ribbon and tailing down. Her soft, full woman body was covered by a man's heavy overcoat and trousers. She moved her chin up to a saucy angle and smiled—it was more smirk than smile—the lamplight showing in her self-amused eyes, an allusiveness that seemed to speak for the feminine fecundity under the neutering masculine clothing.

He wanted to say, What are you doing here? but didn't. Because it didn't matter, and in fact the question quickly vanished from his mind. He felt a soothing all-reaching warmth, a different kind of intoxication from the one that just minutes ago had had him wobbly and disconsolate.

He put the lamp down on the table as she crossed to him and slowly encircled him with her arms. He drew her firmly to him, wrapping her against him, pressing his face down into her hair.

"That was a fool thing to do," he said.

"Are you angry?"

"Furious," he said mildly.

"Sorry you didn't bash me?"

"I still might."

She drew her head back and smiled up at him with her lips. "Do you think," she said, "I'd be chilly if I took my clothes off?"

"Not for long," he said.

Later, he realized it was raining. Given the profound swoon he was emerging from, the realization settled upon him slowly. He listened to the irregular patter on the roof, sometimes fast, sometimes slow, as though a wind was swirling within it. He took a pleasure in it; it made the outside world less hospitable and hence the inside more intimate. He rolled his head on the pillow. She was lying inside the crook of his arm, her head against his shoulder. The one eye that he could see was open and peeping up at him.

"Still mad at me?" she asked.

"Are you still here?"

"Oh yes."

She lifted her head now and smiled at him. She put her finger on his mouth and traced lightly along his softly closed lips.

"What are you thinking of?" she asked.

"The rain."

"That's not thinking; that's listening."

He brought his hand to her nape and she squirmed sensually as he rode his fingers down her back, and then he shaped his hand to the round swell of her buttocks and slipped it around inside her thigh, rousing her to a sudden sharp intake of breath. She put her head down on his chest as his hand came slowly along her back again.

"Have you ever been married, Tom?" she asked.

"No," he said. "You?"

"I'm afraid so."

"Why afraid?"

"Because I wasn't very good at it."

"So you ended it."

"Stopped," she said. "I stopped it. I went away from it. Just left it there."

"So you walked out on him. And he's still there, wherever that is."

"Yes," she said.

"Waiting for you to come back?"

"I don't think so. I hope not."

"Do you have a family?"

"You mean of my own? My own children? No. I wouldn't have left them if I'd had."

"You went away with Bell, didn't you?"

"No," she said. "I met up with him later. It was in Kansas. He was coming through with this other woman. He told me they were going to Baddock, because there'd been a big strike there. He told me he was going to become rich. A lot of men tell you that, of course, but when Lucas tells it, it's different."

"Is that so?"

"You don't have to believe me." Idly, she was making small circles through his chest hair with her finger.

"I believe you. You followed him all the way out here."

"He'd told me in Kansas that he didn't think the other woman was up to it."

"To what?"

"To making the climb with him. That's how he put it. And even if she did make it, he said, the air at the top would be too pure for her to breathe." She tapped his chest with her finger. "You think we're gullible, don't you? Well, it's not like that at all. When Lucas tells you about things—about how they're going to be—he describes them in such a way that you can see them. And what you see has to be true, right? If it wasn't true, you couldn't see it."

"I don't know, Theo."

"Sometimes you might only be seeing what they're seeing, but that doesn't make it any less true, that they're seeing it and you're not. If they weren't seeing it so clearly then they couldn't describe it so that it came up before your eyes."

"They might be fooling themselves," he said, resting his hand in her hair.

"I don't think people can fool themselves so completely."

"So you came out here, followed Bell. Are you glad or sorry about it?"

"Why should I be sorry?"

"Why should you be glad?"

"Let's just say I'm waiting to find out," she said.

"You're putting a lot of faith in him."

"No," she said. "I look at it another way: I'm putting the faith in myself. It's my decision to believe or not. I'm responsible for it."

"So if he walks out on you . . ."

"It's my own fault."

"Jesus," he said, "you've got the kind of faith that could either harness a river or else drown in a dewdrop. I'm not sure which."

"Don't you have any faith, Thomas?"

"I'm careful where I place it. And I surely wouldn't place it in somebody I didn't know."

She laughed. "That's what makes it interesting," she said. "That's what makes it *faith*, don't you see? If it's somebody you know, then it's trust."

"You sound like somebody who's manufacturing wisdom for shape and size."

"It's a woman's feelings," she said with a provocative laugh.

"That's got nothing to do with what's real."

"It's more real than real."

"Because it's what you want to believe, is that it?"

"It's what I do believe," she said. "I think you could do with something like that, something to hold to."

"Maybe I've got it," he said.

It was as if he could feel her thinking, her eyes fixed upon something in the shadowy cabin. It wasn't that she had become absolutely still—she had already been that—but that the stillness had become charged with a deeper stillness.

"Have you thought about leaving this place?" he asked.

"To where?"

"East."

"Why?" she asked. She was still motionless, was only a sound, so much so that he closed his eyes, the better to feel his own conversation and her responses.

"That's where the world is," he said.

"And where you come from. And where you're going back to."

She moved now, slightly, adjusting herself more comfortably, her head still on his chest, her cheek resting flat. He could feel her warm slow breath against him.

"When are you going back?" she asked.

"Soon enough, I would imagine."

"You 'imagine'? Why? What's holding you back? Is there something you have to do?"

"What do you mean?"

"You're like a man who came out here to do something and you haven't done it."

"I've been minding my business," he said. "That's what I've been doing."

"But it's what that business is. That's what I wonder. I have to wonder. I can't help it. Because we've talked so much, close, as we are now; and then later, when I think about it I have to say to myself, 'You still don't know a thing about him.' You say you're going back East; well, that means the law's not after you. But you come out here and watch everybody like a starving chicken hawk, and now you say you're going back."

"And that doesn't make sense to you?"

"It makes perfect sense, Thomas," she said. She brought

her hand up and rested it on his shoulder. "It means there was a purpose to your coming."

"Come on back East with me. I'll show you the Atlantic Ocean."

"I've already seen the Mississippi River."

He laughed. "The Atlantic Ocean could swallow the Mississippi at one gulp and still be thirsty."

"What do you do there, back East?"

"Same as I do here, I guess: stare at people like a starving chicken hawk."

"Why?" she asked. "Why do you do that? What are you looking for?"

He didn't answer. He could feel that stillness settling in her again. Then he said, "Maybe I'm looking for something to believe in."

"You don't seem to be that kind of man. It makes me uneasy."

"What does?" he asked.

"Not knowing what kind of man you are."

"It's not the kind of thing you find out all of a sudden," he said, holding her more closely. "It takes time."

"You should have found that out by now, it seems to me. Unless you don't want to know. Or maybe you do know and aren't too happy with it." Then there was that stillness again, and from out of it she asked, "Were you with them the other night? You know who I'm talking about."

"Why do you ask that?"

"It would tell me something about you."

"It wouldn't tell you anything, one way or the other."

Now she placed her hand on his cheek and raised her head and looked up at him for a moment.

"Oh yes it would," she said with a smile. Then she rested her head on his chest again and he could feel her breath running across him like warm threads. "You must have gone with them, whether you wanted to or not. None of them would have had the stomach for it, not without you."

"What do you know about it anyway?" he asked.

"One of the girls told me."

"Then you're back there?"

"Just to talk. Anyway, it's no secret. People know what happened, but they don't know who did it."

"Maybe they shouldn't know," he said. "Certain things can be dangerous to know."

"Maybe more dangerous not to."

"For whom?" he asked.

She didn't answer. And as far as he was concerned, she didn't have to, for it was just as if he could see clearly into her mind and read the thought and see the consternation. She had spoken the one ill-advised sentence and in the ensuing silence it remained in the air, like a physical thing defying gravity.

Damn, he thought. Damn. *Damn.*

"He sent you, didn't he?" he asked, his voice so evenly modulated it sounded incurious, more like statement than question. He could feel the stillness regathering inside her. "You said you walked out here."

"I did."

"He couldn't bring you because he didn't want to be seen doing it. So you walked. Because he asked you to."

"Are you sorry?"

"What I am . . . Sorry doesn't come close to it," he said with a sigh that she took intuitively as a sign of disengagement even though his arm around her never moved.

"I wouldn't have come," she said, "if I didn't want to."

"Nor would you, if he hadn't sent you."

"He looks after me, Thomas."

"By planting you in a cathouse."

"It's not as bad as you think. I get to pick and choose. I picked you."

"It was the other way around," he said.

"I didn't have to say yes. I have privileges there."

"He told you to."

She allowed a short, uneasy laugh. "I would've anyway," she said.

"Why should he concern himself with me?"

"He's afraid of you. Oh, he never said it. But I can tell."

"Why should he be afraid of me?"

"Because he doesn't know anything about you, doesn't know what you're doing out here, or when you're going to do it."

"You can tell him that it has nothing to do with him."

"Then why are you here?" she asked.

"What's his damned history, if he's so concerned about me?"

"I don't know anything about him," she said, "so I can't talk about him."

"I'll believe half of one and all of the other."

"In some places, Tom, a man's past can foretell his future. But not out here. Out here it's all future. The past doesn't exist. That's the beautiful thing. You can reach out into the future and have anything you want of it. And the man who knows that is going to have what he wants."

"And Lucas Bell knows."

"You don't really dislike him, do you? He has respect for you, Tom. I know he does. You really shouldn't dislike him."

Dislike him, Maynard thought. Maybe. He didn't know. Whatever he felt, it certainly wasn't fraternal.

Maynard would not go so far as to say he didn't understand women; no self-respecting man ever would. It was this particular woman that he didn't understand, because he had allowed himself to become vulnerable to her, allowed her to mystify herself to him. He didn't understand her because he had yielded something deep of himself to her. It was as if this relinquishment, this something of him that was now her aura, had re-created her as mystery to him. And now, as if alchemized, she had begun to fade from around him, a process that would end in nothingness.

My own fault, he thought. When you give what is unasked

for, and, worse, unwanted, you find yourself twice levied, in
the giving and in the returning.

"You'd better go, Theo," he said.

"What shall I tell him?"

"Tell him I'll be leaving soon."

"Thomas . . ."

"Just get dressed," he said, "and go. You've got a long
walk back."

TWENTY-FIVE

What happened around dusk that same evening at a place called Alder Gulch, about ten miles northeast of Baddock, was this:

A Concord stage, carrying a half dozen passengers and a boot loaded with gold bullion in shipment from one of the mines, was making its way up an easy incline toward where a little-used pack road switchbacked across the route. As the stage approached the crest, three masked riders drifted out of the trees abutting one side of the trail up ahead, holding pistols. One moved out to the right side of the trail, the other two remaining on the left, the driver's side.

"Three of them," the driver said later. "Three sons of bitches, wearing masks, long overcoats, their hands loaded. Just came wandering out of the trees like they'd been in there God knows how long waiting. They were at right about near the crest, knowing I'd come slowest there, which I was doing most unusual, given the weight I was carrying. But the minute I saw them I began thinking that once I made the crest there was nothing—assuming I didn't stop any bullets—to stop me snakin' the whip and picking up speed and to hell with them. What the hell, that's why Minty was there, right? So I said to him, 'Partner, here's where you earn your dibs.' "

One of the reasons (*the* reason, probably) the driver decided to make a run for it was because the line had assigned him a gun rider (because of the bullion). This was Minton, a small wizened man of some years who wasn't there for youth or strength but for his prowess with a rifle and a long-demonstrated capacity for steadiness in the face of danger.

The driver turned and yelled back over his shoulder to his passengers, apprising them of both the situation and his intentions, and some of them began bringing out their weapons and taking up positions near the windows. Up on the seat, Minton had his rifle resting across his thighs, one hand three-quarters of the way along the barrel, the other just under the trigger, his eyes like polished brown pebbles as they took sight of the riders. He'd deliver the first shot from the hip—there wouldn't be time to raise and aim. If they were close enough—and they were going to be—he could get his damage in. After that there was going to be hell to pay, a quick and blistering hell, and it would be anybody's game.

"I slowed more than normal coming up," the driver said, "because old Minty told me to. He wanted to make it look like we were going to stop. He wanted that first shot, you see, and he said then I had better crackle that whip and get my head between my shoulders because then the bang-away was going to start, which I knew myself anyway, and not just because of flying bullets but because just as surely as the Lord makes an upgrade he makes the opposite and usually one right after the other. So I was going to be taking a downgrade at good speed and not just any downgrade either but one with a couple of bends that are like a snake trying to look at its own ass, and with a stage so back-loaded its rear end might just take its time in finding out what the front end was doing and then not do it. So I was praying that old Minty would put two of them down right off, because one alone wouldn't come after us."

When the stage was almost at the crest one of the masked riders aimed his pistol at the driver and said, "It's about god-damned time, you son of a bitch. Now just stand her right there and do the smart thing." This was the rider on the right-hand side of the stage, where Minton was sitting, the rifle still across his thin old man's thighs that weren't much wider than the rifle butt, an old man who had done this before and who was now stiff with not fear but tension, because he was about to do it again, and do it quickly, and do it right.

"I knew just which one old Minty was going to go for first," the driver said (he was telling it to Turner and the others who had crowded into the Territorial office in Baddock, listening to the driver, who was sitting under the kerosene lamp, in Turner's own chair behind the desk). "The one who was doing the talking. You always go for the big mouth. You shut him down and then see what the others are going to do; but of course you don't wait, you try to shut them down, too."

The riders were about twenty feet in front of the slowly moving stage, which the driver never intended to bring to a full stop; it was of course easier to run up quick speed from a slow roll than a standstill, and if anything was going to bring them through—aside from Minton's rifle—it was going to be surprise and then speed. The one who was doing the talking shouted at the old man to throw down the rifle, but Minton would say later that he never even heard the command, so set was his concentration on the moment of action, now at its brink, gauging the closing distance, braced for the quick rise and swing of the rifle, calculating the placement of his shot. He wasn't going to have time to truly aim and he was going to have to be better than a guess, because he was facing a man with an aimed pistol, and because the second shot was already formulated in his mind.

The driver was gripping the whip handle tightly, setting it for the wrist action that would snap a pistol shot above the ears of the lead team, even as Minton's finger was cradling the trigger, his white-mustached old man's face giving away nothing, as expressionless as a fireside dreamer's. Then the old man swung the rifle with a snap, his face still impassive as his body stiffened and shuddered with the discharge.

"Took him right off the horse," the driver said. "One leg flying up and then over the side like he'd been lassoed. Goddammit, you want cool shooting, you send for Minty. And then by God it broke loose. Minty said I started a second too soon, said the jolt threw off his second shot, while the bullets started coming in at us. I always said that if there was anything you could say on behalf of road agents it was they shot like their eyes was closed. They splintered the foot rail—I can still see the chips flying—and came so close to my ear I could feel the heat."

The lead team leaped out so fast that for a moment it seemed they were pulling not just the stage but the wheel team as well. The night lantern swung so hard with the abrupt start it slammed Minton sharply in the head and set the old man into a profane outburst as the stage finished mounting the crest and went rushing down the grade. The driver half rose in the seat and cracked the whip again just above the lead team's stiffly poised ears as the horses strained and raced and nodded their heads vigorously as if in time with their galloping legs, the stage's full weight rocking on its leather understraps like a giant cradle.

"After us?" the driver said. "I'll say they were after us. Mad as a couple of scorched bears, you can bet. We were rocking so hard coming down that grade that old Minty was afraid to turn around and try to get off another shot. But some of the boys inside were pegging back at them and the bastards were sending shots right on after us. I had all to do to hold on to my lines and now I was afraid to snake the whip because the road was bending up ahead and Jesus I didn't know how much speed it would take before rolling us over. I'd taken two-wheeled turns before and it's never a happy thing, I can tell you. Maybe those bastards were hoping we'd go over. The lantern kept flying around and hitting old Minty in the head and he was cursing and I told him to take hold of his pecker because here we go. But we didn't—turn over, I mean. We held the road and kept going. We took the next bend, too, and now it was all down and straight for a while and Minty was saying he was going to climb up on the roof and belly-flat himself and pick them off from there, but I told him he was too old for that, and the old fool had the sense to listen. How far did they chase us? I don't know, but I guess they finally came to see that if they caught up they were dead men because we had plenty of firepower and weren't shy with it. So I brought her in, nothing lost, nothing hurt, except where Minty says he's got a headache from being conked on by the lantern. Now, if one of you gentlemen will just fill up that glass again."

One thing had stuck in Turner's mind and he kept running it over and over again. It was the thing that brought him out to Maynard's cabin early the next morning and set his large fist to pounding on the door.

"What do you want?" Maynard asked, standing in the doorway in his trousers and a flannel shirt that hung outside his belt, his hair tossed about, his expression a cross between wary and querulous. He looked like he might have been recovering from a night's drinking, but actually he hadn't touched a drop; what he was showing was the consequence of his conversation with Theo and then a long near-sleepless night of trying to remember and forget at the same time.

"I'd like your help, Maynard," Turner said. He was a big man, bulked even bigger by his black overcoat that seemed to smell of hard weather and by the broad-brimmed high-crowned hat he was wearing. When Maynard didn't answer, he went on. "Then you haven't heard about last night?" And when Maynard continued to stand there, having now added uninterested to wary and querulous, Turner went on. "One of my stages was hit, about ten miles out. By three men. But we had a gun riding, and the driver had guts, and they shot their way through it. Got in all right. Everybody. Not a nick."

Maynard nodded. He hoped that was all of it, though he knew it wouldn't be.

"The gun was an old-timer," Turner said. "Minty. Not afraid of anything that ever walked, man nor beast. He picked one of them off, just before the stage ripped out. Here's what I want to do, Maynard: I want to go back up the route and see if that man is still lying there."

"And what makes you think he might be?"

"I think he probably might not be; but I also think it's too good an opportunity to miss out on. There's more to it, you see; you didn't hear the driver tell the story."

"All right," Maynard said, "but even if he is there, what do you gain? You'll have a dead road agent and the obligation to bury him."

"I'm not worried about that."

Turner was a big man, and blustery and brash and impulsive; but he was standing there in Maynard's doorway now with uncommon patience, willing to explain it all carefully and in detail, because that was the way it had been going through his mind for hours as he panned out of it the logic and the possibility, and that was the way he wanted to tell it.

"Look," he said, "the shooting didn't start and end when the stage was stopped. There was a chase. No telling how far; but when the bastards gave up they were nowhere near where they'd started. They might have gone back for their pal or they might not have. If they thought he was dead they probably wouldn't have. Look, they know there's been a committee organized down here; they might not feel too comfortable riding back up the trail and then fussing with somebody who's probably dead, or who's too badly shot up to move about. They'll want to head for the barn. Anyway, as I say, it's too good an opportunity to miss."

"Yes, you've said that," Maynard said, shifting his weight in the doorway and leaning with one hand against the frame as Turner continued to stand there with a weighty interminable patience that was beginning to make him seem larger than he already was, as if it had expansive qualities. "I still don't see what the opportunity is."

"I'll explain it on the way up."

"The way up?"

"I need somebody reliable."

"You've got plenty of men in town," Maynard said. "And most of them you know better than you know me."

"For this," Turner said quietly, "I know you better than I know them."

"I'm not a goddamned gunman, Turner."

"But you can turn into one, if you have to. You've shown that."

"Those were the first men I've ever shot."

"As you say," Turner said with a flicker of smile. "But I'd feel better, and be most obliged. I'll pay you for your trouble."

Worse, Maynard thought. Not just a gunman but now a hired one.

As if seeing the thought, Turner said, "It'll be like riding shotgun."

"An honorable calling," Maynard said mordantly. "Listen, you've got a sheriff. You're already paying him for this sort of thing. Why don't you take him?"

"He's not around. And anyway, I want him left out of it for the moment, until I see what I see."

His interest stirred now for the first time, Maynard said, "What do you mean?"

"I told you, I'll explain it."

"You don't want Bell to know about it," Maynard said, wanting to get it sure.

Turner looked away for a moment, out to where the tree-covered mountains built up against the pale blue sky. Then he turned back to Maynard.

"It would be better," he said. "For now."

The weeks before winter set in tended to see the heaviest shipments come through, Turner told him as they moved at a steady gallop along the stage road, the bulky man posting in his saddle with surprising grace. An overladen stage could bog down in the snow, and things were chancy enough without that happening. So they were shipping heavily out of the mining camps now, and that was why the line had assigned a gun rider to the last stage that had come in.

"I'd hate to tell you how much bullion she was carrying," Turner said. "And somebody knew it."

"Or maybe just a good guess," Maynard said. "You said yourself the stages tend to pack heavy now."

"I'm talking about more than that. When the driver was telling the story of what happened, something he said jumped out and stuck in my head. I think I was the only one who picked it up; but of course I was the only one there who really cared, who was listening more than to just hear a story."

"What did you hear?" Maynard asked. Awakened before he'd wanted to be, up out of bed prematurely, his body still felt warm and unready for the out-of-doors. He was wearing his heavy overcoat, the collar turned up, his hat pulled low. The air felt chillier than it really was. The stretches of gray-green sage spread out on either side of the road had a sullen look they hadn't had before.

"It was something one of the roadies yelled out at them," Turner said. He thought about it for a moment again before saying it, as though it was pure revelation. " 'It's about god-damned time, you son of a bitch.' Now, what does that tell you?"

"That they were waiting," Maynard said.

"Not just waiting, but waiting longer than they'd expected. It so happens that stage had had a bit of axle trouble at its last station, you see, and was behind time. Do you see what I'm saying?"

"It should have passed that place sooner."

"And they knew it. Now do you see what I'm saying?"

"Yes," Maynard said. "I see it."

Turner looked at him for a moment.

"They knew the schedule," Turner said. He looked ahead again, his face hardening, as it did whenever he got to this point in his consideration of the matter, his beard fluttering in the wind. "You tell me how they knew that. There's only two people who are supposed to know that."

"You and—?"

"We used to give the schedules to John Dunlop so he could ride out now and then and meet the stages, unpredictable like. We thought it might help the situation, and maybe it did."

"And you've continued the practice," Maynard said, "with Bell."

"Yes," Turner said tersely.

"Who've you told about this?"

"Nobody," Turner said. "Just you."

"Well, I still don't see . . ."

"Let's wait on that. Let's wait until we see what we see."

When they approached the site of the attempted holdup a blustery wind had blown up, scattering dead leaves up and whirling against the sky, which was losing its blue health to a spreading gray pallor.

"Up there," Turner said, pointing to the crest as they rode toward it, coming to it from the direction opposite the one the stagecoach had taken. There were trees to one side of them, while the ground on the other was covered with bony twists of bramble that fell away from the road before pitching sharply down the mountainside.

"Just about here," Turner said when they reached the crest. Laboriously, he swung one leg around and dismounted.

"Is your man sure he knocked him off the horse?" Maynard asked, watching him from the saddle.

"Knocked him clear off. The passengers confirmed it. They also said," Turner said as he looked around, studying the ground at the side of the road, "that they were pretty sure they saw his horse bolt when the shooting started, that it blew off back down the road, which means it would have run a long time and a long way before it stopped."

"There's still no telling how bad he was hit," Maynard said, leaned forward in the saddle as he watched Turner, one hand resting on the pommel.

"Minty said it was a good hit. Knocked the son of a bitch right off."

Turner stood still, staring at the ground, a dark path of shadow falling away from him. The wind was whirring thinly in the trees. The sound made the site feel lonelier than it already was, like the flapping of a distant flag might.

"They may have come back for him after all," Turner said. Now he was looking in the direction from which the stage had come.

"No," Maynard said. "I don't think they would have chanced it."

Turner squatted his heavy bulk and pointed to the stains on some small flat rocks embedded in the ground. "Looks like blood," he said. "All around here. He got hit hard all right."

Maynard turned in the saddle, his eyes picking slowly along the side of the road where the wind was rescattering some fallen leaves, lifting them singly and in clusters, floating some, swirling others. Now he dismounted.

"Have a look here," he said, going to the edge of the road. Turner rose and joined him.

"Something busted through here," Maynard said, with one hand pushing his hat slightly back up from his forehead, with the other pointing to where some of the bramble had been broken down.

"Could have dragged himself off," Turner said. "Sure looks like it."

They began breaking through the low, stiff growth, crackling it under their boots, following what looked like a crudely made trail, where some of the branches clearly were freshly broken off.

"He hauled himself through here, looks," Turner said. "No doubt. Look at that." Where the ground cleared briefly there were indications of a dragging across it. Turner pulled his pistol.

"I don't think you'll need that," Maynard said, going forward, raising his knee with each step to break down the growth.

"Makes me feel more comfortable," Turner said sourly.

"If he's here, he's dead," Maynard said. "This fellow's been losing blood all the way down from the road."

The ground was tilting steadily down now, though Maynard didn't think that would have made any difference one way or the other to a badly wounded or maybe even dying man who wasn't sure who might come looking for him, his friends or the law or a band of riders with a rope, or who maybe no longer knew the difference anymore or cared, who was breathing little more than by instinct. It didn't take much to imagine the laborious forward motion through the tough resistant growth, one hand underneath clutching what had to have been a frontal wound, the other reaching out and trying to conjoin with whatever push was coming from a pair of straining legs, like trying to swim through a body of coagulated water.

They found the mask hanging to a thin knotted elbow of low-growing branch, where it may have come off accidentally or not. Turner bent and swept it up with his large hand and then let it hang limply from his fingers, a long black bandanna. He scowled at Maynard, then stuffed it into his pocket.

Then the gnarled growth with its short fierce branches ceded to clearer ground and there were more blood-marked rocks, some of them smeared straight across like an ancient daubing.

"He wasn't walking, that's for sure," Turner said. "And he sure dropped a lot of blood."

Then they found the pistol. It was lying in what looked like incongruous isolation, in tufts of short brown grass, in the circumstances devoid of its lethal character. Maynard picked it up and opened it.

"The chambers are full," he said, closing it again.

"He sure carried it far enough, didn't he?" Turner said.

"Never got off a shot."

"I told you, that Minty knows how to shoot."

They went further, the clear ground tilting more sharply now, until it finally pitched off into a dry ravine. They stood at the edge and looked down at where he was lying on his back, arms flopped out, head lolled to a side, his black overcoat twisted up around his thighs. His hat was hanging from a stick of outgrowth halfway along, where it had caught when he went over and tumbled down. The drop was about twenty feet.

"You know that face, don't you?" Turner said, putting away his pistol now.

"He works for Bell," Maynard said.

"Worked for Bell," Turner said tonelessly. "A slimy bastard. Always in and out of town. Now we know what he was doing when he was out. This is going to be a tough climb down."

The descent was steep, through short prickly brier twigs, some of them broken away where the dying man had rolled through. Turner went first, digging his boot heels in at each short careful step. Maynard followed, the fingers of one hand reaching out to grip Turner's coat collar to steady him.

"We're not hauling him out of here, I'll tell you that much," Turner said when they had completed the descent and were standing in the narrow rock-bottomed ravine. "They can come out from town if they want him, or leave him for crow bait. All the same to me."

Maynard looked along the ravine, to where it swung and dipped precipitously between rock-sided walls. It would be a torrent in here in spring when the snows melted. No saying where a body, or what was left of it, might come washing out.

"Look at that shot, will you?" Turner said admiringly. The bloodstain was wide across the midsection, having bled right through the coat. "Right in the belly."

"I'm surprised he got this far," Maynard said. He opened the dead man's gun now, emptied the chambers onto the ground, then closed the gun and stuffed it into his belt.

"Fear. That'll do it. And I'll bet this son of a bitch had a lot of that, knowing as he did where he was going. I'll bet he's getting jabbed in the ass with a pitchfork right now. Look at that face. Almost too mean to have died. Christ, Maynard, you're born with a face like that you almost have to end up like this."

The turned-aside face with its short dark stubble was a hard one, no question. Its barely open eyes were malign slits of dead light, the thick nose had been flattened in the middle.

About a dozen small cuts and scratches, no doubt the consequence of the tortuous crawl through the undergrowth, covered the face. One hand, obviously the one that had been
clutching the wound, was discolored with dried blood, looking as though it had been scorched.

"All right," Turner said, "that's all the religious service
he's getting."

He crouched and began running his hands through the
dead man's pockets. When he had searched the saturated
overcoat, he rolled the corpse to a side and began on the
pants pockets. When he found the folded-in-half piece of
paper, Turner rose, glancing at Maynard. He unfolded the
paper, studied it expressionlessly, then grunted and handed it
across. In crudely printed block letters was written: 11
MORNING.

"That's the time she was scheduled to leave her last station," Turner said, taking the paper back. "This son of a
bitch knew that. Now," he asked with exaggerated coyness,
"how did he know?"

TWENTY-SIX

I don't have a motive, Maynard thought. I shouldn't even be thinking about it. I have an assignment, and that's what this is about, as far as I'm concerned. There is no other thought, no other matter. I'm a serving officer in the United States Army, acting under direct and explicit orders, and I am, in the best way I know how, carrying them out.

These were his thoughts as he rode late the following afternoon out to the abandoned general store where they had gathered before. He was riding alone this time; Patterson refused to join in, nor had Maynard wanted him to. Patterson's sullen refusal was commentary enough; Maynard did not need any soul searching, particularly any that might cut close to his own edgily balanced considerations. What was set in his own mind had been set rigidly and the fact that it had had to be was bad enough.

Being a soldier gave you an exemption from being overly introspective and self-analytical. It was a kind of moral freedom, because what you were called upon to do was ordained elsewhere, the order being its own sanction and thus subject to nothing more than the occasional wayfaring question from afar, detached and not for preoccupation. A soldier was a man expected to move through the night with no more than sideways glances at lighted windows and no thought for whatever scruples they might imply. He was expected to possess some grainy interior that shaped and pointed his life the same as a skill at carpentry or study of philosophy charted the lives of other men. He followed an itinerary of orders that were his own personal epiphanies, acceptable to the fatalist he had been born to become.

The soldier, Maynard knew, had gratifications that did not have to answer to facile rationales, that precluded envying men who slept soundly and breathed unthreatened air. Four years under the lusty seductions and sundering dislocations of war, and then later time spent under wild skies contending with the Kiowa and Comanche had been years of self-enlightenment. The hard path had cut deeply into him and upon it he had met himself and found no secretions of prosaic yearning, no purposes demanding of definition.

But now, as he rode alone to gather with armed men who (with their coils of rope) were out to clean up their town, he brooded upon what brutally penetrant view of him had been taken, what twisted angle of discovery. There were more than enough of them to get done what they wanted to get done. But something patent and ineradicable that skirted self-contemplation and was visible to him in no mirror was apparent to them, because he was the man they wanted with them, he was the one Turner had wanted along for the ride into the mountains that had ended at the ravine. They had detected in him some innate capacity for this sort of thing that he'd never suspected—still didn't believe—was there. He didn't like what they thought they'd seen, and he resented them for believing they had seen it. He could have explained it to them very simply: he was going because he was a United States Army officer intent on fulfilling his commission. It had nothing to do with Baddock or stagecoaches or Lucas Bell. Or a woman. It had only to do with a former Union Army major. It had to do with obligation and responsibility, with nation and uniform and trust.

He had tried not to think about it, but now he felt the need to prop and reassure himself. What faculties she'd had for love had eroded in Theo's heart long before his arrival in Baddock. From flame to spark to ember to cold ash, it had gone its way to disintegration and unmourned burial. Maybe all Bell had done was to officiate at the rites. They were two people already long cast and hardened by the time Maynard came to Baddock. That's why it had been so easy for him to break into their lives; all he'd had to do was pass through a nothingness.

I'm traveling by an idea now, he told himself, riding across ground patchworked with low-growing shrubbery, wind-blown tumbleweed, and those ubiquitous rocks of all sizes shot to this ground eons ago. Tactics, he thought. That would do it. It always had, whether you were facing one man or twenty thousand. You attacked, you defended; you feinted, probed, lunged; you ran, forward, back, laterally. And always you watched, and evaluated.

They were there when he rode up, at least a dozen of them this time, sitting their horses with portrait stillness outside of the abandoned general store, which stood behind them with its sloping roof and bargeboard and of course beyond that the tree-sided mountains, always the mountains, raised as if to keep the sky from descending. From under every hat brim a face was turned toward him as he jogged toward them.

"Maynard," Pearson said by way of greeting.

Maynard recognized most of them: Pearson, the banker, looking more austere than ever; Turner, with his furnace of anger no doubt aflame inside that large body; Abbot, with a curt nod of greeting; O'Connor, once more prepared to finesse the precepts of jurisprudence. The uncomplicated Duckworth was there, with a pistol strapped around the outside of his sheepskin coat and a rifle butt extending from his saddlebag. And there was Thayer, the barber, normally a diffident man, but somehow galvanized for this. And Callahan, the red-bearded Irishman who ran the livery stable and who was in this because of a stated desire to protect his growing daughters from the spread of violence and corruption and lascivious activity (more interested no doubt in closing down the bordello than in securing the safety of stagecoaches). And Addison, a store owner who had been burned out once by a band of obstreperous roughnecks objecting to the price of his flour. And others, with their accumulated grievances and resentments and perceptions of civic responsibility.

"Who's missing now?" Turner asked, looking around. Two names were mentioned, with assurances they would be along soon.

"We've been betrayed by our own goddamned sheriff," Pearson said to no one in particular. "Made to look like goddamned fools. Well, now we're going to settle the account."

"I want to hear him try and speechify us when it comes to it," Duckworth said.

"When action begins," Abbot said, "talking stops."

Pomposity before the event, Maynard thought, eyes lingering on Abbot for a moment. There were men who believed that a bold thing could not be achieved without some slight flourish of it.

"You'll need a new sheriff," Maynard said.

"You pushin' for the job?" someone asked.

"When a pig learns to fiddle, maybe then."

"We may not even need one," Pearson said. "Not when they see the notices." From inside his coat the banker pulled several large sheets of rough brown paper and opened one to show Maynard. In neatly inked lettering they read:

DEATH TO ALL OUTLAWS

CITIZENS COMMITTEE OF BADDOCK

"We're going to leave those bastards strung right alongside the road," Pearson said, "with these pinned to them." He stuffed the papers back inside his coat, an expression of severe satisfaction in his face. "It's the kind of thing that spreads like prairie fire."

"It'll spread that you hanged your sheriff," Maynard said.

"We elected him," Turner said, "we can hang him."

"Maynard might have a point," O'Connor said. "I suggest that before we send him off we officially divest him of office. That way . . ."

"Jesus Christ," Turner muttered, "will you listen to this?" He turned his head aside and spat extravagantly, whether from need or disgust it was hard to tell. "Goddamned lawyers," he said, running the back of his hand across his mouth.

O'Connor smiled at him.

"Where's Patterson?" Abbot asked Maynard.

"He's standing aside."

"His privilege," Pearson said.

"He rode with us once," someone said, "so he's in, whether he likes it or not."

"He understands that," Maynard said.

"A man of conscience," Abbot said, not without some disdain.

"Not really a dying breed," O'Connor said amiably; "just in continuance at the moment."

Turner looked up at the sky. "We're losing daylight," he said.

"Do you know where he is?" Maynard asked.

"We know all right," Turner said. "And a hell of a lot more. Tell him," he said to O'Connor.

The lawyer leaned forward slightly in his saddle.

"We pulled in one of his boys from the Honest Eagle. The Frenchman. The big ugly one."

"They're all ugly," Turner said in a low, lethal voice.

"We told him we had the evidence," O'Connor said. "And we told him we had a tree limb ready to test his weight."

"Nothing like it to refresh a man's mind," Callahan said, ruffling his red beard with a harsh laugh.

"We knew this fellow had never stopped a stage," O'Connor said, "because of his size—he would have been recognized. So we told him we'd let him leave town under his own power—if he told us what we wanted to know. Otherwise he could take the drop for being an accomplice."

"He didn't make a debate of it either," Pearson said.

"He told us everything we needed to know," O'Connor said.

"Which we already knew," Turner said, steadying his horse, which was beginning to react to its rider's growing impatience.

"Including where Bell is," O'Connor said.

"How many men with him?" Maynard asked.

"Two."

"Where?"

"In a roadhouse about an hour's ride north. It's one of several places where they go to hole up. And it's apparently the place where they've stacked away their loot."

Turner grunted. "Which I'll be sitting next to all night with my rifle," he said, "until some of you bastards come out in the morning with a wagon." He looked up to the sky again. "We can't wait any longer," he said. "I tell you, we're losing daylight."

"Do you know how you're going to handle it?" Maynard asked.

"What do you mean?" Turner asked.

"If he catches sight of us," Maynard said, "he'll know why we're there. You could have some gunplay."

"We want to avoid that," Pearson said.

"Bell's tough," Thayer the barber said.

"And wily," another said.

"He won't be as easy as the other ones," Maynard said.

"You mean," Abbot said, "he might have the place posted."

"We may need tactics this time," Maynard said.

"We can decide on that when we get out there," O'Connor said, "and see how things lie."

"Absolutely correct," Pearson said. "We'll survey the situation and decide."

"Everybody got that?" Turner asked, looking around.

"You better be sure you got it, Turner," Duckworth said. "You present the biggest target." It evoked a round of laughter.

The final two men appeared then, riding hard, waving their hats.

"About goddamned time," Turner said.

"Gentlemen," Pearson said, turning his horse, "let's go."

TWENTY-SEVEN

"The more I think of it," Turner told Maynard, "the madder I get."

They were a mostly silent band of men, riding in a steady clutter of hoofbeats rolling in soft hustling cadence across the ground that skirted the foothills. A pile of gray clouds had floated out from behind the mountains but then been blown off to the southeast, taking with them their threat of rain. The mountainsides were teeming with autumn's pagan rituals, showing bursts of yellows and reds and russets like clarions of vanished summer.

"You see," Turner said, "we built that roadhouse when we first set up here, to have a station there. But then we switched the route and abandoned it. And now that son of a bitch's been using it to hole his men up in."

"Kind of sticking his finger in your eye," Maynard said.

"That's right," Turner said.

"So that road's not traveled very much."

"Maybe by the odd miner coming down from that direction. And he'd have to have some luck getting past it if they happened to be in there when he comes along. God knows how many dead bodies they've thrown aside out there."

"Did the Frenchman tell you anything about Bell?" Maynard asked.

"Not a hell of a lot. He said Bell had done this before, in California and Nevada, where he's wanted for God knows what under God knows what names. So they came out here, because this was going to be the new place. Bell organized the whole thing. Planted his gang in the mountains and ran things from town. Was probably angling to become sheriff from the start, to get his hands on those schedules."

"Then those three corpses he rode in with—?"

"His own boys," Turner said. "To turn our heads."

"I wonder what the rest of them thought of that."

" 'For the greater good,' is what the Frenchman called it." Turner laughed bitterly. Then, wonderingly, "What a bunch of bastards."

"Why not wait for Bell to come back to town and take him then?"

"No good," Turner said shaking his head. "You take him in town you'd probably have to hold a trial, which nobody is interested in doing. Waste of time, for one thing, and for another, he's still got friends there. Once he's gone they'll get the message and scatter. This is better."

Maynard left Turner and rode on up ahead, where Pearson, O'Connor, and Abbot were riding three abreast at the lead. Maynard joined them on the outside. Turning to his right, he had view of three stern profiles.

"I suggest somebody had better keep an eye on Turner when we get there," he said. "It wouldn't be a good idea if anybody starts taking independent action."

"We'll see to him," Abbot said. He was riding on Maynard's immediate right, with Pearson next to him and O'Connor on the end.

"Do you think this bunch will have the sense to listen to and then follow a decent plan?" Maynard asked.

"We're all after the same thing," Pearson said.

"Maynard's right," O'Connor said, raising his voice slightly to be heard. "We can't have any rash action. We're going to have to agree on that."

"One plan," Pearson said, "and stick to it."

"A sensible plan," Maynard said, turning his head to them for a moment as he spoke. "A fellow once told me," he said, looking ahead again, "the war could have been over in a year if the officers had been worthy of the men."

"Not having served—" Pearson said.

"Soldier talk," Abbot said dryly.

"I would imagine," O'Connor said, "that the view from the ranks is not without its distortions."

"That would apply in general to the view from below in any line of endeavor," Pearson said.

"In a soldier's case," O'Connor said, "it's probably a response to the fact of discipline. No one who exerts discipline is ever going to be seen objectively."

"A soldier needs to know only one thing," Abbot said, eyes fixed straight ahead as he rode.

"What is that, Mr. Abbot?" Maynard asked.

"To obey. And you don't need discipline to get that."

"And what *do* you need?" Maynard asked.

"Respect. Trust."

"And if the officer loses those things?"

"A capable officer never does."

"Not even under the strain of battle?" Maynard asked.

Now Abbot passed him a sidelong glance, then looked ahead again as they galloped across a narrow stream, their horses emerging with a toss of small clods from the damp surrounding ground. Maynard could hear the others splashing through behind him. The pace was steady, purposeful.

"A good officer," Pearson said, "—I would imagine— thrives on battle."

"Even good officers can lose their senses," Maynard said.

"What did he say?" O'Connor called across.

"That even good officers can lose their senses," Pearson said.

"That's a matter of interpretation," O'Connor said. "As an attorney, I would plead that one man's lunacy might very well be another's inspiration. A truly inspired man often appears eccentric to others."

"We're talking about the battlefield, O'Connor," Pearson said. "Not a goddamned courtroom. Life and death."

"Yes, yes," O'Connor said, as a gust of wind blew up the brim of his soft white hat and pressed it back for a moment. "Well then, you ought to study some of Alexander's campaigns, or Caesar's. Some of their strategies must have seemed sheer madness to their soldiers."

"You've studied those campaigns, Mr. O'Connor?" Maynard asked.

"I've had a glance," O'Connor said. "Let me tell you, brilliance can be blinding. It has its own singular logic, clear only to the visionary."

"If there can be logic in war," Maynard said.

"The logic begins," Abbot said, "when the war begins."

"I'll gladly debate that with you, Abbot," O'Connor said. "But this isn't the occasion."

"This certainly is not the occasion," Pearson said. "Right now we have to focus our minds on the one thing. Just the one thing."

Soon Turner called up from behind that they were getting close. They were threading through a lightly wooded area, in and out of stands of pine and alder and cottonwood, moving parallel to the abandoned stage road. A pale sun was now in departure behind the mountains, creating long and keenly laid shadows like spears of advancing night.

Some minutes later they drew together and stopped. Through the trees they could see the square-built flat-roofed roadhouse. Built originally to accommodate a stationmaster and occasional overnight travelers, it had an exterior about sixty feet long and slightly shorter dimensions along the sides. Adjacent was a small rail-fence corral and behind that a large stable and outhouse. The stable's roof had caved in. Three horses were grazing in the corral. From the tree line to the building the ground was flat and almost clear. Rising from the chimney were coils of gray smoke that seemed to bow before the thin wind before being blown to dispersal.

"Turner," Abbot said, "tell me what you know about that building."

They were dismounted now, gathered in the tree cover.

"Windows on both sides," Turner said, his voice a quiet monotone, "and a back door. Inside, there's a large front room, a couple of smaller ones, and another large one at the back. As I remember it."

"How strong is that front door, if you can recall?" Abbot asked.

"Just an ordinary door. If it's locked, one or two good heaves will put you through."

"One or two good heaves," Pearson said, "might be time enough for somebody in there to put his hand on a gun. We want to avoid that."

"We could wait till they've gone to sleep," Duckworth said, "then bust in on them, like we did t'other time."

"No," Abbot said with a shake of his head as he studied the roadhouse and the ground around it. "The place is too large. You can't be sure in what part of it they'll be. Or even if they'll all be in the same room."

"That's correct," O'Connor said. "Frankly, I wouldn't relish the thought of crashing into a dark place where Lucas Bell is lying arm's reach from a gun."

"I'll chance it," Turner said. He was holding his rifle now, diagonally across his large chest. "I'll blow his balls right out through his asshole."

"We want to avoid gunplay," Pearson said.

"It's a hanging," somebody said.

"Well," Turner said, "so far it's been all talk."

Abbot looked at him for a moment. "If you talk first," he said, "you might not have to die later."

"That's right," Maynard said. "Tactics, that's what's called for. Let Mr. Abbot work it out."

Abbot looked curiously at him for a moment, then turned back to the open ground, the house, the corral. He folded his arms and took several steps forward, then stood in contemplation, underlip slightly advanced. After several moments, he said, "We're going to have to encircle. There's a back door, windows, too many points of egress."

"What?" Duckworth asked.

"Exits," Maynard told him. "Ways out."

"We're not going to be able to ride up," Abbot said. "They'll hear us. Surprise is everything. But first we've got to be positioned."

"Exactly," Pearson said. "But how?"

"Two men will circle wide," Abbot said, "and assume an angled position that will enable them to cover both the windows on the left-hand side as well as the back door. I want men who can shoot from a prone position and hit what they're aiming at." He turned around.

"Considering the distance," Callahan, the red-bearded Irishman, said, "I can make that shot, if necessary."

"If Callahan lies on his belly," Duckworth said with a glance at the oversized Irishman, "he'll still be four feet in the air."

When the uneasy laughter had made its rounds, Duckworth said, "I'll go with him. What he misses, I'll hit," raising his rifle with one hand.

"All right," Abbot said, returning to his survey of the house. "I'm glad you built this place in open ground, Turner. If they break out they've got a long run to any cover."

"Grazing ground," Turner said. "You always need it."

"All right," Abbot said. "Now, most vitally, we'll need a man to take cover behind the water trough." The storekeeper was pointing to the corral, where the trough was located on the far side of the rails, away from the house. "If they come out they'll be going for their horses. It's absolutely essential they don't get that far."

"Two men then," Maynard said.

"What?" Abbot asked.

"You ought to deploy two men at the trough."

"All right," Abbot said. "We'll deploy two men there." He seemed to caress the word *deploy* with some irony, as if it amused him.

"I'll take it," O'Connor said. "Who's with me?"

"You go with him, Maynard," Abbot said. "If it comes to it, it's going to be vital that we get good shooting there."

"Maynard's probably the best shot here," Pearson said.

Maynard didn't find the accolade either pleasing or reassuring. None of them had ever seen him fire a pistol; the praise made him wonder about the proficiency of the others, if it came to a shootout.

"All right," Abbot said. "And I'll want two men to stay back here, mounted, in the unlikely event any of them get through and try to make a run for it. Who can shoot from a moving horse, if he has to?"

"I can," Turnerame forward to have a look until they formed a nearly straight line, "won't call for any particular skill. I'd rather have a couple of good shots on horseback."

"For God's sake, Turner," Pearson said, "we're not here for glory."

"All right," Turner said brusquely. "But if they come running out be sure to chase their asses up this way. Especially Mr. Sheriff Lucas goddamn Bell."

"Another thing," Abbot said, raising one finger for a moment, "for you men who are going to be in the enfilading position . . ."

"The what?" Duckworth asked.

"On the sides," O'Connor said.

"I mean you and Callahan," Abbot said, "on the one side, and Maynard and O'Connor on the other. If any of them try coming through the window don't fire on them until they're out. I don't want them chased back inside. If we have them out, let's keep them out."

"Dead or alive," Callahan said.

"Dead is better," Turner said.

"All right," Abbot said. "You fellows who are going out had better start now. Circle wide, keep low, and quiet. Once you've taken up your positions the rest of us will move in."

"Suppose we're spotted?" Duckworth asked.

"Hit the ground," Abbot said. "Keep your head down. If

you're fired upon, the rest of us will blast away. Let them know they're surrounded by a superior force. We'll try and talk them out."

"Never work," Turner said. "They'll know what we're here for."

"We could burn them out," Duckworth said.

"This was supposed to be a nice clean, quiet hangin'," someone muttered.

"These are contingency plans," Abbot said. "We've got to be prepared for any eventuality. We've got the advantage of surprise and we have superior numbers. I don't think we have anything to worry about." He looked up through the trees for a moment, where a mass of gray clouds had gathered. Then he spoke to the men again. "Go now. When you're in position, we'll move."

As he and O'Connor began moving laterally through the trees in an attempt to create the large, needed arc to get them safely to the corral and the cover of the trough without being seen, Maynard wondered for how long they were going to hold the advantage of surprise, and what would happen if and when they lost it. It could become very hot. Or maybe, he thought, he was placing too high an estimate on the capacities of Lucas Bell, as if the man who had so effortlessly taken possession of the heart of Theodora Diamond (and seemed so indifferent about it, which only added another, grating dimension to it) had to be more than mere man.

They came out of the trees about four hundred feet from the corral, crossed the road into a field of brown, knee-high, sickly-looking autumn grass, just as a soft rain shower broke out. Maynard never liked a sudden weather change in these circumstances; it was as if nature was too unconcerned to remain still and respectfully curious while he was putting his life at risk. Also, the sound of rain on the roof might bring a man to the window, if only for a moment, and as they ran through the whispery grass even a moment could be too long.

Followed by O'Connor, Maynard ran in a half crouch, pistol in hand, at a pace where he could gauge the setting down of every step, his eyes in constant rise and fall from the ground just ahead to the corral and the house beyond. He could hear O'Connor behind him, panting now, the sound conveying a mixture of exertion and tension.

They had swung out at an arc that now kept the corral between them and the house. The horses inside the corral shifted about for a moment, one flexing a foreleg as it pawed at the ground, while another, a large piebald, lifted its head and looked directly toward the two oncoming men.

Maynard reached the trough first and crouched at one end of the long wooden tub. He could hear the raindrops pinking the surface of the water inside. The wood gave off a moldy odor. Several moments later O'Connor was crouched next to him, drawing breath in short rapid gasps.

"All right?" he asked. His head was well below the level of the trough and he was watching Maynard.

"So far."

"Do you think they've made it to the other side yet?"

"I should think so."

"Then what's he waiting for up there?"

"Let's assume he knows what he's doing," Maynard said, keeping his eyes fixed on the house, watching through the thin unhurried rain. "Are you any good with that gun, O'Connor?"

"I go out now and then and do some target shooting."

"Ever hit anything?"

"Occasionally."

"If you have to shoot," Maynard said, "take your time. Make your aim. Don't just bang away. Toughest thing is making your aim while somebody is shooting at you. But you have to do it."

"I'll be all right. Do you see anything?"

"No."

"Do you think they're on to us?"

"Possibly."

"Why do you say?"

"It keeps you careful," Maynard said.

"That's true," O'Connor said. He was still keeping his head lowered, holding the pistol in his hand as if it was an object he wanted to put down but had no place for. "Christ, I thought this was going to be simple."

"That's a very dangerous man you have in there."

"If he's even in there."

"He's there," Maynard said. "That's his piebald on the other side of these rails."

"Is it?"

"Have a look."

"I'll take your word," O'Connor said. His breathing had restored itself now.

They were out of the trees now, at first vague and undifferentiated in the gray rain, and then becoming more distinctive. One, in fact—Maynard believed it was Addison—was walking across the open ground with his rifle up and aimed, like a strolling executioner. The others were taking long running steps, with the fastidiousness of men striving for stealth, armed with pistols or rifles. Abbot was in the lead, gun in hand, erect, striding on with a most crisp and positive step, as though in an environment of regimental banners and running drumrolls, walking quickly enough so that his pace was equal to the guarded scuttling behind him. His bold stride was in contrast to that of Pearson, some ten feet behind, who looked as though he were hurrying on tiptoe, with an odd side-to-side weaving, which Maynard suspected was to keep Abbot in direct line in front of him.

When he reached the road, Abbot raised the gun into the air and then swung his arm forward as if to hurl the weapon and began running hard toward the house, the others following, closing their scattered ranks as they converged on the door. That was when the shooting started. From his point of vantage, Maynard could not see it, but was told later that they could not get through the door and that the first thud against it had evidently alerted the men inside, who began firing.

"Jesus, somebody's hit!" O'Connor said excitedly as they saw a man go stumbling back and then collapse on the ground.

The others scattered away from the door and windows and crouched for cover against the walls. Shooting broke out on the other side of the house as a man ran from the back door, gun in hand. He was wearing trousers and long john tops, a pair of unraised suspenders flailing brokenly around him as though he had torn loose from a harness. He paused indecisively for a moment, gun raised, and then they saw him shot down by the rifles on the other side.

Two more men ran from the back, cut sharply away from the house, and headed for the corral. As the first one began climbing over the rails, pistol in hand, O'Connor rose to his feet and fired, and missed, discharging four errant shots as the man got over the top rail and dropped inside the corral. From his position at the corner of the trough Maynard had a clear shot, took it, and brought the man down with a jarring plunge. The man looked up vaguely for a moment, as if roused from a deep sleep, then never moved again.

Maynard watched a bareheaded, frock-coated Lucas Bell come running at the corral, seize the top rail, and in a single swooping leap swing himself over, hitting the ground in balance, pistol in hand, the unbuttoned coat flaring around him. O'Connor fired and again missed as the horses began swirling around the corral with panicky aborted jumps. Bell lunged for his piebald but the fractious animal bolted past him. The other two horses set off in blind gallop and smashed through the railings just to the right of the trough. Bell grabbed again for the piebald, missed, and lost his footing, falling to his knees just as Maynard and O'Connor fired in unison, the shots missing. From his knees Bell fired back, sending a series of shots tearing into the trough as Maynard and O'Connor flattened themselves on the ground.

Getting to his feet with a thrust, Bell ran through the break in the corral, the storming piebald giving him momentary cover. In the same slow steady rain, he ran across the road and through the grass, the unbuttoned frock coat swinging around him.

The appearance of Turner thundering out of the trees made Bell look small and hopeless. The bulky stagecoach man had the reins in his teeth and his rifle up and raised, looking astonishingly huge and overpowering. Bell saw him but didn't fire, kept running. Maynard, from one knee, measured his shot through the thin gray rain, one eye squinting along the barrel of his moving pistol. He fired, simultaneously with Turner's crackling rifle. Bell swerved, as if he had been physically shoved, went stumbling awkwardly on for another few steps as if on suddenly deformed legs, and then dropped into the grass as Turner galloped past with a whoop.

Maynard began running as fast as he could, pistol up and steady in his hand, watching for any movement, though he wasn't expecting any, not from the soft, wholly relinquishing way the man had sunk. The others had broken away from the front of the house and were running and yelling, ignoring something that Abbot was shouting at them.

For some compelling reason, Maynard felt it important that he reach the body first, as if to make what would be the lasting and definitive judgment of it. Getting there, he crouched and with his free hand rolled the body over on its back. Bell's white shirt was soaked with blood; his face, with its closed eyes, was as impassive and unrevealing as ever. With a curious sense of detachment, Maynard stared at the narrow forehead under the dark hair, the closed eyes, the finely shaped nose, the soft, almost feminine mouth. *Damn you,* Maynard thought, without rancor, without any sense of emotional expression at all. Simply, *Damn you.*

"Is he dead?" someone shouted.

Maynard turned toward them.

"I got him!" Turner cried out. He had brought his horse

to a skidding halt and then executed a violent demivolte, was momentarily thrown back in the saddle by the reared horse, one hand gripping the tautly extended reins, looking as though enormously awaiting a pedestal. Now he came riding back, holding his rifle up in the air and shaking it like a trophy.

Now they were all there, gathered around the body that lay like an indentation in the high grass.

"Look at that," one of them said breathlessly. "Son of a bitch is wearing his badge."

"Not anymore," Duckworth said, reaching down and ripping the star from the front of the rain-splashed coat.

Maynard drew back, with one final, lingering look at the body, then turned aside, slipping his pistol back into its holster.

"What about the other two?" he asked.

"Dead," Abbot said, walking up. Of them all, he was the only one who had walked to the spot. "Very nice shooting, Maynard," he said.

"I was the one brought him down," Turner said, sitting his horse.

"Yes," Maynard said. "I believe it was Turner." He looked over at the water trough, where O'Connor was still sitting. "Is he hit?" he asked.

Someone called over to O'Connor; the lawyer answered with an indifferent, dismissive wave.

"Not used to being shot at," someone said jocularly.

"You'd think a lawyer would be," Callahan said, his voice droll under his broad red beard.

"We got the first one," Duckworth said. "Me and Callahan. Turned him into rags."

"Who was hit?" Maynard asked.

It was Pearson, he was told, taken by a shot in the leg. The banker was sitting where he had fallen, resting back on outstretched arms. Thayer the barber was bent solicitously over him.

"It was a hell of a hanging, wasn't it?" Duckworth said to no one in particular.

The journey back, made through a softly rained night, was quiet and reflective, all of the risen excitements worn off. Left behind were Pearson with his bound-up, painful, but not serious wound. Thayer remained with him, as did Turner. The stagecoach man had found boxes of stolen bullion in the house, along with other loot. He and his loaded rifle would sit by it until morning, waiting for the doctor and several men to come out in a wagon.

Maynard did not speak to Abbot on the ride back. Abbot, in fact, chose not to speak to anyone, riding well in the lead and always alone. Maynard watched him for long periods of time, wondering what was in the man's mind, how far back his thoughts might be going, how far ahead, if ahead at all.

He thought about Theo, in a musing, detached way, like running fingertips across a portrait of the long lost, speculating upon just how much she had known about Bell and the route of his poisonous ambitions. It was best for him, Maynard decided, to assume she had known everything. It made things easier for him. He wondered about her capacity for mourning, and if she possessed such capacity, what exactly she might mourn for.

TWENTY-EIGHT

The next morning Maynard rode out along the stage road to the small church he had previously visited with Patterson. He found the minister, Mr. Wynston, outside in the sunshine, earnestly at work. In his shirtsleeves, the red-haired churchman was swiping away at the tall grass at the side of the modest nailed-together building with a scythe.

"Good morning, Mr. Maynard," the minister said, pausing in his work, shielding his eyes from the sun with his hand like an inexpert salute as he watched Maynard canter toward him.

"You have a good memory for names, Mr. Wynston," Maynard said, slowing, and then stopping.

"And you," the minister said as Maynard dismounted, "have given me a good excuse to stop working for a bit."

They shook hands, then walked toward a small bench near the front door. When they were seated, the minister laid down the scythe. The roof shadow lay just at their feet.

"If I don't keep at it," the minister said, "the prairie will gradually come in and reclaim us."

"Something symbolic in that, don't you think?"

The minister laughed. "A keen man will find something symbolic in everything. Are you by for some spiritual talk?"

"Should I be?"

"It might be in order this morning."

"Then you've heard?"

"News of that character? In a place like this?" The minister shook his head ruefully. "I've had two people come out

already to inform me. But you aren't here for that, are you?"
He glanced at Maynard's profiled face.

"No."

"It's a nasty business, on both sides of the fence. Lord, out
here," the minister said, gazing across the hard prairie ground
out to the mountains, "it's like starting all over again. The values, the morality, the reasoning. It's a book of blank pages."

"A rare opportunity for a man of God, perhaps," Maynard said.

"Sometimes I feel like a missionary, though I'm not sure if
I'm here to convert, reconvert, or try to hold on to what's left.
But anyway, what can I do for you, Mr. Maynard?"

"I have a question that pertains to monasteries."

"I'm not more than superficially informed there, but go
ahead."

"I once read a book that had some references in it to the
monastic life and it came back to me last night. What I'm trying to clarify in my mind," Maynard said, "is the precise
order of authority in one of those places. Who would the
head figure be?"

"In a monastery? That would be the abbot."

"And next in rank?"

"Most times that would be the prior."

"Prior first," Maynard said, "and then abbot."

"That would be the usual hierarchal order."

"Thank you, Mr. Wynston," Maynard said, rising.

"Is that all?"

"It's exactly enough."

Back in town, Maynard went to the livery stable where he
hired a hanger-on to ride to the garrison at Bear Creek with a
sealed envelope for the commanding officer. In it was his
written commission from General Northwood along with a
note requesting a detail be dispatched to Baddock. He, Maynard, would await them at the Territorial Stage Line office.

After inquiring at several of Abbot's establishments in

town, Maynard learned that the man had not yet appeared at any of them today and was probably at home.

The house was about a quarter mile outside of town. It was a two-story white clapboard, built on a small rise at a point where the ground was beginning to swell up toward the foothills. Large by Baddock standards, and by them even elegant, the house seemed designed for a family, but the storekeeper lived there alone. A low white picket fence surrounded a lawn of uneven trim, while around the sides shrubbery grew free and uncut. Curtains hung over the windows downstairs and up. The lean-to-style roof was crowned by a redbrick chimney. A narrow, chairless front porch rendered a look of lonesomeness. What the house wanted, Maynard thought as he walked his horse toward it, what gave it its look of tentative occupancy, was a woman's hand, a caring attention for detail.

He dismounted, tied his horse to the hitching rail, then swung aside the gate, and walked the dirt path to the front door.

Abbot opened the door to Maynard's knock.

"So you're here," Abbot said. With a peculiar beckoning of his fingers he invited Maynard in, then closed the door.

Maynard walked directly into the parlor, where the sunlight was lightly misted by the white curtains, its light falling across worn, floral-patterned carpeting. There were a pair of twin red velvet–upholstered rockers, several other chairs, a lumpy scroll-backed black sofa, and several small tables with kerosene lamps. The walls were bare.

"Have a seat," Abbot said casually, sitting himself in the center of the sofa and tossing one leg over the other. He was wearing a white shirt, open at the throat, over it a brown silk vest, dark trousers, and boots that bore mud stains from the previous day's adventure. He appeared relaxed, except for his face, which held a slightly querulous expression, like a man who had been disturbed at sleep.

Maynard took a seat across the room from him, in one of the rockers. He placed his hat in his lap and crossed his legs.

"What's happening on Main Street?" Abbot asked.

"You mean in reference to yesterday?"

"I mean that, yes."

"Same as last time; people unwilling to look one another in the eye."

"It was all to the good. You know that."

"I don't think anyone is questioning it," Maynard said.

"The reputation of the committee will hold things in check until we bring in a new sheriff. How is Pearson? Have you heard?"

"No."

"I suppose he'll play the hero for a while. But aside from that, it went smoothly, I felt."

"We've seen much worse," Maynard said.

Abbot studied him carefully, with narrowing eyes, as if trying to decide whether to agree or not.

"You've done well for yourself out here," Maynard said.

"The Montana Territory is a mecca for someone who's got some ambition and isn't afraid of hard work. You ought to stay here, Maynard. Become part of things."

"That's not possible, I'm afraid."

"I think that's too bad. I guess it means that you'll be leaving. Where will you be heading?"

"East."

Abbot nodded and said, "Ah." Then, "You've been something of a puzzle to us, Maynard. To some of us."

"Yes, I know that. There's a peculiar quality to the deep night hours out here, like nowhere else. Something in the silence. Maybe it has something to do with confinement by the mountains, but you can *feel* it when you're being thought about."

"And you've felt that?"

"Clearly," Maynard said.

"And did you have any idea who it was doing this impertinent thinking about you?"

"It could only have been one person."

"And why should they have been giving you such consideration?" Abbot asked. He was sitting with a poise so complete it almost seemed as if designed to upset. "You're a good enough fellow, but hardly anything out of the ordinary, if you don't mind my saying."

"That's the surest place to be," Maynard said, "among the ordinary. If you stop to think about it, it's really a most sublime elevation."

"To see what?"

"All."

"And have you?"

"Well," Maynard said, smiling pleasantly, "here I sit."

"Yes," Abbot said with a brief, knowing nod. "You know, Maynard, you may be right about the quality of a Montana night—I had the same intuition last night, of being thought about."

"It's a phenomenon. Somebody ought to write a paper on it. Do you think it has something to do with there being gold in the ground? It does tend to intensify things, doesn't it? I mean, it blocks out many of the extraneous things we're accustomed to, a lot of the common human feelings. It shows us the best and the worst of us, and not much in between. Like war."

"War does that?" Abbot asked with an innocent curiosity.

"Doesn't it?"

"What led you to my door, Maynard?"

"A word here, a word there."

"Such as?" Abbot asked, guardedly now.

" 'Deploy.' 'Enfilade.' "

"Common enough."

"To certain people, yes. And I heard you say that a soldier needed but the one quality: to obey."

"Anyone could have said that," Abbot said. "It's common sense."

"But it's also so true, and you made it sound so true, because you said it casually."

"You sound like a man who's looking for a white button in a bale of cotton."

"And," Maynard said, "you said, 'The logic begins when the war begins.' "

"A layman's perception."

"Hardly. It sounds very professional to me."

"So you've picked certain words out of the wind and come to some conclusion."

"Oh, it was more than just words. It was the way you handled the men yesterday. Very crisp, self-assured. Tactics."

"I remember you saying that," Abbot said. "You said that tactics were called for and that Mr. Abbot would work it out."

"You gravitated toward it most naturally, and, I might add, most ably."

"It was hardly a very demanding action."

"But you assumed the responsibility," Maynard said.

"Somebody had to."

"And it was you."

"I felt responsible for those men," Abbot said.

"Nostalgia?"

"I haven't offered you any hospitality. Would you like whiskey?"

"No thank you," Maynard said.

Abbot moved about on the sofa, uncrossing and then recrossing his legs.

"Tactics, Maynard," he said. "You've had some of your own, haven't you? You've been like a man trying to slip through a perimeter—there's another good word for you to file. You've been a good one for asking questions. And always interested in the answers. But you weren't just offering conversation, were you? You were building something inside your head. And now you think you have it."

"Yes, sir."

" 'Sir'?" Abbot asked with an amused look.

"I've also added on your private little monastic joke."

Now a frowning interest filled Abbot's face.

"First a prior and then an abbot," Maynard said. "You gave yourself a promotion of sorts, didn't you?"

Abbot laughed easily. "Promotion," he said softly, as if finding a fond memory among a ruin of ideas. And then, vaguely, with a wry smile, "It was irresistible, I suppose. Who are you, Maynard? Exactly."

"United States Army."

"Rank?"

"Captain."

"They set a captain to catch a major? I suppose there's a logic in it. The added spice of hunting something larger than yourself. Where are you attached?"

"I'm on General Northwood's staff, at the War Department."

"All the way from Washington? You poor fellow. You must have done something really dirty to deserve this."

"Actually," Maynard said, "I did. I punched a colonel. Getting me out of Washington for a while was an act of benevolence."

"I wish you would have restrained yourself."

"They would have sent someone else."

"But I doubt anyone as tenacious, who would join a band of vigilantes in pursuit of his duty. Actually, I'm surprised they would send anyone at all, that they would still be interested. But I suppose once that fool notified them they felt obligated to do something."

"Barley Newton."

"Yes, that was his name. Of all the damned fools to show up. God, just think upon it, Maynard. This is a small, remote place. There aren't many people here, and those that are, are not wont to look at faces, at least not very closely anyway."

"Did you shoot him?" Maynard asked.

"Did I shoot him?" Abbot—Pryor now—asked rhetorically. He looked up in the air for a moment and sighed. "Did I shoot Barley Newton? If I didn't, should I have? And if I did, should I have not?"

"Somebody shot him."

"More or less," Pryor said abstractedly. "He was one more who became less. Dead before his time. Or is that illogical? If you're dead, then it is your time, no matter what. I knew it was bad luck the moment he spotted me. He knew me all right, it was across his face like a statement. But he never uttered a sound, and at first I said to myself that he'd embraced the code out here, where tact and discretion aren't just indications of cultured behavior but also ways of remaining healthily alive. But then I kept thinking about it. I kept harping to myself about how I'd come all this way, paid for my derelictions with shame and ordeal, resurrected myself, in a manner of speaking—forgiven myself, which isn't as facile as it sounds. I don't know if you realize it, Maynard, but self-forgiveness is the purest and most sincere act of exoneration. There is no possible self-deception in the matter."

"I understand," Maynard said.

"And now it was all suddenly at risk because of some nondescript miner who sooner or later was going to soak his skin and run his mouth. I'll tell you what view I took, Maynard. I told myself that this man was going to go back up into the mountains where he would either be shot to death in a brawl or freeze to death over the winter. I saw it as an absolute certainty. So you see, in my mind he was already dead when I next saw him. It's not as outlandish as you might think— after all, I was long dead myself, wasn't I? So I knew about these things. You're an intelligent fellow, Maynard, I think you can see it. But it was strictly a chance encounter. I certainly wasn't out looking for him. But all of a sudden there he was, brought around by a friendly providence. I met him on a cross street late at night—I'd been out drinking and, I suppose, brooding upon my predicament. I looked up and saw him. He was staggering a bit. He looked at me and gave me the most inane smile. I was shocked, the same as he must have been when he had first seen me, because in my mind I'd already buried him. Now here he was, up out of the grave.

This may sound callous, but I felt I was within my rights. This man was a threat to my very existence, the same as if he'd drawn on me."

Pryor paused for several moments to reflect.

"Looking back now," he said, "I think it was because he smiled. That stupid, inane smile. It was like a lash across me. For God's sakes, I'd been his commanding officer, remember. I'd had the power of life and death over him before. So I drew on him and finished him off, once and for all. I'll tell you, Maynard, the openness out here has its advantages as well as its disadvantages: a gunshot in the middle of the night doesn't necessarily draw crowds of people into the street. You can get by with it, if you're careful."

"And you were careful."

"Everything was 'deployed' just right," Pryor said with a faint smile, as if mocking Maynard with the word. "But obviously I was too late; the fool had sent off his letter to someone or other, which ended up on the desk of your General Northwood."

"The fact is," Maynard said, "he never told more than that he'd seen you. He wouldn't identify you."

"He still said too much."

"He thought he'd seen a ghost."

Pryor laughed mirthlessly. "Well, he had, hadn't he? He saw somebody who no longer existed, who'd been buried, and," Pryor added wistfully, "no doubt with honors."

"Why did you cease to exist, Major Pryor?"

"I was killed in the war," Pryor said frankly. "It's written in the official records. I've been mourned by kith and kin. I'm a quite posthumous person. I occur after death."

"As well as just before," Maynard said. "You seem to take some relish in it."

"It's the epitome of the private joke, isn't it? You have to enjoy it, or else. Were you in the war, Maynard?"

"From its infancy to its dotage."

"Well, so was I, though not quite all the way, of course. In it and out of it."

"Were you out of it while you were still in it?"

"What does that mean?" Pryor asked warily.

"You lost your way."

"Say what you mean, Captain."

"You went out of your senses."

"Ah. Is that what I did?" Pryor shifted about uneasily on the sofa.

"Hardly a disgrace."

"Desertion in time of war? Hardly a disgrace? I find that statement highly unbalanced."

"You were an unwell man."

"I was West Point, Maynard."

"Anyone's mental binding can come undone."

"Not a West Point officer's. I was educated to a specific purpose, Maynard. I was entrusted with grave responsibilities. I was an officer in a time of war."

"And for a long time," Maynard said, "you carried out those responsibilities with great efficiency."

"A long time wasn't long enough," Abbot said with an air of wistful dejection. "But it seemed to become too long for me. I'll tell you, Maynard, it isn't that there's not a limit to what a man can withstand; it's that there are a lot of small, gradually accumulating limits. It's like clearing one redoubt and then finding another, and then another. You find yourself slipping past each one only to find it there again. It happens piecemeal, you see. A gradual unhinging. You think you can deal with them one at a time, but you aren't, because they're not really going away. You lie on your cot at night and try to listen to what's inside your head. It's a silent, unimaginable ordeal. You're at the bottom of your soul, a place where no man ever expects to visit. You find yourself summoning up conscious resolve, all your reserves of it, all the things that are supposed to serve you by natural flow. And let me tell you, when you start consciously calling upon your strengths— that's when you realize you've exhausted them. Under certain circumstances they become irreplaceable, and I was living under those circumstances, every day. You must have seen this happen, if you were any kind of soldier."

"I saw men break apart all at once."

"That's the easy way. Hardly as dangerous. It can be taken hold of. But the other way is the insidious way, when the poison is leaking in by drops, when you start telling yourself that a good night's sleep will put everything right. When your pride gets in the way. And while it's going on you're being asked to formulate strategy and lead men into battle. You're responsible for those lives, and when you lose some of them—as inevitably you're going to—you start asking yourself what you'd done wrong, even if you'd done nothing wrong." Pryor paused. "I was deeply ashamed of myself, Maynard."

Now he looked aside for several moments, folding his arms, while Maynard never ceased watching him.

"It feels strange talking to a fellow officer again," he said. "I almost feel like I'm back in uniform. I was a good officer, Maynard. A bit of a stickler perhaps, a disciplinarian. My men didn't like me very much; I knew that. Often a sign that you're doing the job correctly, isn't it?" Pryor said as Maynard smiled tersely. "But they respected me. And that was the important thing. A West Point officer must be respected."

He turned back to Maynard, who was sitting motionlessly in the rocker, arms on the rests.

"You're not West Point, are you?" Pryor asked.

Maynard detected the merest tone of superiority. "No," he said. "But I do understand."

"I became a major early in the war," Pryor said. "And so remained."

"Did that offend you?"

"I've always felt that ambition in an officer is a virtue. But," Pryor said, "that had nothing to do with anything; that was a mere skirmish at the edge of the amphitheater."

"It finally did come apart, didn't it?" Maynard asked. "All of it."

"When I think about what severed the last and most delicate strands, well, it sounds like some old whittler's yarn, spun out to pass the time. You see, it had to do with the man who was killed by Abraham Lincoln's hat."

Consciously, Maynard did not smile.

"Yes," Pryor said, as if affirming for himself the gravity of what he had said. Then, with a dispassionate curiosity, he asked, "May I ask what you're going to do? What your orders are?"

"I've sent word to the garrison at Bear Creek," Maynard said, "and they'll be sending a detail to take charge of you."

"Have you told anyone in town?"

"A select few," Maynard said, lying now.

"I was wondering why you came unarmed."

"I didn't think you'd want to shoot your way out, Major."

"You're a cool head, Maynard. I can see why you're on staff."

"Tell me about Abraham Lincoln's hat."

"It was—to me—a very serious story at the time. I had a man in my company named Baker. A good soldier, but a singular sort of man. Whenever we went into action he would put on a stovepipe hat that had become part of his baggage. When I asked him why, he said it was too good a target for the rebels to aim at and consequently they would leave the rest of him alone. Well, what do you do with somebody like that? I chose to leave him to whatever devices he relied on. And the fellow kept coming through, one campaign after another. We were mowed down with incredible ferocity at Second Bull Run, but Baker was never touched, though the fool hat was shot off his head twice, which he claimed proved his point. But then one day—it was toward the end for me—I mentioned to him, jocularly, that his hat was similar to the one popularly worn by Mr. Lincoln and that some rebel marksman might take personal umbrage at the symbol and bear down on him. I suppose this alarmed him, because he discarded the hat, and the next time we went in he was shot dead, wearing his regulation forage cap. It will give you something of my frame of mind when I tell you that I believed that I had killed him; not of my own hand, of course, but with my words. I was undergoing a goddamned eclipse, Maynard, and what little light there was for me was going fast. I had to get out while I still had enough lucidity left to do it."

"But there was more to it than a stovepipe hat," Maynard said. "At the end, I mean."

"I don't understand," Pryor said warily.

"You've omitted your crucial episode."

Pryor said nothing.

"The old woman you shot," Maynard said.

"The old woman I shot," Pryor said, making of it a flat, declarative statement, as though it was the theme of a paper he was about to read. "Yes, I recall that. It has nothing to do with anything, of course. That's not why you're here. I don't think it's worth any discussion. There isn't much to say about it anyway. I remember having done it, but not actually doing it, not that I'm asking for any dispensation, but merely to say this: maybe the person you see sitting before you did it, but that person was not Andrew Pryor at the time. Lord knows who he was, if he was even anyone. That must have been the moment of full eclipse, of the darkest subversion. Look, Maynard, you have to remember who I was. I had the strictest orders against looting. It was well known. For me to enter a home with the intent of looting it was absurd; to steal some old woman's jewel case was ludicrously beyond reason."

"And to shoot her?"

"I can tell you exactly why. She made a move to get out of bed, and I thought—I can still remember thinking it: She wants to dance with me."

"You thought that?"

"I remember it, vividly. And it must have struck me as some kind of mockery, that she saw there was something wrong with me and was trying to humor me, which by extension I saw as ridicule. That's what I imagined her thinking.

Absurd? Today, yes, certainly. But what is sadly laughable now was savage conviction in my head at the moment. You can imagine my fury. I was a lost man, Maynard."

"But you found yourself soon enough."

"Well, there was a corporal present. He witnessed the whole thing. I ordered him to keep silent on it, but you know how far that goes. You know about bivouacked soldiers, sitting around with nothing to do. For God's sake, Maynard, I was an officer who was known to flog looters. There was no possible way I was going to survive this. Thief, murderer, hypocrite, all in the same bow."

"So you lit out."

"Almost immediately, before that damned corporal began spreading his story and before I could shoot him, which, believe me, blew across my mind as part of the storm. (I knew the possibility was there by the apprehension in his face.) I did some solitary riding the next day—we were encamped in northern Virginia at the time—and came across the body of one of our pickets, who evidently had wandered unwisely and been brought down. He had been shot in the face, and I suppose that gave me the scheme. I took out my pistol and shot away the rest of his face, then switched uniforms with him, giving him my papers and identification. I put my ring on his finger. I trusted the chaos of war to do the rest."

"Which it did."

"Evidently."

"Allowing Major Pryor to be buried with honors."

"There's no irony in that, Maynard; I had served extremely well for years. Whatever they read over my coffin was earned, believe me. It's always the past that's buried anyway, isn't it? I had a family, of course, brothers and sisters, and I left them a memory to be cherished."

"Your senses seemed to have restored themselves rather quickly."

"If that's meant as cynicism, I resent it. Let me tell you, when you're desperate to preserve yourself, you become very

cunning and devious, no matter the temper of your mind. I
was a professional soldier, hence resourceful. It didn't take
me long to acquire civilian clothing and I began my odyssey."

"Which ended in Baddock."

"Yes."

"Where you've prospered," Maynard said.

"So I have," Pryor said absently. He raised his head and
closed his eyes for several seconds, assuming a passing look
of spirituality. When his eyes reopened he glanced at Maynard, looked away, and then got to his feet. He left the room.
Maynard heard him in the next room, opening and then closing a drawer. When he returned he was holding a pistol.

"There's always the honorable way, isn't there?" Pryor
said, standing in the middle of the room, holding the weapon
down against his thigh.

Maynard, who had been moving barely perceptibly to and
fro in the rocker, now came to an absolute stillness.

"There's a point where you fight on," Pryor said, "and a
point where you stop. You always know when to fight on, of
course—that's a decision that's almost taken for you. But
when you stop, when you know you've heard the last
chord—that's an intellectual choice. Have you ever witnessed
one of these, Maynard? I suppose not. I would imagine few
people ever have. Call it what you want, but I think there's
something ennobling about it. Something plain, clear, and
dignified. My mind isn't wandering now, Maynard. You can
see that, can't you?"

"I can see that."

"And you've seen men die."

"Of course."

"And when you look back, it seems they all died on the
same day, doesn't it? At the same time, of the same thing. It's
best to remember them that way, a great single heap of them,
with one fine elegy for all. You don't want them littering your
memory. You may have a rougher time fitting me in, but I
won't apologize for it. After all, you came a long way to find

me. Under orders, granted. You found me, and now I'm going to see to it that you don't ever lose me. I'll always be the broken spoke in your wheel of memory. You do understand why this must happen, don't you? All I have left to me now is your understanding. Do I have it? I'm not quite sure that I do, Maynard."

"If it helps," Maynard said.

"It would help immeasurably."

Pryor raised the pistol and cocked the hammer, keeping the barrel pointed away, across his chest.

"When a man can't go back and is unwilling to go ahead . . ." he said. "You see what it is, don't you?"

"Clearly."

"Some burdens should be carried, some not. There are good arguments for both sides. You can see that."

Maynard continued to sit motionlessly, arms on the rests, watching.

"Captain," Pryor said in formal address, and as he raised the pistol and held it a fraction of space away from his temple, staring expressionlessly at Maynard, the latter turned aside and then winced and shuddered at the roar of the pistol.

TWENTY-NINE

"About a half hour now," Turner said, coming out of the office, looking at the large stem-winding watch that lay in the palm of his hand.

"Thank you," Maynard said. He was leaning against a post outside of the Territorial office, his back to Turner, his suitcase on the boardwalk next to him.

"If it's on time," Turner said. When he received no response he walked back into the office, looking over his shoulder for a moment at the lone figure who had the infernal stillness of one who might have been standing there for an eternity, while at the same time in its slouch against the post evoking a sense of long-ago departure.

Main Street was quiet this evening, continuing what had been the town's careful, self-regarding mood since news of Lucas Bell's death had spread, followed later by word of the stunning and unaccountable suicide of one of its most prominent citizens.

Baddock, Maynard thought, his eyes moving without interest or curiosity along the buildings across the street, coming to rest briefly on the building at the far end known as Paradise West, where no lights were showing this evening. A handful of icy stars were dispersed delicately above the Montana mountains. Baddock: it made a dull and lifeless sound in his mind. Another point of arrival and departure on a soldier's sheet, already recessive, fading into whatever would come next.

He listened to the slow approach of boot heels on the boardwalk. Near him, they stopped.

"So it's good-bye, and I suppose it's good luck, whatever meaning that might have for you."

The voice was sardonic. He shifted position against the post, watching the street with that same solitary detachment. "She's gone, you know." Simon Patterson was speaking with a slight slur. Maynard didn't have to smell the whiskey to know it was there. "Went out on the early stage. But you probably already know that. I helped her load. I wished her luck. She kissed me on the cheek and said thank you. I didn't ask where she was going, nor did she say. She heard he was dead and she left. Nothing left to stay for, I guess. Nothing. Gone now, somewhere beyond the mountains. She didn't mention you, by the way."

Maynard turned his head till his cheek touched his raised coat collar. Patterson looked as though he was having to make an effort to remain steady, tipped slightly forward, his hands slid into his coat pockets as if to provide ballast. The crown of his Stetson was dented in on one side, like a signal of his condition.

"I wouldn't go chasing after her, either," Patterson said, and after a brief snag in his breathing, adding, "if I were you. Which I'm happy to say I'm not. Have you worked it out in your head yet, Thomas? I mean, which man you were *really* after? Was it your sad major with his stricken conscience, or was it Lucas Bell, of no conscience at all? Did you go along hoping the major would smoke himself out, or was it Bell you were after, for your own private reasons? Don't say it makes no difference, because it does. It does, Thomas, for whatever conscience you might have. Were you being a soldier or were you part of a mob?"

Patterson came several steps closer, almost within arm's reach.

"They could have brought those men in, Tom," he said quietly. "They had evidence. There was no need to set up a slaughter. No need to go outside the law again. How are we going to get anywhere out here, for God's sakes, if we have to depend on vigilantes? You could have stopped them, Captain. You could have made them work it out differently. You should have told them who you were. They would have listened to you. But you wanted that murderous bastard dead right now, so you let them go outside the law. Well, congratulations, you got them both. But she's gone. Over the hills and into the night, and no good-bye."

"Just what are your regrets, Simon?" Maynard asked.

"My regret is that I may be the only man in this town tonight who's mourning the absence of civil decency. And maybe I'm mourning a poor sod who—whatever his sins— was driven to blow his brains out."

"Then you ought to be more careful, Simon. Remember, it all began when you wrote that letter. You took on a responsibility. You started something. What did you think was going to happen?"

Patterson said nothing.

"When you choose to remove yourself from the world, Simon," Maynard said, "and sit yourself down in some remote place, you shouldn't then send out letters of invitation. But," Maynard said, turning back to his contemplation of the street, "if you want to stand high and condemn it all— if that'll help get you through the winter—then by all means, go ahead."

"And what will get you through, Thomas?"

"I'm a soldier; I'll get through."

THIRTY

General Northwood seemed compassionately inclined toward the late Major Pryor.

They were sitting in the general's office, where Maynard had come to give a verbal report, to be followed by a written one. The autumn late afternoon had dimmed the room, but Northwood seemed to prefer the fading light. He held a smoking cigar between his large fingers.

"It didn't happen that often," he said. "Which probably is surprising of itself, given the character of that war, particularly. But it did happen. Usually a few weeks back home turned the trick. Mental fatigue."

"This was more than that, sir," Maynard said. "He said it happened by degrees. He would slide back and forth."

"Until he was only sliding."

"Sometimes, sir, when I think back on those years . . ."

"You wonder why it didn't happen to all of us. Maybe you think there's something deplorable about remaining sane and stable throughout a long war." Northwood smiled privately. "No, Tom, you can't look at it that way. Just because somebody can't carry the burden as well as the rest proves nothing. It really doesn't. You see all sorts of things in war; it provides for the demonstration of every human trait and characteristic. Savage by day and by night pious. You do a thousand reprehensible things and you're not supposed to repent a one of them. It can unhinge a man."

"That's true, sir."

"Christ, Tom, it must have been unsettling for you, having the man blow his brains out right in front of you."

"He was oddly composed."

"You wonder," Northwood murmured.

"He said it was the honorable thing."

"To him maybe; it's certainly not part of the manual."

"What would have happened to him, General, if he'd been brought in?"

Northwood shrugged, puffing on the cigar. "I don't know," he said, the words following on a cloud of smoke. "It would have been a delicate matter for handling. And anyway, you say he'd committed a murder out there. Those people might have claimed a jurisdiction."

"There isn't much jurisprudence out there, I'm afraid."

"A hell-raising town, eh?"

"Lord knows what it's going to become."

"Well," the general said, "they'll settle down sooner or later. They all do."

"General, do you think I was wrong to ride out with those men?"

"You had to make an on-the-spot decision, Tom. You couldn't be absolutely sure about what they intended to do, could you?" Northwood asked, giving him a meaningful look.

"I guess not."

"And you say it led directly to you getting your man."

"Yes, sir," Maynard said quietly. "I got him all right."

"Then that's all that matters. It was a difficult assignment and you handled it well. But, imagine, the goddamned sheriff being the head of a gang of road agents. It's a hell of a country."

"Out there, yes, sir."

"I meant out there," Northwood said. "And as far as back here is concerned, you'll be interested to know that your friend Colonel Zachariah is dead."

"Is he, sir?" Maynard asked, with interest.

"A few weeks after you left. Died of a seizure. In bed."

"His own?"

"Not unless he carried it across town with him. No, it was in one of those places. Which I'd advise you to stay out of, young man, if you don't mind the avuncular word or two."

"Not at all, sir."

"They can only bring you grief, in the long run."

"In the short run, too, sir," Maynard said.